BULLETPROOF LOVE

<u>VENGEFUL HEARTS</u>

Dark Romance Series

Book 1 - I'm Not in Love (I Promise)

Book 2 - Bulletproof Love

Book 3 - Love Bleeds Red

<u>PALM COVE</u>

Small Town Interconnected Standalones

Book 1 - Fight For It

Book 2 - Fight For Her

Book 3 - Fight For Us

<u>GREYRIDGE</u>

Small Town Holiday Themed Novellas

Book 1 - Holiday Heartstrings

Book 2 - Holiday Hook-Up

AUTHOR'S NOTE

Hey loves! Before you dive into Jasper and Falin's story, I want to be upfront with you about the content. This book is definitely intended for mature readers (18+) only, and I want you to be able to make an informed decision about whether it's right for you.

This story contains themes of:

VIOLENCE & CRIME

- Organized crime and criminal activities
- Gun violence and weapons
- Murder and death scenes
- Human/sex trafficking
- Physical assault and violence
- Blood and injury
- Police interactions
- Cult-like organizations
- Stalking behavior
- Abuse of power

PSYCHOLOGICAL & EMOTIONAL

- Substance addiction and drug abuse
- Withdrawal symptoms
- Trauma and depression
- Grief and mental distress
- Intrusive thoughts
- Suicidal ideation
- Self-harm behaviors
- Parental neglect and death (mentioned)
- Child abuse (mentioned)
- Sexual assault/non-consent (not between main characters, and not graphically depicted)
- Dubious consent situations
- Pedophilia (mentioned, not depicted)
- Hospitalization and medical settings
- Anaphylaxis and severe allergic reaction

SEXUAL CONTENT (All scenes between consenting adults 18+)

- Explicit sexual content including oral sex, fingering, and anal play
- BDSM themes including dominance/submission
- Rough sex and impact play
- Spanking, flogging, and other impact play
- Sadism and masochism
- Pegging
- Barebacking/unprotected sex
- Praise and aftercare
- Degradation and begging
- Edging and orgasm control
- Tribbing

• Biting

This isn't a complete list of everything you might encounter in the book, but I wanted to give you a good idea of what to expect. Your comfort and safety while reading means everything to me, so please make sure to check in with yourself and practice self-care while reading.

If you have specific concerns or triggers you're worried about, please don't hesitate to reach out to me on social media – I'm always happy to provide more detailed content information.

Take care of yourselves!

Lauren

*To all the prickly flowers who have learned that it's not your
roots that define you, it's where you choose to bloom.*

SPOTIFY PLAYLIST

PROLOGUE

I was never meant to be saved.
Wandering aimlessly,
A broken, bleeding heart.

But you—your touch ignites my veins,
A new addiction I never expected,
A feeling I can't explain.

Control is your mask. Chaos is mine.
Unwilling or unable
To surrender what we've become.

We circle this city,
Hearts shrouded in armor,
Bulletproof against the world.

I'd end it all to keep you safe,
So pull the trigger, Trouble,
And watch me bleed for you.

CHAPTER ONE

JASPER

THE CHILL IN THE AIR HAS MY SHOULDER ACHING LIKE a son of a bitch. It's stiff as hell, even after going through those stretches Blake swears will help. I've been trying to lay off the painkillers despite what a certain platinum-haired brat may think.

Really, I have. Her side-eye and sass pisses me off too much to not at least give it my best go.

Unfortunately, the cravings are winning tonight. I can deal with pain; it's been a constant in my life since I started playing football in high school. Does it fucking suck? Hell yes. But it reminds me that I'm resilient. I'm still alive and kicking through every hit, every concussion, every broken bone. Getting shot brought my threshold to another level, though. All those movie action heroes make it look so easy.

Back in college, I was able to take a pill or two the first couple days after an injury and never think about them again.

But that was before my sister vanished.

Before my world shattered like a city hit by nukes.

My life was ground zero. My own personal apocalypse. Bailey was gone. Getting shot was the excuse I needed to surrender to the sweet bliss the pills provided. I could be numb. Forget the pressure from my parents. Tune out the guys and their constant planning. Even suppress the guilt that weighs me down each time I realize I'm not doing enough to find her. Nothing will ever be enough.

Nausea roils my gut as I make my way to the meeting point. We've only been living in the city for a couple weeks, so I'm no expert, but the night seems unusually quiet. It makes the skin on the back of my neck prickle in alarm.

My footsteps echo against the cracked pavement as I open my phone to double check the text. My memory's been shit lately. That coupled with the move has made it exponentially difficult to get around. But it seems I'm heading in the right direction.

A gust of wind rattles the loose metal fire escape on a graffiti covered building nearby. The sound is like a warning bell in the night. I pull up my hood and keep going.

Stop being a pussy. This will be the last time.

It has to be.

I spot my landmark—Mr. Clean 24/7 Laundromat—and turn down the adjacent street. Every step feels as if I'm plodding through a mountain of mud. The relief is near... I'm so close.

I pick up a flicker of movement out of the corner of my eye and stop, resting my hand on my gun tucked in the side of my jeans. "Hello?" I call out. "I know you're there."

No mistaking it, there's someone hiding in the shadows. Fuck. Grabbing my phone, I tap the screen to wake it up, squinting from the brightness. The space ahead gains a faint glow, revealing an empty alley. I'm alone.

Great, now I'm seeing things. What would Falin think

if she were here with me? I stifle a scoff. She'd definitely bust my balls, no doubt about that.

I release a breath and turn back toward the street. At least there's a bit of light coming from the laundromat windows. Texting my contact in a dark alley feels a bit too criminal for me.

Well, what do you expect? You're about to buy drugs, dumbass. Not a smart move, but it is what it is.

My phone vibrates against my palm, so I stop to see who's calling, hoping it's the dude I'm supposed to be meeting. Gotta love burner phones and Telegram. It's so much easier now than when I was in college trying to score weed.

As I rub my eyes, blinking away the moisture forming in the corners from the assault of bright light, a harsh voice cuts through the quiet street. "You got two seconds to tell me who you are and what you're doing on my street."

My eyes adjust, revealing two forms in front of me. They're both tall guys—not as tall as me, maybe about Damon's height. One's a thick dude with a large sagging gut. The other, his gun aimed at my face, looks fit enough to cause trouble if I make a run for it. Gaiters partially cover their faces, leaving only dark, narrowed eyes visible.

I hold my hands up, phone still grasped in my palm, and smile. Time to do what I do best—talk my way out of this shit. "Hey man, why don't you lower your piece and we can talk. I'm not here to cause trouble. "

My phone vibrates again, and both sets of eyes zero in on it.

"Make that shit stop and answer my question," he says, gesturing to my phone. My pulse pounds as I nod and slowly lower my hand to peek at the screen. *Falin.*

Why is she calling me at 1 AM? It kills me to side button her, but I don't have a choice.

"Better?" I ask, raising my hand back up.

"Answer the question. What are you doing here?"

Goddamn, I think his voice made my nuts retreat all the way up into my body. Is that even medically possible? Balls can drop, but can they un-drop? Maybe Dr. Blake knows.

"I promise you, I'm a great conversationalist. We can walk outta here, hand in hand, new best buddies. But you gotta do me a solid and lower your weapon, then I'll tell you why I'm here."

Did I think I'd be sweet talking a gun-wielding criminal tonight? Nope. But I guess this is what I deserve.

His buddy, we'll call him Big Guy, taps him on the shoulder and he legit growls. I'm talking a cross between a rabid dog and a feral zoo animal. "What?"

"Maybe we can see what he's gotta say?" Big Guy offers, looking me up and down. "Seems like he's alright."

I nod vigorously. "He's right."

Growler lowers his piece and I breathe a sigh of relief. "Fuck's sake," he says. "Just answer the goddamn questions."

"I'm J. I'm here for a pick up." My phone vibrates again but I angle it so they can't see. I'm worried something is actually wrong. Falin's only used my phone number once before...the night of the haunted show last month.

The two turds look at me like I have an extra eye coming out of my forehead. Are they going to make me spell it out? "Oxys? This is the spot he told me to come to."

Another wave of nausea has me closing my eyes for a moment. I'm so damn over these two idiots. If they don't give me what I came for, there's a strong chance—maybe ninety-nine percent—that I'll have to kill them. My mind wanders, imagining all the ways I could do it. There's my gun, but that's too easy...

Growler interrupts my thoughts. "So you're saying you're here to buy pills?"

Holy shit, they don't have two brain cells to rub together. My eyes dart between the two of them, checking to see if they really need me to repeat myself. When they keep the same dumb head tilt and wide eyed stare, I huff and confirm. "Yes, that's exactly what I'm saying."

Growler inclines his head in a subtle nod and all at once, shit hits the fan. Both men pull out their weapons, pointing them directly at me, and Big Guy shouts, "Police! Get your hands up where we can see 'em. You're under arrest."

Fuck me.

There's no way I'm getting snagged for buying a couple pills. Not happening. I slowly raise my shaky hands, silently praying for a miracle.

Maybe I should stop by a church to show my thanks because an engine suddenly squeals, drawing their gazes away from me. I know I only have a split second, so I make the best of what I can and shove Growler hard in the gut, knocking him into Big Guy.

"Fuck!" one of them bellows. I don't hang around long enough to see who. Taking a breath, I sprint around the corner as fast as my out of shape ass can carry me.

There's no gunshot ringing out in the dark. No thunder of footsteps behind me. Only distant sirens and mumblings of conversation coming from a few drunks smoking cigarettes across the street.

Hell yeah. I'm in the clear.

My phone vibrates yet again and I finally answer it, hitting the speakerphone icon. "Fal... in," I force out between panting breaths. "You oh... kay?"

The next block is up ahead and I try to remember if

that's where I need to turn. Come to think of it, maybe I should find somewhere to hide out. Leading them back to the apartment is asking for trouble.

"Christ, you finally answer the damn phone." She sounds thrilled to speak to me, as usual. I can almost see her eye-roll.

"Kind of busy at the moment," I say, my words bouncing with each pound of my feet against the pavement.

"Yeah, I know. I'm trying to save your dumb ass." I hear faint clicking in the background as I take in her words. There's no way she knows. How could she?

"Don't know what you mean." Wind whips at my face, stealing what little breath I have. I lean against a rough brick wall and bend at my side, heaving.

"Don't stop, they're not as far as you think they are," Falin says. "See the old phone booth up ahead? The one with the flickering light?" She doesn't wait for me to answer. "When you reach it, turn left. *Left*," she repeats. "Not right. You go right and you'll run right into a cop car."

"I thought Damon was the stalker," I say, clocking the phone booth. It's close. Maybe I'll make it home unscathed.

I take off running again, keeping my phone in my hand at my side. Falin repeats "Left," again.

Whatever she's doing, I'm grateful for her. I'd never tell her that though. It doesn't fit the little game we've been playing. I like to call it *who can get under the other's skin the most?* I think it's a tie so far.

"Okay, see that door with the barred up windows?" I glance around and spot exactly what she's talking about.

"Yes," I pant out.

"The door should be open. Go inside and stay there for at least an hour. I'll monitor those cops and let you know when it's safe to head home."

"But where—"

"Just listen to me. You think I'd go out of my way at almost 2 AM to prank you? That's something you'd do, not me. I'm a mature adult." She sounds so smug. I know the exact face she's making. The one that gets my dick hard. Fuck, she'd look incredible hovered over me, that bratty look on her face, while she berates me for being a bad boy. I could come in my pants just thinking about it. "Jasper?" she asks when I don't answer.

"10-4, boss. I have one question though." I reach the door and yank it open, covering my nose at the invading stench of cat piss and rotten garbage. Now I know why this place is vacant.

"What's that, dummy?"

"You still got access to cop uniforms? I'm picturing you in those starched linen pants and it's giving me a semi." A smirk spreads across my face, but it's short-lived. It smells God awful in here.

"Wouldn't you love to know," she teases. "I'm hanging up. Don't get yourself arrested. Or killed. Blake would be sad."

"What about you? Would you cry for me, sweetheart?"

"I might shed a tear or two... when I see all the extra work I'd have to do to cover for you."

"Damn, that's cold. What did I ever do to you?" I make my voice smooth as silk, laying on the charm.

"Goodbye, Jasper. Keep your phone on. I'll tell you when it's safe to leave."

With that, the line goes dead and I'm left to find a spot to sit in this hovel. From the empty shelves and faded signage, I'm guessing this place was a store of some kind. Wonder what happened. I kick old used cups and empty trash aside and spot a semi-clear looking place to sit in the corner.

Catching my breath, despite the cat piss stench, I play the events of tonight back in my mind. Where the hell did it go wrong? My hands shake and now that I'm "safe", that aching hunger takes over. This is perfect, fucking perfect. I thought I found a legit plug here. It was going to be my last time. *Scout's honor.* And now I feel like shit in more ways than one.

I vibrate my leg, restless energy coursing through my muscles, and hum this Sleeping With Sirens song that's been stuck in my head all day. I wish I had my guitar. I'd play it and get it out of my system. I wonder what Falin would say? She likes that band. In fact, she's the reason the song is stuck in my head to begin with. Her incessant humming can drive a person to insanity. Just proves how much of a nuisance she is in my life. To put it poetically, she's my personal buzzing earworm.

I scoff out loud as the thought enters my head. *Wonder if playing her will get her out of my system.* Doubtful, but I'd be willing to test the theory.

How long have I been sitting here? It feels like days. The smell of this place will be forever burned into my nostrils. I pull out my phone, lowering the brightness as much as I can, and text Falin.

> Me: Am I good to go yet? It smells like death in here.

A few minutes go by as I scroll through my favorite social media site.

Car video. *Swipe.*

Football recap. Painfully *swipe.* Why are all my teams sucking this season?

Hot chick showing off some teeth whitening gel. Hmm, linger...

Nevermind, she's too clothed. *Swipe.*

A text notification pops up and I grin.

> Falin: Better to smell the dead than be dead. Keep your ass planted until I say.

> Me: That's debatable... with all due respect, you're not here breathing in the scent buffet that my sniffer is suffering. I may never be the same again.

She's so pissed. I know it.

Three dots show up and disappear four separate times. Yup, she's going to eviscerate me with words. Hell, I'll take it. It's better than focusing on the withdrawal symptoms. And to be honest, my dick gets hard when she's mean to me. Still trying to wrap my brain around all the reasons why. I glance down at my crotchal region and whisper to Jasper Junior. "You and me have some serious soul searching to do, big guy."

> Falin: Aww, poor baby Jasper. I know! I'll send you a scented candle... in the city that never sleeps, one of those delivery services has to be going strong. Hmm, but what scent? Eau de not dead yet because of me sound good? Pull up your big boy panties and stay put.

"Fuck," I say, shaking my head and chuckling. And there's Jasper Junior waking up to say hello, right on cue.

I tap the screen and think of a witty response, an action that doesn't come as easily as it used to thanks to the fucking brain fog.

Me: What if I don't wear big boy panties?

That sounds dumb as shit. Also, it's a lie. That's Damon and his freeballing. I'm too scared of zippers for that. Plus, ball sweat is a real issue.

Delete.

As I tap out another intellectually stimulating banger, a scratching sound from behind the wall startles me. I jump to my feet.

My pulse picks up and I instantly pull out my gun. It can't be those cops. Not unless they can become invisible and phase through solid objects. Goddamn, I wish Damon was here. I'd even take Leon, although he'd be giving me the silent treatment. They're better at this than I am. Better at everything, to be exact.

My ears prick as the sound repeats, this time a bit louder. I suck in a breath and call out. "Who's there?"

Please don't let someone answer. I feel like shit and killing someone in this dump will mean I have to spend more time in here cleaning up my mess.

"Hello?" I repeat louder, waiting a moment before I step quietly around the space.

Then I hear a completely different sound. Pitiful meowing. Oh fuck, there's still cats in here. I laugh out loud and put my gun away, searching the space for the culprit. The meowing grows louder, like a song made up of tiny, pleading cries.

"Where are you, buddy?" I whisper, still trying to keep myself hidden. I stop and point my phone's flashlight at a hole in the bottom of the wall, no bigger than my fist. "Of course. Alright, I'm going to get you out."

The cries reach a level of desperation that motivates the hell out of me. I'm a damn hero tonight. Rescuing a cat and shit. I rip at the crumbling drywall, taking out chunks that scatter like piss-stained confetti, revealing the rotten studs beneath. "Almost there."

Knocking the wall with the butt of my gun gives me the opening I need. Right there, between old electrical wire and water lines, are two of the dirtiest, skinniest kittens I've ever seen. They cower once they realize I've spotted them, but I scoop them up before they can dart further into the wall.

The first one is all black with bright green eyes that stare into my soul. She's meowing quietly, fur puffed. The second little one is the hellion. I can tell already. Its cries turn to incessant wails now that it's in my arms. It looks black like its sibling, but as I take a closer look, I notice it's just filthy.

"Where's your mom?" I shift them to the crook of my arm and bend to shine my light back inside the wall. The only crying comes from them, and the rest of the opening looks clear.

I turn my light off and take a quick picture of them, adding it to my text thread with Falin.

> Me: You can call me daddy now.

Send.

Don't care what she has to say. These two babies are all mine.

"You ready to get out of here and get something to eat?" They quiet down like they understand my words. "Me too."

Without waiting for Falin's reply, I stick the babies in my hoodie pocket and slink out the door.

CHAPTER TWO

FALIN

My eyes are bleary as hell, but I'm stuck awake at 2 AM, staring at multiple screens while I track Jasper's movement through a rough part of town. This damn man will be the death of me. Did he actually think he could sneak out to buy pills without my knowledge? He must be dumber than I thought.

At least I know he's safe in that abandoned storefront—for now. As long as he doesn't make any stupid moves, everything will work out fine. Well, except me missing out on much needed sleep.

My phone buzzes from its spot on my desk and I roll my eyes, already sure he'll have some ridiculous comeback for my last burn. What pops up on the screen is entirely unexpected. A photo of two scraggly kittens, small enough to fit in his massive palm. My heart melts for a moment before my brain catches up. *Aww* switches to *oh no* so fast it gives me whiplash. He's going to bring them back here. To our apartment. Which is already housing five extremely different people despite it being slightly larger than a shoebox. Okay, maybe that's an exaggeration. It has three closet-sized bedrooms. But the walls are so thin. Way too thin to be sleeping next to my best friend and her obsessive new boyfriend. Where the hell would we put two kittens who probably have a plethora of diseases and parasites?

The text comes through next.

Jasper: *You can call me daddy now.*

I snort in the most hideously unladylike manor. Not like I've ever been much of a lady anyway. *Why do I have a soft spot for this buffoon?* As I pick up my phone to reply, I get an alert on my screen. Jasper's on the move. "Is he serious?" I ask out loud to no one at all. I told him to stay put. My palm itches to beat the ever-loving shit out of him—but then that thought has my face flushed and breath quickening. *No. You will not get turned on at the thought of punishing Jasper Shea.*

I check my screens, showing small images of nearby street light cameras. Making sure he's not in imminent danger, I call him. It goes to voicemail on the first ring. "Oh, hell no."

I press call again as my pulse picks up. Fucking voicemail for a second time. I push up from the creaky desk chair we bought at a flea market last week, and pace the three steps of my bedroom. The generic, *please leave a message* recording plays in my ear and I make a split second decision to give him a piece of my mind.

"Do you want to get arrested? Or maybe it's a death wish, I can't quite decide. Either way, you're being stupid. I told you to stay put." I heave an aggravated sigh and continue in a resigned tone. "If you absolutely have to head home, call me back so I can give you the best route. Oh, and the cats... good luck getting everyone to agree on keeping them."

I hit end, feeling more frazzled than before I left the

message. My muscles ache from being at my uncomfortable desk all day, my feet are ice cubes since the heat in this building is spotty if on at all, and I'm goddamn horny. Add on dealing with Jasper's incompetence and I'm standing here questioning if leaving my job and life was the right decision.

My life there was put together. I had control of every aspect—where I lived, which projects I worked on, when I traveled, and most importantly, who I slept with.

Ah, the sex was beyond good. Always a new guy to make me come. Love 'em and leave 'em. Never get attached and I'd never be hurt or abandoned.

To have every modicum of control slip through my fingers the way it has been this past month has been difficult to say the least. My carefree mask has started to slip. Even Blake's begun to notice the changes in my mood.

I try to call Jasper again while watching his dot on the screen move from block to block toward the nearest subway entrance. No answer, like I figured. I could go to bed. Force myself to not care. *Yeah, right.* That's not who I am. If I was that person, I'd still be in San Francisco, sitting in my office overlooking the bay.

I'm here for Blake. She needs me. Plus, with my help, maybe we can finally find Jasper's sister and my best friend can get her life back in order.

As the thought leaves my mind, the familiar sound of her bed frame knocking against my wall starts. Just like every other night since we moved here. I swear, I don't think I've known anyone who fucks as much as those two do. I don't know if I'm jealous, or concerned for her vagina.

And *there* goes the moaning.

"Christ on a cracker," I groan. Phone in hand, I make my way to the small open concept kitchen and living area. I almost slam straight into Leon's shirtless chest, jumping back a step in shock.

"Fuck, sorry I scared you." He drags a hand over his tired eyes.

"Damon and Blake's wake up call get you too?" I ask, shuffling past him to the fridge for a bottle of water.

He makes a sound that's somewhere between a groan and a chuckle. "I don't think I've slept a proper night in weeks."

"Should we have a family intervention?" I joke, wiping my hand over my wet lips.

"You might be onto something," he says with a smirk. Damn, he's attractive. He has these smoldering hazel eyes that hide all his secrets. That lip ring too. He's always nibbling it between his teeth. Something about a pierced guy gets me going.

I realize I'm staring up at him and blink, focusing my gaze at a discolored spot on the wall. "Remind me to never hang pictures in my room."

"Oh yeah, that would be asking for broken glass every-where." He stretches his arms over his head, showing off his lean muscle. "Hey, I noticed Jasper's gone. Is he in your room?"

I'm mid-sip when water almost spurts from my lips. "What? Why would you think that?" My voice drips with indignation.

Leon grabs me a paper towel from the counter, that smirk still visible. "Come on, I know you two are hooking up. It's obvious."

What the hell did Jasper tell him?

"We're not hooking up. That man drives me insane. Plus, he's not my type," I lie. "I go for older guys... with their lives put together."

Leon scratches his chin, scrutinizing me far too closely for my liking. "What about Blake's birthday?"

Damn him. I knew he'd bring that up.

"That—That was—I—That had—Nothing. Nothing happened." From the way I mangle my own words, any bullshit detector would know it's a bold-faced lie.

Truth is, we made out that night. That's it.

Well... okay, maybe there was some dry humping too. But I swear that's where it stopped.

Thing is, only one of us actually remembers what happened—and it's not the guy who was so wasted on pills and booze he could barely stand up straight.

I knew it was a mistake the second I woke up and saw him passed out on the floor beside me. If he wasn't going to bring it up, neither was I. Lucky for me, he never said a word.

Leon, being the smug jerk that he is, only shakes his head and lets out a dry chuckle. I'm glad he thinks this situation is so funny. Before I have a chance to think of a witty retort to his mocking, we're interrupted by an earthquake.

Not really... but holy hell it sounds like those two are going to break the floor. I clench my thighs together and take another sip of water.

"I'm surprised we haven't gotten a write up from the building manager yet," Leon says. He heads over to the couch, where his laptop sits folded on the coffee table.

"Oh, I think we have. Blake told me that Damon took care of it. Whatever that means." I shrug and organize a few random objects on the kitchen counter. Not like I'm getting any sleep tonight. May as well straighten up.

"So if Jas isn't in your room, any idea where he is?"

Leon has his phone out and is texting someone. Probably Jasper. The brightness on his screen is like a spotlight in the dim room.

"No idea," I lie again. I'm not getting in the middle of Jasper's addiction issue. If the guys haven't seen what's right in front of them, then they're far less intuitive than I thought.

Looking at Leon's expression, he seems to believe me... but there's concern written all over his face. I've got a feeling he knows exactly what's up. I sink into the other end of the couch, tucking my legs beneath me. Even with my thickest socks on, my toes feel like tiny icebergs.

Unease makes my chest constrict. There's no use in calling Jasper again if he's on the subway. But if I timed his route correctly, he should be getting home in a few minutes.

Leon and I sit there wordlessly, each lost in our own thoughts while our friend's... enthusiastic noises... fill the silence. I'd bet any amount of money that he's just as worried for Jasper as I am. Living here is going to give me premature aging. Crow's feet before I'm even thirty. I better hit up Sephora for some new skin care.

Fifteen tense minutes crawl by before the front door knob rattles and Jasper's unmistakable heavy steps have us both turning to look. An ache gnaws at my chest as I take in his disheveled state. His black balaclava is scrunched up on top of his head, with strands of his dirty blond hair poking through the bottom. He's wearing a black hoodie, and baggy dark wash jeans—both covered in what looks like dust and dirt. There's a dull pallor to his skin, despite being outside in the cold for the past hour. Even his ocean blue eyes are foggy, like the sea in a storm.

He notices us sitting there and suddenly the mask he wears for the world slips back into place. "Lee, what are you doing up?" He tilts his head, picking up the sounds from Blake and Damon's room and laughs. "Oh. Right on time."

"Where were you?" Leon asks, getting right to business.

My knee vibrates while I watch Jasper try to bullshit an excuse. Before he can open his mouth, the sound of mewling echoes through the apartment. Damn, I'd almost forgotten about the kittens.

"What the—" Leon scrunches his face as Jasper pulls the two scraggly kittens from his hoodie pocket.

"Shhh, babies. Daddy's going to feed you," Jasper says to the kittens, completely ignoring Leon's question.

I break my gaze away from Jasper and turn to Leon. "You don't even want to know."

"You're right. It's too fucking late for this," Leon says with a sigh before pushing up from the couch. He steps closer to Jasper, peering down at the kittens. "They're not staying in our room."

He holds a black kitten up so it's eye level with Leon. "Don't say that. Look at this face."

"I'm going to bed." In the dim light, I catch the ghost of a smile on Leon's face as he heads back to his and Jasper's room.

Jasper makes himself busy, pulling out a dish from the cabinet. I join him in the kitchen, wondering what the hell he's planning on feeding two feral kittens at nearly 3 AM. I don't have to wonder for long as he grabs a can of cat food from his hoodie pocket.

"Are you Mary fucking Poppins?" I ask. "What else do you have in that hoodie?"

"Nothing else in the hoodie, but I have something magical in my pants," he says without missing a beat. I smack his arm, which only garners a smirk from him. He hands me the can. "Here, can you open this? My hands are full."

"Yeah." I guess I'm an accomplice to his cat crimes now. They are pathetically cute. Poor little things.

"One second guys, Mommy's opening your num-nums," he says in a baby voice that weirdly does it for me. Goddamn, I need to find a normal guy to fuck in this city.

"Please never say num-nums ever again. I think my ears are bleeding." I grab a spoon and dish up the cat food onto a small plate while Jasper snickers. "Let's bring them to my room."

His brow raises. "I'm finally getting invited in, and all it took was some starving kittens." He holds them up in one hand so they meet his eyes. "I knew I loved you two."

"Come on, dummy. Let's get them fed so I can yell at you for being stupid tonight." I head toward my room, noticing that Blake and Damon finally seem to have quieted down. Once we're both inside, I close the door.

In this tiny room, Jasper's size is overwhelming. His presence seems to swallow up every inch of space, every breath of air. I shimmy around him and bend to put the dish on the floor, being acutely aware of just how teeny my sleep shorts are. Jasper gently places the kittens down in front of the dish and we sit on the edge of my bed, taking a moment to watch them go to town on the gross wet food.

"I think I'm going to name the black one Mayhem. May for short." He leans back on his forearms, stretching his long legs out in front of him. "And the other one, maybe Chaos. That one's a hellion, I can tell."

I ignore the pang in my chest. "What the hell happened tonight?"

He bends at the waist to scratch the kitten on the head. "Or maybe Havoc. Yeah, I like that name."

"I know what you're doing," I say, crossing my arms.

"I should go grab a washcloth. They're filthy." He hums to himself and starts to stand.

"Jasper." I grab his bicep—or try to. The thing is massive.

He releases a long sigh and meets my gaze. His brows draw together and his face sags like it's weighed down. "What do you want me to say?"

I'm acutely aware of every feeling coursing through him. He thinks he can hide from me, but he can't. He can't hide his trembling limbs, or how he worries his lip until it's raw. I see his restlessness. The way his thoughts drift away when the cravings take hold.

As much as I want to berate him for being stupid, I know that's not what he needs. "Take off your hoodie and lie back."

The corner of his lip tips up and he tilts his head to take me in. "Oh, really? I didn't think we were going there, but yes ma'am."

I shove his arm playfully. "Shut up and do as I say."

"Fuck, at least buy me dinner first." He yanks his mask from the top of his head, tossing it on the floor, before pulling the dirty hoodie off. He's left wearing nothing but a white cotton undershirt that clings to his pecs like a second skin.

And my mouth is suddenly dry as hell.

"Lie back and close your eyes. I'm going to do some acupressure points on you."

I cross the room to hit the light switch as he repositions himself, laying his head on my pillow. The kittens have polished off their meal and my mind drifts to the fact that they'll now have to use their non-existent litter box, but once I see Jasper finally listening to me, I ignore the thought.

His chest rises and falls slower already, a telltale sign that he's starting to relax. I climb into bed beside him, scooting as close as I can so I don't fall off the edge. Being this close, his masculine scent overwhelms me. Goddamn, why do I have to be so horny?

"Falin?" he whispers. "Should I sit up?"

"Such a good boy, asking for permission," I joke. It gets a quiet laugh out of him. "No, stay just how you are." I take hold of his hand and start with the point in the webbing between his thumb and index finger, exerting gentle pressure. "I lived in China last year. It was only a few months, but I learned a thing or two."

"Oh yeah?" he mumbles. "Feels good."

I can't help but smile from his praise as I continue holding the point. "There's a belief that we have a life force inside us called Chi. There's points throughout the body where the Chi can get stuck, which leads to all kinds of uncool shit."

As I move my hand down his wrist to the point on his inner forearm, he hitches a breath and trembles slightly. I spend about a minute, quietly holding the point before gently massaging in a circular motion. The skin on his arm breaks out in goosebumps.

"There's one last point I want to get." I look him over, trying to figure out the best way to reach the spot. There's really only one way with him laying the way he is.

"Uh, huh," he says, barely coherent. Without overthinking, I climb on top of his torso, my knees on either side of him. Of course, his head snaps up, eyes wide. "We doing this?"

"Shh," I say, pushing his shoulders down. "That's not what's happening here. Just close your eyes again."

"You expect me to relax with you straddling me?"

"I'll stop," I warn.

"No, don't." He sounds so desperate that warmth spreads through my chest... and other places... lower.

I press the point between his brows, trying my best not to press my tits into his face. *But, fuck.* I really want to press my tits into his face. His body is so damn perfect. Abs like a goddamn washboard. All I'd have to do is scoot down a bit.

No.

The kittens start crying, breaking me from my train of thought. Thank fucking God.

Jasper starts to sit up again, but I push him back down. "Rest. I'll go see if we have a box and some old newspaper from the move."

That'll have to do for a makeshift litter box for now.

"You hear that, girls? Mommy's taking care of you."

I let out a soft scoff, tucking my chin to hide the traitorous smile tugging at my lips. Whatever fantasy world Jasper's living in, it must be quite the vacation spot. I almost want to join him. It would sure beat our current reality.

CHAPTER THREE

ALEXANDER

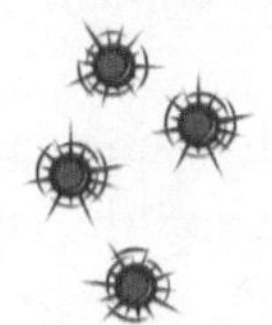

THE BEAUTIFUL MELODY OF MY FIST CRACKING AGAINST Dominic's skull helps my foul mood. His brother, Bruce, paces the perimeter of my high rise office with his head hung low.

Dominic's body slumps, but before he hits the floor, I grab a fistful of his dark hair and yank him up. "Bruce, get over here and hold him."

"But—"

"Now. Or would you rather I call Ace and tell him to pay a visit to a certain nursing home?" *Ah, that gets his attention.* Bruce shuffles over, the pathetic piece of garbage that he is. "Hold him up. I'm not done with him."

He hesitates, but I widen my gaze, showing him I'm not messing around. These useless animals screwed everything and now Brennan is dead and my uncle is breathing down my neck for answers. I've been holding off our meeting for weeks, but I've run out of time.

"Please," Dominic pleads. "I'll do anything... I can find them."

I stretch my arms over my head and rub my sore fists. "Shut the fuck up and be a man."

I reel back and punch him along the corner of his eye, smiling as his head reverberates against the wall. Adrenaline floods my veins, and a laugh escapes my lips. This is exactly what I needed.

"Boss, I think he's had enough," Bruce says, not meeting my gaze.

"I'll say when he's had enough." Blood streams down Dominic's cheeks, saturating the collar of his tan Carhartt jacket. The sight only fuels my rage.

I draw my fist back and punch his gut over and over again until red stains his lips. His moans echo in the cavernous space.

A knock at my office door stops me mid-strike. I nod to Bruce. "Check it."

The moment Bruce takes his hands off his brother, Dominic crumples to the floor, only partially conscious. I grab a few tissues from the box on my desk and dab my split knuckles. "It's the girls," Bruce mumbles as he closes the door.

"Well," I say. "Don't just stand there, let them in."

Kicking Dominic out of the way, I round the corner of my desk and perch on the edge. Bruce opens the door wide, and two gorgeous girls drag their feet inside. One redhead and one blonde, both barely legal, just like I wanted. The uncertainty in their eyes tells me they're new. *Perfect.* I'll have to thank Yuri later.

"Come on in, I don't bite." I flash a grin, and spread my arms wide in a show of goodwill. "Bruce, why don't you get my new friends a drink?"

"Yes, Boss."

Dominic attempts to sit up behind me, groaning.

"When you're done, take your brother and get him cleaned up. I'll need you both back here in an hour. We have work to do before I meet my uncle for dinner."

Bruce nods and pours vodka from my bar cart into three shot glasses. He hands one to each girl before bringing the third to me. I take it and shoot it back, sucking air between my clenched teeth.

"Anything else, Boss?"

Making my way around the desk, I pull open my top drawer and gesture to the contents. Bruce is a good trained dog. He knows exactly what I'm asking for. While he's busy, I motion for the girls to come closer. "I want to look at you."

They're holding hands, the tremble in their limbs evident. "What do you want with us?" the redhead quietly asks. I love the fiery spirit of a redhead. Makes them so much more fun to break.

"We're just here to have some fun. You like fun, don't you?" I reach out and run my fingers over their supple skin. So young and pure. "Bruce?"

Bruce may be a fat fuck, but he's fast when he needs to be. While their wide eyes lock onto mine, Bruce jabs them one at a time with my favorite concoction—a sedative that'll make them my pliable playthings but won't completely knock them out. What would be the fun in that?

He's set up a few lines on my desk for me like a good dog. I need the pick-me-up.

"Where do you want them?" he asks, as the girls heads nod and legs give out.

Sniffing, I point to the couch in the corner. Fucking new office. I need to get this place in order if we're going to be here for long. I had the perfect setup in the back of Velvet, before those scumbags ruined it.

Flexing my fists, I let the anger wash over me. It's too

bad Brennan's dead. He would have enjoyed these two. He was always up for some fun. That's about the only thing I miss about the whiny ass kisser. It's for the best that he's gone. I just need to make Ivan agree.

"Get out, Bruce. And be back in an hour. We have work to do. Ivan expects every detail for that fucking New Year's Eve party." Like I need to waste time on some politicians and their dicks. But their wallets never run dry... and that makes them our most valuable customers.

I'm hovering over the blonde, belt off, before Bruce and Dominic are out the door. Her eyes flutter open, and she whimpers. "Please..."

This is where I come alive.

CHAPTER FOUR

JASPER

THROUGH THE WINDOW, I WATCH THE MASSES OF people passing by, each one busy living their ordinary existence. Wrapped in their own world of grocery lists and scheduled meetings. Picking up dry cleaning or rushing home to pay the babysitter. Wonder what that would be like?

"What if I try to... No, they thought of that too. Whoever encrypted this knew what they were doing." Falin and Leon are side by side on the couch, doing the same shit they've been doing everyday since we moved here. My leg won't stop shaking and it's driving me crazy. I need something to take the edge off.

"Well, it definitely wasn't Brennan. He was absolute garbage when it came to tech stuff," Blake says. She's on the end of the couch, lacing up her boots for her date day with Damon.

Falin turns to meet her gaze with a sad smile. "Who knows? I mean, he *was* living a double life."

Blake tucks her head and sighs. "True." She stands and grabs her coat from the hook behind the front door. "Are you sure you don't need our help today? I don't mind staying in."

"Go have fun. Please... there's already too many of us in here. We're going to start killing each other soon." Falin glances my way before bringing her attention back to her screen.

I'm reminded of how I woke up in her bed, with her body cradled against my chest, the kittens asleep in a cuddle pile at our heads. Fuck, it was nice. Probably the single best way I've woken up in the past few years.

Too bad as soon as her eyes opened, she was back to pretending she hates me.

"We got one part at least—the breadcrumb that led us here. Now if I could just crack the rest of this mess and figure out where in this city to look." Leon taps away at his keyboard, head slumped. We all look exhausted, except Blake. She's goddamn glowing.

Damon makes his way over from their bedroom, freshly showered and dressed in black. I bet he used all the hot water... That would be so Damon.

"You two look adorable," I say. "Like the perfect emo couple. And so well rested, almost like you weren't up all night screwing each other's brains out."

Damn, I'm grumpy. I wish I could blame it all on lack of sleep.

Blake's cheeks flush pink as Damon puts his hand on her lower back. "I'm going to take your compliment and leave the rest for another time. Did you eat? You sound hangry."

"Not yet." I huff. "You can't just shove food at me whenever I'm pissy."

"I'll order something," Falin says, swapping her laptop for her phone. She looks at Leon, adding. "Thai?"

"That works," he answers.

Am I fucking invisible?

"What if I want something else? Like Mexican or Italian," I snap, crossing my arms.

"Oh, this place has five stars. The best Pad Thai in the neighborhood," Falin says, ignoring me.

"We're going to head out," Blake says carefully. "See you guys later."

"Call if anything comes up," Damon adds. They're out the door before any of us get the chance to say goodbye.

"I'm gonna go check on the kittens," I grumble.

Leon finally notices that I'm in the room. "Did you mention them to Blake and Damon?"

I stop halfway to Falin's door and turn. "Not yet. They weren't exactly *available* this morning."

He stretches his arms above his head, settling them far too close to Falin's shoulder for my liking. "I'll look up the nearest shelter. We can take them in after we eat."

All at once, emotion floods my system. With my teeth clenched, I grit out a simple, "No."

Falin cocks her head, eyeing me closely. "Jasper, you know we can't give them a good life."

"She's right. You can't possibly want to keep them." Leon adds.

"Try and take them," I say. "You won't like what happens."

Maybe I'm being a dick, but I'm tired of having no say in what goes on around here. I haven't been of much help since before the accident and I need something, anything to keep me going.

They exchange glances. "Alright... Well, maybe you should go pick up some stuff for them. A litter box, real food bowls."

"We'll see what Damon thinks," Leon says, keeping his voice level. I'm not stupid. What he's really saying is, '*I don't want to be the bad guy, so I'll let Damon take one for the team*'.

"They stay," I repeat. "We don't just give up on the people—animals—we love."

Falin stands, eyeing me like I'm a flight risk. "How about we go get them some supplies? I'll come with you."

I can read her expression. She doesn't actually want to come with me. She wants to make sure I'm not going to score again. Well, I don't need a babysitter. Especially one who looks at me with pity eyes.

"Stay here, eat your Pad Thai or whatever it is you ordered. I'll be back later."

"Brother—" Leon starts. I put my hand up.

"It's fine. I'm a grown ass man. I don't need your food and I don't need a babysitter."

I cross the room and slip out the door, not caring that I haven't showered or changed.

It's fine. I've got this. It's a simple task—find a pet store, buy some shit, and come back. I don't need to find a plug.

The cold air hits my face and I release a long breath. I can do this.

I make it a few blocks before I realize she's behind me. I've memorized the way her Doc Martens sound on pavement, learned the subtle hints of her perfume. She smells like roses, but not the cheap kind vendors sell on street corners—darker, richer, like they bloomed in a night garden behind iron gates, their stems wrapped in the sharpest thorns. So fitting for her personality.

I veer to the right, passing a couple hand in hand, and turn at the next corner. Should I bring her on a little adventure? That would be fun, but I don't want to leave the kittens too long without food and litter. Instead, I duck into an alcove, some restaurant back entrance, and wait.

Her body comes into view seconds later. That perfect hourglass, making my mouth water. I swear she wears those tiny crop tops just to fuck with me. This one is decorated with metal studs and black hearts. My palms itch as she steps closer, glancing around. She turns in a full circle, missing out on what's right in front of her. *Can't forget the shadows. That's where us monsters hide.*

With her back turned, I step forward and wrap my arms around her waist, lifting her until her back presses flush against my chest. My palms spread across her bare midriff as she kicks her feet in the air, thrashing in my hold.

I lean in and brush my lips against her ear. "Where's your jacket? You'll freeze out here in this tiny shirt."

"Jasper, what the fuck? Put me down." The fire in her voice has me fighting back a smile.

"Why are you following me, sweetheart? Miss me too much?" I linger against the shell of her ear for a second, loving the way her body squirms against mine.

"I swear to God, I'm going to slice your balls off in your sleep if you don't let go right fucking now."

"Okay, okay, no need to bring the baby juice storage into it." I slowly place her feet back on the ground, crossing my arms and leaning against the brick building. She stands motionless, only her shoulders rising with one quick breath. The movement is so fast I almost miss it—her body pivoting, closing the space between us. Suddenly she's pressed against my chest, holding the sharp edge of her switchblade against my throat. Her eyes pin me, hard and deadly. I don't know whether to moan or piss myself. "Quit flirting with me, or I just might fall in love with you," I say in a playful tone.

"I don't make empty threats, Jasper. You ever grab me like that again and this blade will look like a butter knife compared to what I'll use." She presses the blade closer and I feel the sharp sting of my skin splitting. We stay like that for a few long moments, heartbeats thundering against each other's chest, eyes locked in a silent battle. She's waiting for me to relent. To tuck my tail between my legs and tell her "Yes, Falin," like an obedient puppy. And I will, but not before I've memorized every spark of fire dancing in her smokey eyes.

I reach for her hand and pull it away from my throat. "I believe you." She blinks and steps back, glancing down at the blade in her fist, dotted with my blood. I cup my neck, wiping at the crimson beads that made their way to the surface.

Falin digs through her purse and pulls out a tissue. "Here." Clearing my throat, I take it and attempt to wipe away the blood. I notice a few pedestrians staring at us from across the street. "We should go," she says, probably noticing the same people I do.

"Yeah, one sec." I take off my hoodie and pull it over her head. "Don't fight me on this. It's cold." A cute scowl lines her lips, but she slides the hoodie down the rest of the way. It stops at her knees, and I'm momentarily bummed that I don't get to ogle her anymore. But then again, neither does the rest of Manhattan.

We walk side by side, toward the independently owned pet supply shop I found on Google. Falin seems to be deep in thought as she toys with the ribbed wrist cuff. "I didn't need a babysitter. I wasn't going to buy pills."

"I'm too tired to deal with this argument," she says, not missing a beat.

The pet shop is a few feet away, just past a pedestrian

tunnel where a group of workers crowd around brick siding, making repairs.

"What's the argument? All I'm saying is, you can trust me. I'm not going to make that mistake again." I hope I sound more sure than I feel.

She sighs and turns her head in my direction. "I know more about this than you think, okay? I don't want to get into it right now, but trust me on this. You're nowhere near ready to be left to your own devices."

As my brain wraps around a response, she quickens her pace, stepping around the crew of workers, and heads into the pet store.

Thirty minutes, three hundred dollars and two arguments later, we leave the sweltering pet store, arms full of bags, a pre-assembled hot pink cat tower, and a self-scooping litter box.

"We should buy one of those cart things people use to lug their groceries around," I say, adjusting the cat tower against my shoulder.

"Or order online like normal people," she says. I notice she's shoved my hoodie in the bag, after taking it off in the store.

"You're not cold?" I ask.

She rolls her eyes. "Are you kidding? Their heat had to be broken. It was like a sauna in there."

"True, but it's cold out here." I shrug, leaving it alone. Don't need to piss her off yet again.

"What's with your obsession over my body temperature? I don't need a big, strong man telling me to cover up. I'm not going to catch the plague from a little cool air." She tosses her hair over her shoulder in an extra show of sass.

Yeah, but I won't have to kill every person in the tri-state area for looking at you. Exhibit A: the creepy contractor who's eye fucking her right this very moment. *Stay calm. You know how most men are.* Disgusting animals who can't keep their eyes or hands to themselves. My jaw clenches and fist balls around the base of the cat tower hard enough to crush metal.

"Looking good, blondie. Can I get your number?" the dude calls to her as she passes by.

"Fuck off," Falin snaps, giving him the finger. That's my girl.

"Come with me and I will," he replies, loud enough to be heard over the chuckles of his coworkers.

I stop in my tracks, only a foot away from the bastard, forcing air in through my nose and out through my mouth like my therapist taught me last year. But it's not doing shit to calm me. Only one thing will.

"Hey, fuck face," I call out. He whirls around, giving me his toughest expression. He's gotta be shorter than six feet at first glance and a hell of a lot smaller than me, not that it matters.

I don't wait for a response—my body acts on its own accord. I swing the hot pink cat tower, the hanging bell toy jingling like a soundtrack to my rage, and smash it over his head.

Caught off guard, he loses his balance and stumbles back against the wall. I barely see the other contractors standing at attention beside him through my tunnel vision. But I hear her, Falin, as she calls my name. "Jasper, what the hell?"

I ready the cat tower to strike again, but she grips my arm and yanks me toward her, ignoring hollers from the guys.

"Call the cops, Gino. This fucker just hit Miller."

Pulling from her grasp, I advance on my target again, wanting to see him crumple to the cold, hard ground.

"Come on!" Falin yells beside me and I finally come to, blinking and taking in my surroundings. "They're calling the cops. Let's go!"

"Fuck," I say under my breath. Hoisting the cat tower on my shoulder, we break out into a run and don't stop until we're two blocks away from home.

CHAPTER FIVE

FALIN

MY THIGHS BURN AND LUNGS ARE READY TO EXPLODE by the time we reach our building. Jasper climbs the steps behind me, oddly quiet. Is it possible he's actually thinking about his actions?

"You're pretty quiet for a guy who just assaulted someone with a cat tower," I say through labored breaths.

As I turn the doorknob to our apartment, he says, "Cat-callers get the cat tower... it's only fitting."

I shake my head. "How have you lived on this earth twenty something years without serving jail time?"

"Twenty-five years, and I don't know... My good looks and charm seem to help." My eyes roll back before I can stop them.

"I cannot with you."

We're interrupted by Leon striding toward us with an arm full of kittens, a wild look in his eyes. "Take them. One of them clawed me."

"Why were you holding them?" Jasper asks.

"They wouldn't stop meowing." Jasper grabs the babies, and Leon curses under his breath. "I'm going to get rabies now." He stomps off toward the bathroom, but not before stopping to stare at our pet store haul. "A *pink* cat tower?"

"Ask him," I say, pointing at Jasper.

"What? They're girls, they wanted pink," Jasper says, as if he's said the most obvious statement ever.

Leon shakes his head and leaves us to our mess of shopping bags and hungry, demon kittens.

I SHUT MY COMPUTER, more forcefully than I mean to. These encryptions are testing every bit of my knowledge and patience. Between Leon and I throwing everything we have into it, we've still only managed to figure out the first bit that led us here. I've stared at the list of seemingly inconsequential patterns so much in the past few weeks that they're engrained on the back of my eyelids.

RH-MEXP4521937-12-1022-NYC,
PN-MEXP4521882-07-2230-NYC,
HH-MEXP4521756-16-1845-NYC ,
PJ-MEXP4521664-09-0215-NYC

Port names, container numbers, times. At least that's what we all seem to agree on after studying the patterns. The problem is, the list ends abruptly, and we haven't been able to gather any more intel from Brennan's hard drive. My stomach churns thinking about how they're using this information for heinous shit.

I've been tempted to call my dad for the first time in months, and see if he has any colleagues in the human trafficking department that could lend us a hand. He may be in rural Ohio, but weirdly, the law enforcement community has ties that run deep in more jurisdictions than I would have ever imagined.

There just so happens to be three brooding pains in my ass that would kill me if I got him involved. Which, okay, I get that they're closer than they've ever been to finding Bailey, and that they need to lay low with Alexander still out there, but I can't sit here and do nothing. It's not in my nature.

Thinking of my dad makes me remember the email I got earlier from that DNA matching site I joined last week. Something about all this searching has made that itch to find my birth parents come back stronger than ever.

A knock at my door has me spinning my desk chair. "Come in."

"Hey, how's it going in here?" Blake looks around my disheveled room, holding my favorite kitten, Havoc. Her and Damon took to the kittens as soon as they saw them, much to Leon's aggravation.

"Wonderful," I say, slumping further into my chair.

"The guys are heading out to Brooklyn later. That terminal, I think it's called Red Hook. Damon's been itching to get his hands dirty. To ask around. I'm not sure if that's the best idea, but of course, they're not listening to me."

"I don't blame them. We're all going stir crazy. Not sure what they think they'll find. We've already combed through their database a hundred times. Those container numbers never existed."

I hold my hands out and Blake plops the kitten into my arms. I love how she always knows exactly what I'm thinking.

"You're right. I'm just nervous. Who knows where Alexander is, or who he has working for him. Those codes meant something to Brennan, which means they must have meant something to Alexander and Ivan, too." She wraps her arms around her chest and taps her foot.

"They'll be okay." I straighten my back, hoping that'll help bring any small semblance of confidence to my words. "It pains me to say this, but I know they can take care of themselves. Jasper may not know how to brew a pot of coffee, but I've seen him handle himself, and we have nothing to worry about."

Did I sound convincing? I hope so. Blake doesn't need more on her plate.

Blake narrows her eyes in a look of all knowing mischief, a small smile lining her lips. "You've seen him 'handle himself,' huh? And how good was his 'handling'?"

I scrunch my lips and glare. "Trust me, there's been none of that. I'm actually dying for some dick... I think my vagina's going to dry up and wither away." She raises a brow, not buying my distraction. "We should go out tonight. Just the two of us. Get some dinner, blow off some steam, maybe find some hot guys to flirt with." I wiggle my brows until she laughs.

"Yes to the first few ideas. I won't stop you from finding a hook-up. I'll even help. We can bring back our system from college."

"The hand signals?" I laugh. "Okay, remind me again."

"You don't remember?" she asks, shocked. "Two thumbs down for 'save me right now from this mouth breather.' Jazz hands for 'eh, I'll make out with him but that's about all.' Finger guns for, 'clear out of our room tonight because this bitch is getting some.'" She tilts her head to the side, thinking. "I feel like there was one more, but I can't remember."

Little Havoc meows at the exact moment the memory comes back to me. "Wait! That time you got pissed at me because I went out back to that really fucking hot guy's car and you had no idea where I was. You made another sign that meant, 'I can't wait until we're home, I'm doing this now.'"

"The fist pump!" She shakes her head. "I was so mad at you. Jealous, but also mad."

I wince. "Yeahhh, I wasn't the best at communicating then."

"And you're a master at it now." Her voice drips with sarcasm.

"Very funny," I say, matching her tone. "So, do we have a date?"

Standing and stretching her arms above her head, she smiles. "Sounds perfect. I'll tell Damon so he's not a worried mess."

I flip my computer back open, feeling better than I did ten minutes ago. "Yeah, you probably should, although, I'm sure he'll know exactly where we are every second of the night."

She huffs and heads for the door. "Oh, maybe we can make a pit stop to see the tree at Rockefeller Center. I haven't gone since I was a kid." Her voice trails off but I barely hear her through my pounding pulse. My eyes are fixed on a notification on my screen.

"Holy shit, Bee. Brennan just got an email."

She hurries to my side. "What? How?"

"No fucking idea. It's not encrypted or anything, just a normal email. Sent from someone named Fairfax. It looks like an invitation." I stare at it like it's a ticking time bomb. "What if it's some kind of trap? They could hack my system. We need to tell Leon so we can open it with one of his devices."

I bend to put Havoc on the floor while Blake lets out a

sound that's a mix between a gasp and a squeal. "I'll go get him."

The room is graveyard quiet as we crowd around one of Leon's monitors. If I'm this anxious, I can't even imagine how they must be feeling. "Does the name Fairfax ring a bell?" Damon asks Blake.

She shakes her head. "Not at all. But Brennan was involved in a lot of charities the past few years. He went to events all the time."

Damon pulls her against his chest, and I notice the moisture gleaming in her eyes. "It's okay, Angel."

"Let's open it," Jasper says. "What's the worst that could happen?"

Leon and I exchange similar looks, dread mixed with anticipation, and I nod. "He's right."

"Alright, let's see what Fairfax has to say." Leon rubs his hands together before clicking the email open.

From: events@fairfaxassociates.com

Subject: Annual New Year's Eve Masquerade - The Fairfax Estate

Dear Mr. and Mrs. Brennan Whitaker,

Harrison and Evelyn Fairfax request the pleasure of your company at their Annual New Year's Eve Masquerade Ball.

Join us as we welcome the new year in elegance at our upstate home, Fairfax Manor. As always, this exclusive gathering brings together New York's most distinguished leaders in business, politics, and philanthropy.

Details are as follows:

Date: December 31st, 2024
Time: 8:00 PM until after midnight
Venue: Fairfax Manor
44 Riveridge Road
Bedford, New York
Attire: Black tie
Masks required for the midnight unveiling ceremony
This year's charitable focus supports youth education initiatives across the state. Your generous contributions have made significant impacts in previous years.
RSVP required. This invitation is non-transferable.
Security protocols will be strictly enforced.
Regards,
Office of State Senator Harrison Fairfax
Chairman of the Finance Committee

I read over the email two more times before pacing the length of the room. This has to be significant. As soon as I open my mouth to speak, the room explodes with questions.

"Finance committee?" Leon asks, bewildered.

"What the fuck is an unveiling ceremony?" Jasper adds at the same time.

Blake takes a few steps toward Leon's bed and sits. "This is something he must have attended before. We have to go."

I spin to face her. "Wait a second, Bee. We need to think this through."

"I agree," Damon adds. Him and I never agree on much, but when it comes to Blake's safety, we're of the same mind.

"I'm going to run their names through every database I can," Leon says, already typing. "We need to find out more before we make any kind of rash decision." He turns to meet Blake's gaze. "I'm just as thrilled with this bit of intel as you are, Blake, but after everything that happened recently, we need to be careful."

"I'll help," I say. Finally, something to work with. My hands shake with anticipation.

"We still gonna go to Brooklyn tonight?" Jasper asks. He's looking straight at Damon, conveying a silent message with his expression. He wants to go. *Needs* to go. I can't blame him. He's been idle too much lately.

Damon turns to Blake and she nods. "You should go. This could be nothing. We shouldn't abandon all our plans."

As much as my fingers itch to glide over my keyboard, I can't take seeing Blake so sad. "We'll still go to dinner too."

Her lips curve upward, but the smile doesn't quite reach her eyes. "Sounds good."

We spend a few more minutes rereading the email, brainstorming what it's all about. I have too many theories running through my head. Most of them lean toward this party being a trap, or at the very least, something more nefarious than a normal charity gala.

I leave Leon to his work, grabbing a few empty Red Bull cans on my way out of the room he shares with Jasper. Damon and Blake follow me out into the kitchen.

"Where are you thinking of going tonight?" Damon asks. He's leaning against the counter, feigning nonchalance, but I know he's already anxious at the prospect of Blake and I unaccompanied in the city.

"Oh, you know, first I figured we'd hit up the nearest crack house, then go to a bar and grind up on every guy that approaches us, and maybe end the night hopping into a strange white van, see where it takes us. I'm feeling adventurous." I flash him a wry smirk.

Jasper steps in, coming up to Damon's side. "Why does he look pissed?"

"He's not," Blake says. She softens her expression and wraps her arms around Damon. "What she means is, we'll probably stay in the neighborhood, grab dinner and a few drinks. Nothing crazy."

"You're such a killjoy," I tease, pouting for extra flair.

But she doesn't register my jab. She's too busy swapping saliva with Damon. When they keep going, grinding into each other, the awkwardness grows thick enough to slice with my switchblade. My eyes drift to Jasper and I catch him already watching me. Time stretches into an infinite void with his intense gaze locking me in place. My skin tingles and heat pools in my core. Blake lets loose a small moan and finally the spell breaks. Jasper pulls a hand through his hair, shuffling back a step. "Think I'll go get some air."

"Yeah—I'm gonna—" I mumble, feeling my cheeks flame. Turning on my heel, I speed walk into my room and flop face down on my bed.

What the hell was that?

I'm literally panting and all he did was look at me. I've gotta find a hook-up. This is a five alarm emergency, I need an orgasm stat situation. I'm in one of the biggest cities in the world. It can't be difficult to find someone decent to fool around with.

I flip over and grab my phone from my desk, tapping my favorite dating app. While it updates my location, I close my eyes and replay that moment in my mind. Holy sexual tension, Batman. Except, I *can't* mess with Jasper Shea.

He'd be a fun time, for sure. I had a small taste on Blake's birthday. Holy crap, I'd love to climb him like a tree. But we're stuck here, living together. On top of that, he's a mess right now. Neither of us need the complication of a "relationship" or whatever we would call it. I couldn't live with myself if I caused him any more pain. That is, if he's even capable of being serious for more than five seconds.

No.

What I need is a complete stranger. Someone hot who knows where the clit is.

My screen loads with an array of options. I'm like a hungry bitch at a buffet. Within two minutes, I find someone.

Hello, Hot Jake who works in finance and loves to mountain bike.

> Me: Let's meet up.

I wait approximately ten seconds before his reply pops up.

> Jake: When and where?

> Me: Now. Night Shift Bar.

I quickly type out the address of the nearby dive bar and jump up to get ready. I haven't fucked in a dive bar bathroom since college, but where there's a will, there's a way.

CHAPTER SIX

JASPER

I suck in a cool breath of air as my feet pound the cracked pavement. That should help lower my body temperature a degree or two. Goddamn. I was two seconds away from initiating a whole house orgy right there in the living room.

Memories from that night run through my mind, like they have every day since. The haunted show and the party after. Falin and that prick scare actor all over each other, until I took care of him. She'll never know, of course. I crave the way relief washed over me the moment he passed out, his eyes rolling back in his head and his body slumped against the cold dirt.

Then I had her to myself.

Her lips were fucking lethal. I'd trade my last breath for another moment lost in her kiss. The way she molded against my body, the needy moans that spilled from her. Hell, I'd never been so gone for a woman before. Every ounce of suffocating pain evaporated while she was in my arms. I could breathe, could imagine a happy ending to my dumpster fire of a life.

Until the moment that absolutely wrecked me.

We crash onto the couch side by side, my body hanging off the edge. I feel so fucking incredible. And not just from the pills and the booze. It's Falin. The whirlwind who barreled into our lives and became the only woman I can think about. I'm finally going to feel her warm skin against mine. Finally going to sink into her. Claim her. I've wanted her since I laid eyes on her. Even more since she opened her smart mouth.

She scrambles closer, lifting her dress and grinding against my hard cock. "Fuckkk," I groan. Her fake vampire teeth graze against my neck as she nibbles and sucks. I need to slow down or I'm going to come in my pants.

I roll, flipping her onto her back, and make my way down her perfect body. I'll admit, I'm wobbly. This isn't my best, but I won't let this opportunity go.

"This pussy is mine," I say, hiking her skirt up and gliding my palm over her black fishnets.

"Wait—" She pushes up onto her elbows and gazes at me with a look of pure, unfiltered emotion. Her glassy eyes bore into mine and I swear her lip trembles.

"You okay?" I ask. Please God, let her say yes.

"I just need to—It's just been so long since I could actually trust someone, y'know? Like, the kinda trust where you don't have to check their phone or wonder why they're not answering..."

I sit back on my knees, listening. What the hell could I say to that?

"God, I've just been hurt so much. Too much. And I just... Is it stupid that I just want someone good? Just like... Just a genuinely good person?"

She rubs her eyes and snorts a laugh while I stare, dumbfounded.

"You're... You're good, Jasper. You're actually good. Like, deep-down good. Not fake-good. Real good. And I don't... I don't usually say stuff like this cause it's scary but... the drinks and you kissed me, and you're just... You're just good."

She flops back on the couch and pulls her skirt up higher. "M'kay, my pussy is all yours."

I blink more times than I could count. Is there moisture in my eyes? What the ever loving fuck? It feels like someone dumped a bucket of ice cold water over my head.

I clear my throat. "Uh, be right back. Bathroom."

She singsongs something as I book it down the hall, holding onto the wall for balance. When I stare at myself in the mirror, I don't even recognize the man looking back at me. Dark puffy bags under his eyes. Sallow skin, scruffy facial hair. Smile nowhere to be seen. What good does Falin see in me? I'm not that guy. The one to keep. I've never been him.

I splash cold water on my face and groan. "Fuck, I'm going to regret this."

Turning, I head back to the living room, ready to tell Falin all the reasons why she shouldn't trust me. Why I'm not the guy she thinks I am. But she's curled onto her side, eyes closed, and lips parted while soft breaths escape them.

I grab a blanket from the other side of the couch, cover her, and turn to head into my room when her soft voice pulls me back.

"Stay," she whispers.

I fight with myself for a moment before finally giving in and sliding against her on the couch.

We haven't talked about that night since. What is there to say? She opened up to me, told me exactly what she needed, and I ran. Well, only in the metaphorical sense. But still, I can't get her out of my head. I crave her more than those fucking pills and that's saying something.

My skin is tight, like it's stretched over a body it doesn't belong on. I run a hand through my hair and open the door to the deli down the block from our place. The clerk nods his head at me while I step around a mother and little kid browsing the candy rack. I go immediately to the sweets section, grabbing a pack of cookies and a fucking Twinkie. Sugar has helped with the cravings, although I don't know what's worse for my body. I head down the aisle and grab a Monster from the cold case before getting in line to pay.

"Hey, man," the clerk says. "That all?"

"Yeah." He rings me up and I grab my wallet, remembering how long it's been since I actually took a paying job.

"Fifteen seventy-two," he says. I hesitate and hand him the credit card I swiped from one of those pricks at Blake's house. So far it hasn't been flagged, but I've been waiting.

After I pay, I head outside, immediately stuffing my face. The sweetness hits my tongue, sending the pleasure signals I needed straight to my brain. I wonder what Falin's doing right now. And what's the deal with that party invitation?

We'll have to go, even though I'm not in the mood to deal with a bunch of rich assholes. But it could lead us to my sister.

A girl passes by with the same long chestnut hair as Bailey, and I stare for an extra second. It's become a habit, especially since moving here. I see her face everywhere. It's maddening. There's little reminders no matter where I go. Her favorite song playing at a gas station. Someone wearing a shirt I swear she had. A hint of the body spray she used to overload herself with when she was in middle school.

I can't catch a break. Bailey's gone and the ghost of her won't let me forget it.

Leon swears she's still alive. Says he'd bet his life on it. Damon agrees, but not as intensely as Leon. I think he's just trying to keep me from losing my shit.

I don't know what to believe. I'm lost, and finding answers is the only thing keeping me going. What else is there anymore?

The sound of a door shutting pulls my attention. It's Falin leaving our place. She changed from her leggings into a black skirt and it looks like she straightened her hair out. "Where are you going, Trouble?" I say to myself.

I watch her cross the street, her eyes locked on her phone screen. Whatever messages she's reading have stolen all her focus. I follow her, keeping just enough distance between us to remain unseen. My heart drums against my ribs. What can I say? I live for moments like this. Hunting my prey. Not that Falin is truly prey, but she's giving me exactly the chase I crave.

She slows, her steps stopping once she reaches a shitty bar called Night Shift. Why the hell is she going there at two o'clock in the afternoon?

I hang back for a few minutes, giving her time to get settled, before heading inside. The place is narrow, but long with sticky floors and cracked stools crowded around a wooden bar. Falin's perched on a stool at the very end of the bar, phone in hand, texting.

I have a few options here. There's the Damon way—slinking back into the shadows to wait and watch. I've never been one for the shadows though. I make my way down the bar, past a few blue collar looking guys nursing their beers, and pull out the stool next to Falin.

She looks up from her phone and an instant frown lines her lips. "What are you doing here?"

"Thought I'd get myself a beer." I signal to the bartender, a smoke show with long legs and glossy dark hair. If I were myself... or I guess my old self, I'd have her number before I left here. I flash her a smile and watch her cheeks blush. "How's it going today?"

"Not too bad. What can I get you?" She fiddles with the rag in her hand.

"I'll take a beer, whatever you have on tap." I turn to Falin. "What would you like?"

She purses her lips. "I'm not here with him."

The bartender darts her gaze between us. "Oh, okay. I'll go get your beer."

"That wasn't very nice," I say, purposely irritating her.

She sighs and picks her phone back up, ignoring my needling. "You should go, Jasper."

"But our date just started." The bartender picks that moment to slide a beer in front of me. I nod and thank her, taking a long sip. "Now that's delicious. You should get one."

Falin ignores me, tapping her heel against the barstool. She's got her phone in her hands again and is furiously typing. I crane my neck slightly to get a peek at who she's texting, but she catches me. "Can you take a hint? Wait, I forgot, you only have two brain cells left."

I clutch my chest. "That was mean. Truly. I'm hurt."

She finally turns and meets my eyes. "Come on, I'm serious. You need to leave."

Her pleading tone has me concerned. Could she be in trouble? Is this part of the job? Maybe the guys sent her to meet with someone and didn't want to tell me. That has to be it. They're shutting me out again. Well, I'm not moving a fucking muscle. If Falin's getting herself into some kind of trouble, she needs me here.

"What did they ask you to do?" I scan her face for any changes. *That's right, I'm onto you guys.*

She scrunches her brows. "What?"

I shake my head. Leon must have told her to keep it from me. I squeeze my fist around my glass. I don't know if I should be hurt or pissed. They all know I'm a mess right now. There's no doubt in my mind.

I'll prove that I can handle our shit.

Just then, the door opens, letting light into the dim space. I look over to see a guy lift his sunglasses on top of his head as he comes inside. He immediately looks out of place with his shiny dress shoes and perfectly tailored suit, covered by a long tan trench coat. I even get a whiff of cologne—the kind I've only ever smelled on testers at the mall.

Falin squirms in the stool beside me and I instantly know—this must be the guy. I don't recognize him as one of Orlov's dudes from the warehouse, but he has the same air about him.

"Follow my lead," I say to Falin under my breath.

"What?"

Mr. Suit stalks toward us, a sly grin lining his lips. I sit up straight, pushing my chest out. If he wants to talk to Falin, he's gotta get through me.

"Jasper, you need to leave now," she hisses through clenched teeth, her voice barely above a whisper.

"Falin?" Suit asks as he reaches us. His smirk lifts into a full grin, showing off expensive-looking, stark-white veneers.

"Who are you?" I ask in my most menacing tone.

"Am I *interrupting* something?"

I move to stand but she grips my bad shoulder, digging her long nails in, and pushes me down. If I wasn't so distracted trying to figure out this sketchy guy, I'd be incredibly turned on right now. Ah, who am I kidding? I'm always half-mast when Falin's around.

"Not at all." Standing, she adjusts her skirt and squeezes herself between our stools. I reach my arm out, effectively blocking her. She lets out an unamused laugh. "Give me one sec to talk to my *friend* here. Meet you outside."

Suit's smile falters and he checks his watch. "Okay, but make it quick. I only have fifteen minutes left on my lunch break."

"I thought you were a CEO?" she asks, her brows narrowed in that fierce expression I've grown to obsess over.

He clears his throat. "I meant between meetings. I have a meeting with, uh, China soon."

Even my bullshit detector is on red alert. She gives him a hard look and sighs. "Just wait outside, Jake. I'll be right there."

Once *Jake* is out of earshot, she lets her grip loosen. I rub my shoulder. "Damn, that's gonna leave a mark." I raise a brow and add, "Not that I'm complaining."

If looks could kill, I'd be a pile of brittle bones.

She rubs her temples with the tips of her fingers, letting loose a long sigh. "Are you determined to interfere with every single guy I try to meet?"

I stare at her, blinking, as my jaw practically unhinges. "This was a hook-up?" Pointing out the door, I laugh. "You and that dude? Are you serious?"

She shoves my shoulders hard enough to knock me off-kilter and pushes past me. "And what's wrong with him, huh?" Her voice grows louder. "He has a cock and I bet he knows how to use it."

I laugh. "Right? Because mind-blowing sex is going to happen during his ten minute lunch break from his 'CEO job.' The dude has probably never made a woman come in his life. Jesus, Falin, I thought you were meeting someone for..." I lower my voice. "For the job."

"Why would you think that?" Her arms cross against her chest, pushing her tits together. I can't help but stare. Did I say half-mast? I'm dangerously close to a fully up the flagpole situation. "My eyes are up here!"

I blink and meet her stormy gaze. "I don't know. What else would you be doing?"

"Wow. So you think the only life I have has to involve you and the guys? Classic narcissist." She checks the time on her phone. "Jake has a few more minutes and I intend to *fully* use them. Do not follow me."

I grab her arm. "The hell you will. You think I'm gonna let you screw that lying piece of shit? Think again, sweetheart."

"You don't own me. I decide who I fuck, not you." Her tone is full of venom as she struggles to pull from my grip.

The bartender, who until this second I'd forgotten existed, clears her throat. "Is everything okay?"

"No," Falin says.

"Yes," I say.

"Um, I think you two should leave," she says tentatively. "I don't need any trouble here. It's only my first week."

"I was just leaving," Falin says, digging her nails into my hand.

"If she's leaving, I am too," I say.

"The fuck you are." She glances in the direction of the door as Jake sticks his head in. "I'm coming, Jake."

I chuckle. "That's the only time he's ever heard that phrase." That earns me a punch to the gut.

Okay, I'll take it.

"Why are you doing this?" Her tone softens but is still full of contempt.

Here's where I can come right out and say any number of the reasons why I can't let her hook-up with another person. None of which have anything to do with me trying to control her.

I like you. More than like... but I'm fucking terrified of hurting you. I'm not the "good guy" you think I am. I want you more than I've ever wanted anyone or anything. I can't look at you without wanting to sling you over my shoulder and drag you into my bed.

I struggle to find the right words as my mouth opens and closes uselessly. "I—uh—"

Before I can let out a coherent thought, Jake's head pokes back through the doorway. "Hey, um, I gotta get going. Hit me up later."

Her face falls, but only for a moment. I catch it though and I don't know if I want to kick myself or pat myself on the back now that I've effectively gotten rid of Suit. "Yeah, okay," she calls out to his retreating head.

"I'm sorry?" There's no way in hell I sound sincere. By the evil glare I get, I know she doesn't buy my apology. "What can I do?"

"Nothing. You've done more than enough already. Let's just go home so I can take out my frustrations on my keyboard."

"You can take your frustrations out on me." I don't mean for my words to drip with innuendo. They just naturally do when I'm talking to her.

She sizes me up, leaving me wondering what's going on inside her head.

CHAPTER SEVEN

FALIN

Since I was old enough to remember, probably shortly after my dad found me and my parents adopted me, I've had a hard time expressing my frustrations. An even tougher time calming myself down.

There were many attempts to curb my wild, volatile side during my childhood years, most brought about by my parents not knowing what to do with me. They signed me up for soccer, karate, archery, competitive swim... even a short stint in cheer. I can't say those were the worst ideas. Physical exertion was always good for clearing the mind. Except cheer... I hated that shit. They realized nothing worked, and after my mom died, he didn't care anymore.

But when I turned seventeen, I figured out that sex helped. Of course, in our small town, there were only so many people to choose from, so that form of recreation was limited.

Right now, looking at Jasper, all the horny feelings I felt an hour ago morph into a tingling wave of anger. Now that Jake's gone and I can't fuck my frustrations away, I'll need another way to calm down. There's no way I'll fool around with Jasper. He had his chance and turned me down. That night together wasn't even important enough for him to remember the next day. It doesn't matter that we have insane sexual tension. I care too much about myself to sink that low.

"Why are you scary quiet? And what's that face you're making?" His head tilts as he studies me.

There's only one thing I can do to calm my mind and ease my frustrations.

He follows me like a puppy across the street and down the block until we reach our apartment door. I purposely stay quiet, letting him stew. I hate to admit it, but not all the horny feelings left. His discomfort makes me wet. Knowing he has no idea what I'll do or say gives me that feeling of control I desperately crave. He feels bad for screwing up my afternoon? Well, I'll teach him not to interfere with my plans.

BLAKE KNOCKS lightly and cracks my bedroom door open while I circle Jasper. I keep my eyes fixed on my work, watching his shoulders tense with each step I take.

"Oh, wow," she says, drawing out the word. "I—Um, I'm sorry for interrupting."

"One second, I almost have it right," I say. "There." I let my hand fall, almost brushing Jasper's arm with the scalding hot glue gun, and face her. "What do you think?"

Her eyes widen as they dart between me and Jasper. "You're crafting."

"Yes," I say. "His mask needed some pizazz."

"What happened? You only craft when you're ready to commit murder."

I rummage through the open bin next to me, tossing random bits of ribbon and string onto the floor. A creak from behind makes me turn to find Jasper slowly rolling toward the door. "Where do you think you're going?"

"Nowhere. Just, uh, saying hi to my good buddy Blake." He lets out a nervous laugh while fidgeting with the ski mask covering his face.

"Good, I have these metal studs somewhere that would be perfect." My hands shake slightly as I dig deeper, scattering more supplies.

Blake grabs one of the kittens, stopping her from spreading even more rhinestones around the cluttered floor. "Maybe we should get ready for dinner?"

"I'm almost done." The words snap like a rubber band. My fingers press another rhinestone into place so hard there will definitely be an indent in his forehead.

Deep breaths.

It's Jasper and his presence. I should have crafted in peace and solitude instead of trying to torture him via hot glue gun.

I step back to examine my masterpiece and freeze. There, right in the center of his forehead, a crooked heart made of metal studs catches the light, surrounded by a scattering of broken rhinestones and splattered paint. A snort escapes before I can stop it. I double over, wiping tears from the corner of my eye.

"I swear I didn't do anything," Jasper mutters to Blake.

"Falin, sweetie... are you okay?" Blake places a comforting hand on my shoulder and I finally meet her gaze.

"Honestly... no." I gesture to Jasper's abomination of a mask covered in metal studs, rhinestones, and white fabric paint. "But this helps."

"Glad I could be of service?" he says, voice lilting up like it's a question. "I'm scared to look, but I should probably go put something on these hot glue welts. Blake, you have anything?"

"I think so. Let's go check the bathroom," Blake says.

Jasper eyes me tentatively while slowly raising himself from the chair. Am I really that scary that this giant grown man is afraid to get up? I mean, yes, I did threaten his manhood multiple times today. And yes, I scalded him with hot glue. And maybe I kind of, sort of, enjoyed it. But I'm not a monster.

"Go ahead," I say, plopping on the edge of my bed. He jumps up and leaves the room before I even get the words out. Blake lingers for a moment, nibbling her lower lip. "I'm fine. I promise."

"Okay. But this," she waves at the craft explosion, "we'll discuss later."

She cradles Mayhem to her chest and backs out of my room slowly, leaving me sitting in a mess of glittery shame.

As I pick up the remains of my meltdown, my mind replays the afternoon at the bar. Jasper stopping me from hooking up with Jake. As frustrated as I am, I didn't hate the way his voice dripped with dominance. I don't see that in him often. Not since Blake's birthday, when he stepped up to Ian. What ever happened to that guy? That night is fuzzy, but I remember how Jasper pressed me up against the side of our Uber, trapping me with his hard body. He wrapped my hair around his fist, tipping my face up to meet his lips.

Holy shit, I'm wet. Wet and thinking of Jasper.

Huffing, I slam the lid on the craft bin and shove it back under my bed. Time to get cleaned up for a night out, away from him.

CHAPTER EIGHT

JASPER

DO I WANT TO LEAVE FALIN IN THE STATE SHE'S IN? No,
not at all. Especially not to freeze my jewels off in Brooklyn.
But Blake's right. We can't put all our eggs in one basket. If
this New Year's party is a bust, putting all our eggs in that
basket will leave us fucked.

I'm waiting outside for Damon to finish saying goodbye
to Blake. It's been five minutes already and I'm sure it'll be
five more. The cold breeze against my face helps to relieve
the sting from where Falin burned me. Who knew a
goddamn hot glue gun could get that hot? Certainly not me.
I think the craftiest I've ever gotten was when I made a
laughable phallic vase for my mom in high school ceramics
class.

As I lean against the brick wall, my phone vibrates in
my pocket. Curious, I pull it out, spotting a notification
from Telegram.

You still want to meet up? I've got pinks.

It's the same guy I was supposed to meet the other
night. I pound my fist against the wall to keep myself from
cursing in front of an old lady walking by. Once she passes,

I push off from the wall and pace a few steps. It's been a couple days, and the worst of it has subsided. The shakes, the nausea, the skin crawling edge. But if anything, the craving to be numb has grown. I don't like feeling this raw. Like every word said, every second of me being powerless to help, burrows into my skin like a splinter that I can't pull free.

Fuck it.

I type out a quick response, telling him to meet me on the corner near the deli in ten minutes. Then I text Damon.

> Me: Hey, running to the deli for a coffee before we leave. You want anything?

While I wait for his reply, I pull out my frayed wallet and count the cash. One hundred and three dollars. It's not much, but it'll do. I'll have to talk to Leon about some side work. I can't rely on these stolen credit cards forever, and there's no way in hell I'm asking my parents for money. They've already cashed out their retirement and taken out a second mortgage on the house to pay for Ray and the other useless private investigators.

> D: Yeah, grab me a Monster. I'll meet you over there with the car.

Shit. That doesn't give me much time. This asshole better be quick. The last thing I need is Damon on my ass. By the time he leaves Blake, walks over to the lot where he parks his car, and meets me, I've got maybe twenty minutes, tops.

> Me: Got it.

A notification pops up from the dealer.

Be there in five.

Something's going my way today. That's a first.

I keep my head down and eyes up as I weave my way through a few slow walkers, probably tourists. I'm hyper-aware of every passing car, every siren in the distance, every stare that seems to linger on my face. The bells on a dry cleaner door jingle from a person exiting, making me jump out of my damn skin. I quicken my pace.

Goddamn paranoia.

Every step I take has my stomach clenching.

It'll be worth it when that blissful wave washes over me.

The meetup is quick. No more than two minutes. I barely even register what the guy looks like before he's taking off on foot down the street a hundred bucks richer. It doesn't matter, I got what I came for. Only three pills though. I'll have to make them last.

I grab our drinks from the deli, taking a plastic straw from the box on the counter. Once I'm back outside, I shove the energy drink cans in my hoodie pocket, and head to the bus bench around the corner. My hands tremble as I go through the motions. Unwrapping the straw and bending it at the end. Carefully slipping the pill into the bent end, and chewing it until it feels like a fine enough powder between the plastic. With a quick glance around to make sure no one is watching me, I snort, feeling the burn that hurts so good.

My eyes instantly water and my nose drips, but none of that matters. Fuck. The head rush feels incredible. My limbs are light, my head is clear. Everything slows down as I move toward the corner again. Like I'm wading through ankle deep water. The world gets softer somehow—the lights, the sounds, even my own thoughts, all wrapped in a warm blanket. I finally remember what it feels like to be okay. To be normal. To not worry about all the bullshit.

But deep in the back of my mind, that familiar whisper starts up again, like the nagging bitch it is. How long will this last? There's only two left now.

I push the thoughts away. Right now, I'm floating, untouchable, safe. At least until it wears off.

I shove the straw into my pocket, along with the baggie, and right on cue, Damon pulls up, the rumble of his engine louder than the thoughts in my mind. I rub my nose with the back of my hand and hop in the passenger seat.

"No Lee?" I ask, handing Damon his drink. I keep my eyes trained forward, hoping he won't notice my dripping nose.

"Nah, he wanted to stay back and research those politicians some more." Damon's knee vibrates in his seat as he speeds forward. He seems just as jumpy as I was ten minutes ago, and I think I know why.

"The girls leave yet?"

"Not yet. They were heading out right after I left." He glances in his rearview like he expects Blake to be behind us, waiting for him.

"They'll be fine, brother. Just relax."

Does my voice sound normal? I hope so.

"I can't relax. I fucking hate this city. Too many damn people everywhere." His fist tightens on the steering wheel as he barely misses hitting a jaywalker.

"I feel you, but hey, we got the night to ourselves. Been a while, huh? Let's turn up the music, open the windows, and make the best of it." I mess around with his stereo, the only upgraded thing in his classic Chevelle, but he swats my hand away. I raise it in mock surrender. "I forgot, no one touches your precious music."

"Damn right," he says, with a hint of a smirk. He pulls his phone from his back pocket and taps a few times. The opening of "A Day To Remember, The Downfall Of Us All" blasts through his speakers. This song always hyped us up, and right now is no different. I let my head nod back and forth as the wind whips my hair in front of my face. If I close my eyes, I can almost imagine we're back in college, when life was simple. I hold onto that feeling the entire way to Brooklyn.

"MY DICK IS GOING to get frostbitten," I groan, rubbing my cold hands together. The wind coming off the bay assaults the sliver of skin exposed in my mask.

Damon shakes his head. "I can't take you seriously in that thing."

The thing he's referring to is my now bedazzled balaclava. He laughed for a full minute straight when I first put it on. "Yeah, well, I volunteered yours for her next creative burst. You're welcome."

"Oh, hell no." He pokes at the studs along my forehead. "I'm hiding my mask when we get home. The whole point of masks is to be incognito. This," he gestures to my face, "is the opposite."

"What was I supposed to do? Tackle her to the floor, glue gun and all?" I smirk beneath my mask. "And hey, at least it's not boring anymore."

A gust rattles a nearby container and Damon instinctively grabs his gun. "It's nothing," I say.

Tonight has been a bust. The place is pretty dead—only a few ships getting unloaded. Looks like shipments of produce. That's going on far enough away from where we're camped out that we haven't gotten close to any employee. The only living things near us are a few relentless pigeons poking around a nearby dumpster. Between the cold, and Damon's shitty mood, I've lost most of my high. The rest of my pills gnaw at the back of my mind like an unscratched itch. My thoughts are swimming again, mixed with the weight of guilt sitting on my chest.

"I'm gonna take a walk around, see if we missed something west of here." I have to move my body, do something other than stand in the shadows.

"We should stay together. It's too quiet. I don't like it."

"Bro, this place is fucking huge. There's acres that we haven't checked. I know you want to focus on the area Lee told us to, but he's not always right." I don't know where this speech came from, but from the look in Damon's eyes, he might relent.

"Go ahead. I'm gonna check on Blake, but call me if you see anything." He pulls his phone out and holds the screen in front of his face to wake it up.

"Sounds good." I shove my freezing hands in my pockets and step toward the darkened space between containers. "Check on Falin too," I add at the last second. I don't wait for his teasing remark before I slip between containers.

This place is fucking creepy. I feel like I'm a character in a mafia movie, finding the perfect spot to off someone. Come to think of it, I'm going to stash that idea away for the next time I need to do that.

I make my way to a broken down crane sitting in an empty lot. Far enough away from Damon that he won't easily find me. Once I'm behind the wheels, I pull my pills out and crush up another, my heart pounding with each passing second.

I know I shouldn't. With the straw pinched between my fingers, I lean my head back and count down.

"Five." *What the fuck am I doing?*

"Four." *Is this who I want to be?*

"Three." *Damon might need me.*

"Two." *If I'm high, I'm no good to anyone.*

"One." *Fuck!*

As I bring the straw to my nostril, my phone vibrates in my pocket. In a split second decision, I throw the straw containing the crushed up pill as hard as I can into the darkness. My chest heaves and hands shake as I pull out my phone. It's Damon. "Hey, man, miss me already?"

"We need to go."

He sounds like something sharp is lodged in his throat. No hint of humor or casualness, just fear and urgency.

"What's wrong? Is it the girls?"

"It's Blake. She's in the ER."

What the fuck?

CHAPTER NINE

FALIN

I PACE THE WAITING AREA OF THE EMERGENCY ROOM, too scared that if I take a moment to breathe, somehow Blake will take a turn for the worse. Damon showed up a few minutes ago and I've never been so grateful to see him rush to Blake's side.

I lift my eyes to find Jasper maneuvering his large frame around a family who look to be in a similar state as me. When we lock eyes, I can't hold in the emotion anymore. It all comes pouring out like a fucking floodgate. Tears spill down my cheeks, smearing my makeup, and my body shakes uncontrollably.

This isn't me. I'm the one to keep my cool. But seeing Blake that way was the single worst thing I've ever seen in my life, and that's saying a lot.

Jasper quickens his pace and wraps me in his arms. His scent envelops me, calming my frayed nerves. "Shh," he whispers. "It's okay. She's going to be okay. You did so fucking good, Falin."

"I-It all happened so fast," I say as I suck a breath in through my clogged nostrils. "She was sitting across from me, laughing and talking and then... she just... stopped. Her hand went to her throat and she got this look in her eyes... this terrified look. I knew something was wrong when she started scratching at her neck. Red splotches... like welts. They spread on her skin. She tried to tell me something, but her voice came out all hoarse and wheezy. Her lips were swelling up right in front of me, and her face... God, her face got so puffy. She knocked over her water glass trying to stand, her legs couldn't keep her up."

Jasper's reassuring hold tightens. "I can't even imagine how scared you must have been."

I nod, burying my face in his chest and taking a deep breath before going on. "I screamed for help. Someone shouted about an EpiPen. Her face got so pale except for the welts. I can't stop thinking about her eyes—they were so wide, so scared as she slumped forward. That's when it all got crazy. People running, shouting, the manager calling 911, someone saying they were a doctor. I just... I just kept holding her hand. Even after they got her on the floor, even while they were jabbing her with the EpiPen. I kept telling her to stay with me, to keep breathing, that help was coming. The minutes before the ambulance arrived felt like hours. I've never felt so helpless in my life."

"I know, baby. You did so good. I'm so fucking proud of you." He rubs my back with his palm, sending a shiver through me. I didn't know how much I needed this until now. The praise, the comfort, it's everything.

"How did she look when you were back there?" I had to step out when Damon and Jasper arrived. I needed a minute and there's only so much space in the small curtained off area. When he doesn't answer immediately, I back away to look into his eyes. They're wide and vacant. I'm sure I look just as scared. "Still the same?"

"I don't know how she looked when it first happened." He swipes his palm down his face. "She's still covered in hives and puffy. They've got her on oxygen and an IV. I'm sure it'll be a long night."

Our conversation is interrupted by a man in scrubs yelling from the check-in area. "You can't go in there, sir! You need to sign in!"

I look up to find Leon, pushing his way past multiple employees. "Shit," I say. "Did anyone call him?"

Jasper hurries over, and I watch him smooth the employees over with a few words. He talks animatedly to Leon, gesturing toward the corridor right off the waiting area. I should go to them, fill Leon in, but I can't bring my feet to move. Leon's shoulders slump and he chews his bottom lip while he takes in what happened tonight. The weight of almost losing Blake. Jasper talks to the employee again and within seconds, Leon is led away toward Blake's side.

I grip the arm of the chair next to me as another bout of shivers make their way through my body. Jasper's hand wraps around my waist, once again holding me up. "I've got you. Come on, I'll take you home. Damon and Leon are here with her."

"No," I argue. "I'm fine, just cold."

He tightens his hold around my waist with one hand and tilts my chin up to meet his eyes with the other. "You're not fine. None of us are. It's okay to rest. She's in good hands."

She's in good hands.

I let those words mull around in my mind. A few weeks ago, I would have immediately protested. There was no way these three guys could possibly be good enough to take care of Blake. But right now, I have no argument. She *is* in good hands. Damon would spill his own blood if it kept Blake safe. And Leon, as quiet as he is, I know he cares about her in his own way. Jasper does too. And really, what can I do that the doctors and nurses aren't already doing? I'd just be in the way.

I nod slowly, and the corner of Jasper's lip tips up. I hate to admit it but that small smile sends a pang to my chest.

"Let's go say goodnight," he says, leading me out of the waiting area toward the beds. "I'll get the keys to Leon's bike."

IT'S BEEN a long time since I've ridden on the back of a bike. I'd forgotten how incredible it feels. That surge of adrenaline as the bike speeds up, the wind whipping against my chest and helmet, that feeling of complete freedom. The engine vibrates through my entire body, a steady rumble that matches my racing heartbeat. With my arms wrapped around Jasper's waist and knees pressed firmly against his hips, I'm all too aware of how good it feels to let myself touch him. To have an excuse to hold him close. His body radiates warmth against the cool night air, flooding my senses. After what I witnessed tonight, I need him more than I want to admit.

When he pulls up to the curb outside our apartment building and turns off the engine, I feel my muscles tense up again. I hesitate to get off, knowing that for the first time in weeks, I'll be walking into complete silence. Jasper pulls his mask off, and holds his hand out. "I got it," I say.

Accepting any more comfort from him might give him the wrong idea. And tonight, after everything, I don't have it in me to argue or push him away if he relents. I'd thoroughly soak up anything he'd give me and that would just complicate things.

"You need help with the helmet?" he asks, reminding me that I still have it on. I shake my head, pull it off, and hand it over. Once I swing my leg over the bike and stand on hard earth again, every ounce of energy I have disappears. I wobble, grabbing onto his chest for balance.

His palms wrap around my shoulders, steadying me. "Shit. I'm fine," I say.

"Clearly you're not." I shrug to loosen his grip, but he holds firm. "Come on, Trouble. Or do you want me to carry you? Promise I won't grab your ass... unless you ask nicely."

I scoff, and step toward the door. "Don't even think about it. Remember what I can do with a switchblade."

As we climb the stairs, I feel his gaze burning into my back. Or maybe that's just my body on fire from how much I'd love to stab him. Or fuck him. One of those... I haven't decided which tonight.

The kittens run to us, meowing, and rubbing against our legs. "You hungry?" Jasper asks.

"They're not you, they don't need to eat seventeen times a day," I say. I swear Jasper's been feeding them every hour.

"How dare you body shame them," he says as he picks up Havoc. "You're growing girls, aren't you?" And there's that baby voice again.

"That was a dig at you, not them." I rub my eyes and grab a water from the fridge. "I'm going to go shower and lay down, but first, let's text the guys and check in."

He opens a new bag of kitten kibble and pours some into their bowl. "Go ahead, I'll text them and let you know when you're done." I stand rooted in place, watching him feed and pet the kittens. He pulls out his phone, and looks up, realizing I'm still there. "Need help in the shower too? I volunteer, and you don't even have to ask me to grab your ass. I'll do that and more."

I snap out of it and give him the finger. "Be right back. And make sure they tell Blake that I love her."

"Anything else, dear?"

God, he's irritating. "Yes, go play in traffic."

"Might be too late at night for that. Will have to wait for rush hour." He smirks and turns away, leaving me scowling at his retreating frame.

I take an extra long shower, letting the hot water loosen some of the tension in my shoulders. It helps, even if only for a few minutes. Wrapped in a towel that barely covers my ass, I open the door, letting the steam billow out.

"Jesus Christ," I yell, almost losing the grip on my towel. Jasper's leaning against the wall opposite the bathroom, waiting for me. "Why are you standing there like that?"

He shrugs. "Why not?"

"Well... don't. It's creepy." I pull my towel tighter and head toward my room, Jasper following close behind. "Did the guys answer?"

"Yeah, no changes. They're keeping her for the night to watch for a secondary reaction. I guess that can sometimes happen hours later. Leon answered the text. I think Damon's still losing his mind." His voice hitches, sending a flutter through my chest.

"Thanks for checking in." We linger at my bedroom door, both drained from the day, but not quite ready to breathe yet. I don't know whether to feel relieved that all is well, or hang on to the anxiety. My body wants to decide for me—worry. "Let me know if you hear anything else."

"Yeah, of course," he says. He turns to go, but pauses. "Try and get some sleep, okay?"

He sounds so gentle, so caring, that I want to pull him

by his shirt and throw him onto my bed. But I don't. I nod, and close the door before I do something I'll regret.

Sleep won't come no matter how hard I try. Every time I close my eyes, I see Blake's terrified face. We're always so careful with her allergies—checking labels twice, grilling waiters, carrying her EpiPen. Yet somehow, I failed her today. I can't believe I let this happen.

Needing a distraction, I grab my phone from the floor where it's charging. Not having a bedside table isn't something I'll ever grow accustomed to... but at least my bed is near an outlet.

The pull to analyze that party invitation is strong, but work mode means thinking and thinking means no sleep. I dive into mindless scrolling instead.

Teenager lip-syncing. *Swipe.*

Amateur standup. *Swipe.*

Baby hippo learning to swim... Okay, that's fucking adorable.

I swipe up and something familiar catches my eye. My heart stops. What in the hell? Someone recorded us at the restaurant. There's Blake laying on the floor. Me kneeling beside her, holding her hand. That doctor who appeared out of nowhere like a guardian angel.

The view count makes me dizzy. It's got over one hundred thousand views and counting.

I jump out of bed and race down the hall toward Jasper and Leon's room. Before I reach it, I hear the shower going. "Jasper!" I call from outside the door. No answer. I knock and call again. Is he alive in there? The water doesn't muffle sound *that* much. "Ah, screw it," I say as I twist the handle and push the door open.

Steam escapes the small space as I step inside. My eyes dart from the closed shower curtain to the clothes scattered across the floor to a small plastic baggie on the vanity. My blood runs cold. I snatch up the pill. The video will have to wait.

The curtain rings screech against the rod. I meet Jasper's eyes right before my gaze betrays me, dropping to his wet, sculpted body. Holy crap, he looks good.

"See something you like?" His smirk fades as he takes in the baggie in my shaky hand.

"What the hell is this?" I hold the bag up in front of him and watch his eyes shift to the wet tile floor. The silence stretches until I can't stand it. "Jasper? Talk to me."

"It's nothing," he finally answers as he reaches for the towel on the rack. "As much as you yelling at me normally turns me on, can we just *not* right now? I... can't."

I close my eyes, let out a long breath and release some of my initial anger. "Fine, but you're not getting this back." I shove the baggie in my pocket until I can get rid of it later. His head snaps up, his eyes wide. Something in my chest cracks from his look. When I speak again, I soften my tone. "I'm here for you, okay? You can do this."

"You don't know that." With the towel wrapped low on his hips, he bends to pick up his clothes.

I place my hand on his bare shoulder, offering some connection, hoping he can feel the truth in my words. His hand covers mine, warm and calloused from years of playing guitar. "Yes, I do."

We stand frozen in that moment, the steam curling around us mirroring the cloud of emotions in my mind. There's too much that we refuse to talk about. Fear and hope and want all tangled up in a jumble of unspoken truths.

His thumb traces small circles on my skin, and I can't

tell if he's trying to comfort me or himself. Maybe both. "Okay," he finally whispers.

My forgotten phone buzzes, breaking us apart. I remember the reason I came in here. "Shit," I say. "I need to show you something." A ghost of a grin lines his face and I know where his mind is going. "Not that. How are you thinking about anything even remotely sexual right now? You know what? I don't need to know the inner workings of your mind. Just look."

I restart the video, taking notice of the additional fifty thousand views and dozens more comments from when I first watched it. As much as I want to turn away, I force myself to watch the entire thing again with Jasper.

"Shit," he mutters once it's played through. "Hold on."

He rushes out of the bathroom, his towel barely holding on, and grabs his phone from his bed. "What are you doing?" I ask, utterly confused.

He taps away at the screen and brings up a video. When I look closer, I see it's a local news channel that does live streams and recaps. "If it's gone viral, there's a chance the news picked it up. Did you see any press there when you got outside?"

I rack my brain but the events of the night are such a blur. There were people everywhere, everything happened so fast. "I don't know. Maybe. This is bad."

As the words leave my lips, a headline flashes across the screen, along with a video of me and Blake getting into the ambulance.

Drama At Downtown Bistro: Off-Duty Doctor And Restaurant Patrons Rally To Save Woman In Anaphylactic Shock

"So fucking bad," he says.

CHAPTER TEN

JASPER

BLAKE GOT HOME AN HOUR AGO, LOOKING AND FEELING much better. The swelling in her face has gone down but some of the welts still remain.

Falin and I spiraled last night, going back and forth on whether or not we should tell the guys about the news head-lines. I wanted to, but she argued that they had enough on their minds and didn't need the added stress. She wasn't entirely wrong, but I know my brothers. They'd want to know.

When she took a bathroom break, I texted them from my burner. As expected, they flipped out.

With Falin keeping Blake comfortable, the three of us opt to climb up to the rooftop to talk. The cool winter air chills my face, but it's exactly what I need.

"There's nothing you can do to scrub that shit off the internet?" Damon asks Leon. The steam from his cup of coffee billows around his face.

"No. Plus, the damage has already been done. I can't make people unsee it." Leon grips the metal handrail, staring off at the dusting of snow on the rooftop across from ours.

"What are the odds that *they've* seen it?" I ask. I want to be optimistic, but by the look on both their faces, I'm the only one. "No one really watches the news anymore anyway. And we don't even know if that King asshole is looking for us. He could have moved on."

"That's not a gamble I'm willing to take. Until we figure this out, I want Blake home with at least one of us at all times," Damon says.

My eyes dart to Leon while I wait for him to acknowledge what Damon said. He finally looks up. "We can't abandon our reason for being here, and there's that gala. Blake will fight us on this."

"I don't care if I have to chain her to the bed. She's not fucking going. The doctors said she needs to rest for a week. Added stress on her body could land her back in the hospital." Damon scrubs a hand over his face and paces a few steps.

"I'll go," I say. "Schmoozing a bunch of rich pricks is what I do best." Damon stops pacing to stare at me while Leon chews his lip. I wasn't imagining it. They really think I'm useless. Aggravated, I ask, "What's with the looks?"

"Are you sure you're up for this?" Damon asks. His tone loses its edge. "Don't think we haven't noticed the pills, J. You haven't been at your best."

"Why are you just telling me this now?" I let out a harsh laugh. "It doesn't matter. Yeah, I've been taking pills. Yeah, I've been off my game. But schmoozing these assholes is muscle memory at this point. Unless you've got someone else who can pass for Blake's brother while also searching the place for answers?"

Damon shoots Leon a look that only pisses me off more. "Lee?"

"If I could I would, but don't think I can pass for a middle-aged white dude, even if I wear a mask."

"Right," Damon huffs. "I didn't think of that."

"I'll be fine," I say. When Leon raises his brow, I add, "I'm off the pills. Falin found my stash and tossed it last night. I want to do this. Fucking need to."

"I guess we don't really have a choice," Damon says. "But you'll have to take Falin as your date."

My stomach does this weird flip thing at the thought of Falin beside me all night in some fancy dress, which immediately pisses me off because I need to keep any feelings I have for her at bay. She's a complication I can't get involved in, especially when I'm trying to keep my head straight. But there's also this traitorous part of me that wants her close. That wants to listen to her voice in the back of my head that tells me to be good, to get my shit together.

"She'll just slow me down," I say, but it comes out weaker than I mean it to. "You really want to put her in the middle of this?"

"She's already in the middle of it," Damon says. "And the invitation is for Brennan and his 'wife.' It'll be suspicious if you show up alone."

"I don't like this, but I can't see another option." Leon turns to me. "I'll be in your ear the entire time. And I can park nearby, like always."

"I already told you I want to go. It's bringing Falin that worries me." I rub my palms together trying to get some warmth back into my tingling fingers. Leon must notice, since he asks if I want to go back inside. "I'm fine. Let's finish figuring this shit out."

By the time we make the bare bones of a plan and head

back to the apartment, my extremities ache from the cold. For the first time since I got shot, I finally feel useful, and that fills me with hope I thought I'd lost all together.

Leon and I head into the room we share to get cleaned up and changed. "We have a few days to prepare," he says. "We can't afford for this to go south. They find out you're not Brennan, and I don't know what will happen."

"Lucky for us, we have someone who knew Brennan well," I say. "I'll just find out as much as I can about him from Blake. I know it'll be hard for her to talk about him, but maybe it'll make her feel needed."

He eyes me with an all knowing stare. "I'm glad you're doing this. I didn't want to tell D, but I think this is what you need. Plus, we both know he's shit at parties."

"Can't make small talk to save his life," I add. My chest loosens as we laugh.

"Don't worry about Falin. She's tough. I think she'll be an asset." He grabs some clean clothes from the closet and heads to the door, ready to shower for the day. "If you two can keep from fighting for one night."

"It's not me," I say, putting my hands up in surrender. "I don't know what I do to irk her."

That's a lie. I love to fuck with her. It's what I live for lately.

He smirks. "You're so full of shit, mate."

I shrug. "I thought she liked me."

"You two need to fuck already. I'm tired of the tension around here."

He says that as if I'm the only one with the power to make that decision. "I thought you were against us being together? If I remember correctly, you said and I quote, 'If you and Falin start fucking, I swear to Christ I'm going to hurl myself off this building.' And something else about being the only one alone. Speaking of, why haven't you dated? Or at least found a hook-up?"

The teasing light in his eyes vanishes and his smile fades. "That's the last thing on my mind."

I instantly feel like shit for bringing it up. I guess I didn't realize what a sore subject it is for him. "Sorry, man. Not my business anyway."

He looks away toying with the clothes in his hands before silently heading out the door and down the hallway to the bathroom.

Now that I'm alone again, my mind won't stop bringing up flashes of the pills. I close my eyes and they're beneath my lids. I open them and they dart around the room, searching. I know I don't have anything, but my brain won't accept that as an answer. How the hell did I let it get this bad? It's no wonder the guys won't trust me with anything, I'm a fucking mess.

I pull out my phone and cycle through the same three apps multiple times, hoping something will pull me in and grab hold of my attention. Anything that my mind can latch onto to dull the craving. Then Falin's laugh travels through the plaster walls. It's a sound I could listen to all day, every day. Her husky voice starts rough-edged and crackling, but as the laugher takes hold of her entire body, it grows lighter. Pure unfiltered joy. Wild, like lightning I could catch and keep it in a jar.

I spot my reflection in the darkened screen and notice I've cracked a smile—slight, but it's there. She's pulled it from me with nothing more than the sound of her laugh through the wall.

Tossing my phone on my bed, I follow her voice to Blake and Damon's room. No idea what I'll do when I reach it, but that doesn't matter. I just need to be near her.

Once I'm outside the open bedroom door, I stand to the side and listen in on their conversation.

"I can't believe that happened," Blake says, laughter playing at the edge of her voice.

"Oh, I'd never lie about something that humiliating. Food poisoning is a bitch, but hey, at least I have a funny story now." The bed creaks as one of them adjusts their position. "But trust me, as horrible as almost crapping myself during a date was, there's been others that have bruised me even worse."

She almost shit herself... Now that's fucking funny. Too bad I missed the whole story. I crane my neck, making sure I don't miss a word from her lips.

"Like? Come on, you have to tell me now that you brought it up. Don't be a tease." Blake's playful tone has the corner of my lip pull up in a smirk. She's got one thing right... Falin loves to tease.

After a few seconds of quiet, Falin finally answers. "Another time. I should go get us something to eat so you can take your next dose of meds."

"Fal," Blake pleads. "What is it?"

"It's nothing, Bee. You rest. I'll just be a minute."

Whatever was in her mind couldn't be nothing. I know her voice, the way her husky tone drops low, turning hollow with unspoken thoughts. I'm so caught up in my head, I don't think to move away from the door. Or maybe subconsciously I don't want to. Either way, as Falin leaves the room, she stops with barely an inch between us.

"Jesus Christ! Jasper, you scared me. Why the hell are you creeping outside Blake's door?" My eyes follow the path of her palm as she rests it over her chest. The swell of her breasts rises and falls rapidly as she gets her bearings. Fuck, I'd love to pin that palm over her head and bury my face in her chest. "Hello? Did you need something?"

I blink and realize she's talking to me. *Whoops.* I can't help myself from daydreaming about her incredible body. Especially when she's this goddamn close to me.

"I need a lot of things. Thanks for asking." I force myself to meet her gaze. Sharp narrowed eyes. Of course. I can't help but smirk.

"Like a few extra brain cells?" She brings her arms across her chest, pushing her tits up, testing every ounce of restraint I possess.

I step closer, crowding her against the wall. My heart pounds and senses feel alive for the first time since I last used. It's her... my trouble maker. She makes the blood roar through my veins. Makes my vision clear. Hell, she's the only one who makes me feel anything strong enough to stop the cravings.

"Jasper?" Her voice catches in her throat and I love it. I love that I'm rattling her as much as she rattles me.

"Yes, Trouble?" I say, my voice dropping low as I drink her in. Those smokey eyes that match the rasp of her voice. The scattering of freckles across the bridge of her nose. Those perfect fucking lips. Each second with her this close pulls at something primal within me, makes me want to abandon everything and take what I want. Before I can think better of it, I lean in slightly, drawn to her like a moth to a flame. My gaze drops to her lips, lingering there with clear intent. Then her palms come up to my chest, the heat of her skin searing through my shirt. I freeze, unsure if I should step back or lean into her touch. She's not pushing me away, but she's not *not* pushing me away.

"Hey, I was thinking burgers for dinner," Damon says from the kitchen. He's coming toward us from the sound of his footsteps, but I don't move. Falin's chest heaves and she shoves me backwards just as Damon rounds the corner in the hallway. He stops and his gaze darts between us. "You guys good with burgers later?"

Falin nods and I let out a low "Yeah." Damon doesn't question what we were doing in the hall, but I can see that knowing look in his eye.

"Did you talk to her about the party?" Damon asks, gesturing toward Falin.

"Party? You mean the gala?" she asks, turning from me to Damon.

"Guess not," Damon says, looking mildly uncomfortable. He cranes his neck to peek at Blake, and quiets his voice. "Jasper can fill you in, but we have a plan. I just—I don't think Blake will like being left out, but she needs to be kept safe. We have no idea what we're walking into."

Just then, Havoc scampers down the hallway and into Blake's room with the other kitten close behind. Falin keeps her attention on Damon. "Can't you tell me now? What plan?"

Damon hesitates, but I have no reason to. She needs to know. "You're my date for New Year's Eve. Excited?"

The annoyed look she gives me makes me instantly hard, not that I wasn't there already. "What is he talking about?" she asks Damon.

"The gala, we need you to go with Jasper. Now that Blake's been flashed all over the media, we can't risk her leaving. I didn't want her to in the first place, but we all know how she fought that. We need a Mr.," he points to me and then to Falin, "and *Mrs.* Brennan Whitaker, if we're going to pull this off."

My lips curve upward without realizing. But I guess I'm not surprised. No part of me is dreading this gala with

Falin. I'm almost hoping some shit goes down so I have an excuse to get out some aggression. As long as Falin's safe, of course, but I'd never let anything happen to her. I just need this—the social energy, the adrenaline coursing through my veins.

Falin presses her lips together and shrugs. "I don't know why I hadn't thought of this myself." Her eyes meet mine, gaze fixed. "I'm in."

CHAPTER ELEVEN

FALIN

Every word of caution that I've heard from Blake and the guys plays on a loop through my mind as we pull up the winding drive toward the massive stone mansion owned by the Fairfax's. It has to be the most opulent home I've ever seen, yet it looms ahead through the gently falling snow like a monster lying in wait.

We pass a circular fountain, ice-covered and dusted white. The statue's vacant eyes seem to follow mine, a warning in them to stay put. I can't do that, even if I wanted to.

I keep my eyes trained ahead at the warm light spilling from the tall windows, and the smoke drifting from one of the chimneys blending into the darkening winter sky. As we approach the main entrance, I see the other cars ahead—all black luxury vehicles, making Damon's 1970 muscle car stand out like a sore thumb.

"Are you ready?" Jasper asks, his voice lower than normal. He seems to have soaked up some of the anxiety that's been radiating off of me since this afternoon, when all of this became real.

I'd shopped for the gown and mask. I'd gone over the details of the plan with the guys. I'd even voiced all my concerns to Blake in private, except for those nagging personal thoughts about a night alone with Jasper, pretending to be his wife. Those were living rent free in my head—little images of Jasper in a black tux and mask, offering me his arm like my own personal dark knight. I know it's ridiculous, but the thoughts persist, no matter how many times I try to shove them away.

I've never done anything like this before. Dangerous activities that were actually quite safe, sure—like skydiving, or cliff jumping, or even picking up random guys in bars. But nothing like walking into a lion's den with a gun strapped to my thigh and my trusty switchblade hidden in my cleavage.

I've been behind a desk, where I have complete control over my surroundings. Where the scariest thing that's happened to me was my hard drive crashing. I breathe in a large gulp of air, letting Jasper's fresh scent calm my nerves. "Yeah, I'm ready. Are you? You've been quiet for the last twenty minutes."

He nods slowly. "You don't have to do this, you know? I can go in there alone." His eyes meet mine, sincere and pleading. If he thinks I'd bail on the group, then he doesn't know me like I think he does. Once I put my mind to something, I follow through, nevermind if it tests my boundaries or even scares the hell out of me. I've chosen to be a part of this team—to help them bring these assholes down and find Jasper's sister, and that's what I'll do.

"No, I want to do this." Hearing my own voice say those words strengthens my resolve. "Plus, you'll need me in there," I add in a teasing tone.

He leans closer, the deep rumble of his voice sending a

shiver down my body straight to my core. "Oh really? Want to bet on that?"

"That I'll end up saving your ass? I like my odds." I cross my arms and lift my chin, the picture of confidence. Am I bluffing? Yes. But he doesn't need to know that.

He plays with a strand of hair that hangs loose at my shoulder before brushing it back. My breath hitches, but I force myself to stay still, to not let him know how much his touch affects me. "And what should we wager?"

I think for a moment. What would I want from Jasper Shea if I could have anything? Then it comes to me. "Winner gets to ask one question, the loser has to answer honestly. No bullshit."

This could bite me in the ass, but maybe it'll help me get closure about Blake's birthday. Knowing he can't feed me some excuse or lie about why he turned me down. Why he hasn't said a word about that night. I'd finally find out if he really doesn't remember us hooking up, or if it's more than that.

He blinks, his deep blue eyes zeroing in on my lips, before meeting my gaze. "You sure about that, Trouble?"

"That's the only thing I want."

"Okay then." He holds his hand out. "Shake on it?"

I take his hand, the rough calluses of his palm and warmth of his skin sending a rush through me that I desperately try to hide behind a confident smile. The reality of what we're walking into leaves my mind as his fingers envelop my hand, gently squeezing. A silent gesture that says *I'm right here with you, we've got this.*

A younger looking man dressed in a warm winter coat with reflective stripes down the arms taps on the outside of the window, and I pull my hand from his grasp. "You have your weapons strapped in?" he whispers.

I pat my upper thigh, feeling the outline of Damon's gun. "Yes."

I roll down the window using the manual knob, and the man peeks his head in. "Good evening. I presume you're here for the gala?"

"Yes, my wife and I were invited personally," Jasper says.

"May I see your identification?" Jasper's features arrange themselves into a mask of entitled annoyance, and I have to admit he's surprisingly good at channeling trust fund brat. We planned for this though, and I'm so glad that we did. "I'm sorry, sir. It's a mandatory precaution set by Mr. Fairfax."

After some grumbling, Jasper produces the false ID that Leon got for him from his jacket pocket. "What are they hiding in there? The Hope Diamond?" Jasper jokes, a slippery edge to his voice.

"I apologize again, Mr. Whitaker." He hands Jasper the ID back. "And I'm assuming this is... *Mrs. Whitaker?*" The way he asks has me wondering if we're not the only ones pretending to be husband and wife tonight.

Jasper rests a palm on my thigh, scorching the skin beneath the silky fabric of my dress. "Of course. My lovely wife, Mischa."

I can barely concentrate on their exchange with his hand so high up on my thigh.

"Give me one moment, please." The man pulls a device out of his pocket and scrolls, likely checking the guest list.

I whisper to Jasper. "You can move your hand now."

He gives a gentle squeeze, spreading his long fingers out so they cover the majority of my thigh. "I don't know, *wife*. I think we should play it safe until he comes back."

"You know I have a blade between my tits, right? Don't

make me pull it out." Whispering ruins my chance of sounding as menacing as I intended, but I can't risk raising my voice with that guy in earshot.

Jasper lets out a low laugh. "Don't tease me like that."

"There's something wrong with you," I say through gritted teeth, and shove his hand off me. In the seconds it takes for the guy to direct us to valet parking, I picture all the ways I'd love to make Jasper unravel.

Paddle his bare ass.

Paint him in hot wax until he learns to ask nicely before his hands wander.

Edge him until he's crying like a baby, begging to come.

I smile, and it must look evil. He'll never know the thoughts behind it, or the way heat pools low in my belly.

"You don't know the worst of it, sweetheart." He turns the wheel, driving slowly toward the rest of the guests exiting their cars. "Let's do this thing. Turn on your earpiece so Leon can hear you."

I pull the small device out of my palm-sized clutch purse and fit it into my ear the way Leon showed me earlier. I click the miniscule button, and adjust my hair over my ear. "Leon? Can you hear me?"

"Copy," Leon responds, sounding official. Once that's in place, I pull on my mask. It's black to match my gown, with silver embellishments that I added myself the other night. I'm happy with how it came out. At a passing glance, it almost looks expensive.

"All good?" Jasper asks, as he adjusts his own communication device and black mask. He'll have to be careful not to get too close to anyone, as his hair doesn't fully cover his ear like mine. I nod while he whispers to Leon.

Once we're ready, I move to open my car door, but his hand shoots out and grasps my gloved wrist. "Let me."

Huffing, I nod. Might as well let him try to act like a gentleman. It'll be interesting to see, at least.

He steps out of the car, and as he passes by the headlights, I'm struck by how damn hot he looks in his tux. It could have been custom-tailored just for him, the fabric hugging every muscled curve of his chest and arms as if straining to contain him. The pants hardly restrain his thick thighs. I can only imagine how good his ass looks in them. Shit, am I drooling?

He opens my door, letting in a blast of cold air that chills me to the bone. My breath hitches but I force myself to climb out of the car, taking Jasper's outstretched hand. "Thanks."

"Of course," he says, flashing me an obnoxiously gorgeous smile.

He hands the valet the car key and we follow another couple into the house. For a girl like me, who grew up in rural Ohio and has bounced from city apartment to city apartment, walking into a home like the one towering in front of us is absolutely wild. But then again, my life's been a wild ride since Jasper's come into it.

We're asked for our names again at the door, but this time the whole ordeal takes less than a minute. No one questions us about our identities, at least not yet. I release a breath, feeling the tension I've been holding leave my shoulders.

"We're in," Jasper whispers to Leon. He takes my hand and we follow the couple ahead of us down a wide hall lined with gilded oil paintings and brocade window treatments toward the sound of instrumental music.

"Do you find it odd that apart from the music, it's super quiet?" Jasper asks. I'm impressed by his observation skills. I hadn't noticed until he said something, too busy taking in the artwork covering almost every spare inch of wall.

"I didn't before, but I do now. Do you think we're early?"

He checks his watch and shrugs. "We're right on time. Maybe in their world, that's early. I guess we'll see." As we round a corner, a woman appears seemingly out of nowhere. She's not wearing a mask, and is dressed in black pants and a white button down. Must be a staff member.

"Right this way," she says, in a singsong voice, gesturing toward the large door ahead. I decide to take a chance and talk to her.

"Are we early to the party?" I let out a nervous laugh. "It's our first time here."

Her eyes dart between us and she smiles, definitely a practiced expression. "Not at all. You're right on time. Here you are."

She opens the door and it's as if we're looking at an entirely different space. A jazz quartet plays upbeat music from the corner of the large ballroom. Rhythmic bass line and piano melodies float above the hum of conversation. Crystal chandeliers cast a warm, intimate glow throughout the space, almost fooling me into believing the people here are warm too. About fifty of them, masked and elegantly dressed, cluster in groups around high cocktail tables draped with midnight blue linens, while silver and gold New Year's decorations shimmer throughout. Ice sculptures glitter on silver stands near the busy bar, and servers walk around holding trays packed with delicious looking hors d'oeuvres. The room manages to feel overwhelmingly huge and intimate at once, with plush seating areas tucked into alcoves and corners, offering quieter spaces away from the main floor.

Normally, I'd appreciate that about a party, but now I just think of all the nooks and crannies Jasper and I will have to keep eyes on.

"So what should I look for?" Other than getting in, the guys didn't have much of a plan.

"Nothing in particular. We'll know when we see it. Let's get a drink." With my hand still folded into his, he leads me toward the bar. I know I shouldn't drink. My reflexes need to be in top form, but it is a party, and I don't want to look out of place. Maybe just one to help settle my nerves.

Jasper orders for me—a vodka cranberry with a splash of seltzer. My usual drink. I pull my hand out of his and run my fingers over the edge of the bar. "How did you know?"

His eyes shine brightly through the mask as he turns to look at me. "What?"

"My drink. That's what I always order."

We're interrupted before he can answer. A broad-shouldered man knocks into Jasper, making him stumble against the bar. His face is fully concealed by a silver mask, the only visible features being his dark hair with graying temples, nearly black eyes, and hard lips.

"Sorry." He sticks a hand out to steady Jasper. "Party just started and I'm already tripping to get to the bar. Don't let the wife know." He laughs too hard at his own joke.

"No harm done." Jasper nods and smiles in a perfunctory way, but I notice how his eyes wander, assessing the man without making it obvious.

After ordering a whiskey neat, the man turns back to us, giving us a once-over. "I don't believe we've met." He states it as a fact, not a question, before sticking his hand out toward Jasper again, completely ignoring me. Not that I want his attention, but it's hard to keep my eyes from rolling with how blatantly sexist this man is. "Harrison Fairfax, party host and owner of two left feet apparently."

Ah, so this is Mr. Fairfax. He looks harmless enough, but there is something about his demeanor that makes me want to run for the hills. Jasper shakes his hand, slipping back into his Mr. Charming act. "Thanks for having us. What are you drinking?"

Avoiding giving his name. Nice touch.

Jasper leans against the bar, pulling Fairfax's attention away from me. I figure now is a better time than any to do a lap around.

With my drink in hand, I stick to the perimeter, taking note of my surroundings. The first thing I notice is the lack of women here. Other than servers bustling around, I've only spotted two or three other women compared to at least thirty men. That's a red flag if I've ever seen one.

"Leon, you there?" I try to speak without making it obvious. When he doesn't answer right away, I bring my drink close to my lips, using that as a way to cover my mouth and raise my voice. "Leon?"

Still nothing.

"Shit." There's got to be something up with the connection. "Jasper, can you hear me?"

Nothing. Not even static.

And this is why there always needs to be a backup plan and then a backup to the backup plan. It's fine though. There's nothing so terrible going on that I need to panic. I'll find the restroom and see if I can figure out what's up. It actually feels good to have something to focus on. Tech, I can do. Mingling with creepy dudes, hard pass.

It doesn't take me long to find the restroom. Once I'm in, I remove my mask and take way too much time trying to figure out the problem. So much time that I jump out of my skin when someone knocks at the door.

Frustrated that I'm unable to fix the problem, I shove the earpiece into my purse, adjust my mask, and slip out past a grumbling man. "It's all yours."

"About time," he says.

"Friendly crowd," I murmur as the bathroom door slams shut inches from my face.

I spot Jasper talking animatedly with a group of men around a cocktail table. They're laughing about who knows what. How does he make it look so easy? I down the rest of my drink in two gulps and make my way toward the bar. He finds me in the crowd, his eyes locking onto mine, sending a spark through my veins.

He places a hand on one of the men's shoulders and excuses himself with a smile. Each step he takes in my direction has my chest loosening and my heart beating extra fast. I look closely at the ice in my glass to keep myself from staring.

As he reaches me, the music changes tempo and a voice sounds above the noise of conversation. "This one is for the couples. Come on up to the dance floor." The band begins to play "At Last." As the vocals drift out in a sultry, almost hypnotic way, a couple nearby gravitates toward the dance floor. I know there won't be many couples out there, and already all eyes are on that lone pair, but when Jasper holds his hand out to me, brow raised and corner of his lip turned up, I don't hesitate.

"Dance with me, Trouble."

CHAPTER TWELVE

FALIN

His hand settles on the small of my back, warm and reassuring, and we weave through a few occupied tables to the dance floor in front of the band. There's no time for me to take stock of how I feel or if I even want to dance with Jasper. He takes charge, pressing against me so close that the fresh scent of his cologne invades my senses, as he wraps both arms around my waist. We begin to sway to the music, and I close my eyes to try and ground myself back to reality. I can't push him away, not here and not now, when we're on display for all these vultures to gape at.

His lips brush the top of my head, sending a shiver down my spine. "Don't hide those eyes from me."

"I'm not hiding."

Yes, I am.

I can't look at him when his body is against mine, wrapped in his arms, tucked beneath his chin. He feels too safe, too right, when inside I know that's bullshit.

His hand trails up the column of my throat until it reaches my chin. He rests the tips of his fingers beneath it, tipping my face up and lightly rubbing his thumb against my bottom lip. A ragged breath escapes me and my eyes drift open, meeting his intense gaze in the dim light. I hate that my knees weaken and I'm forced to clutch him tighter.

"There you are." His voice is barely audible, but I hear it through the noise of the music, the clinking of glasses, the hum of conversation. I'd hear him anywhere and through anything.

There's a dozen ways I could respond, but they all stay stuck in the back of my throat. Instead, I lean into him, letting him lead as our bodies sway to the soulful melody. This is a first for me. I've danced in clubs where sweat-soaked bodies ground against each other without any sense of intimacy. Those moments were nothing more than letting the music take me. A tangling of heat and hormones, chasing the rhythm in the dark.

This is different. His steady heartbeat against my cheek, the gentle dominance of his hands holding me in place like I'm precious to him. It's more dangerous than anything we'll encounter at this party.

When the last note trails off, his arms stay locked around my waist, like he's reluctant to let me go. I clear my throat, breaking the spell, and quickly back away a step.

I glance around the room where most people have gone back to paying the dance floor no mind, except for that same man with the dark eyes—Fairfax. "We need to talk," I whisper. "There's something up with the earpieces."

He takes a moment to snap back to reality. "What?"

I move off the dance floor and back to the side of the room, passing by a few wandering eyes. Jasper follows, close enough that I still smell him. "Try yours. Mine isn't working."

"Lee?" he says quietly. "You there?" When he gets no

response, he curses under his breath. "What do you think it is?"

"I'm not sure. Some kind of signal jammer probably, but that's not really my area of expertise."

"Leon's probably freaking the fuck out," he says, grabbing a glass of champagne from a passing server.

"You think?"

"Yeah." He lets out a long breath. "You haven't seen that side of him yet, but he can lose it when shit goes sideways. Check your phone, see if it has any signal."

I didn't think of that. I open my clutch and pull out my phone at the same time that Jasper takes his out. "No signal."

"Same," he says.

His eyes wander over the guests as a muscle in his jaw ticks. "Stick close to me. We just got the confirmation we needed that this party is more than it seems."

I follow his lead, making small talk with other guests and listening in on conversations. I notice right away that the only individual who introduced themself by name all night was Fairfax. Every other person we've had the displeasure of speaking with has stayed anonymous. Masks, no names. Can they be more obvious? On the plus side, no one has asked for our names since we checked in at the door.

After at least an hour and two more drinks, my patience is thinning. The jazz music settles at the base of my skull, and I'd love nothing more than to be back at our place, curled up in bed with the kittens on my chest.

I put my arms around Jasper's neck and nuzzle him, pulling his attention from the stock market conversation he's faking his way through. "We're not getting anywhere," I say against his ear.

He breathes out shakily and rubs the rough stubble on

his cheek against mine. God, it feels good enough to be a major distraction. "I know. These old fucks aren't taking any of my bait."

I stretch onto my tiptoes and murmur against his lips, ignoring the way my blood rushes in my ears. "Maybe we should snoop around?"

The idea has my stomach twisting, but it may be the only way we find out what's going on. His lips graze mine, and a rush of warm whiskey-scented breath fills my senses, making me dizzy. "Lead the way."

"You two are making me feel ten years younger," someone croaks from the other side of the table. I can almost feel his eyes lingering on my ass. "I'm enjoying the show."

Jasper tenses, his eyes sharp as he puts a few inches between us. I take that as our cue to leave. "I need to use the powder room. Babe, will you help me find it?"

Jasper slides his mask back in place, a smile pulling his lips up. "Of course. Gentlemen, let's catch up again later about that round of golf."

The three men at the table chuckle and the same croaking voice speaks again. I now see it comes from a man with liver-spotted hands clutching a silver cane and combed over white hair. "Take your time with that one. If I were younger, I'd join you."

I squeeze Jasper's hand, knowing without looking at him that he's about ten seconds from losing his shit. "Not worth it," I say for only him to hear.

Once I pull him from earshot, we stop in the hallway near the restroom. He leans against the wall, clenching his hand into a tight fist, breathing heavily. "I wish I could kill that wrinkly old piece of shit."

I pull on the lapels of his jacket, capturing his attention. "I know."

My palm unfurls against his chest as his breathing starts to slow. "Are you okay?"

"I'm fine. Pervy McPerverson just bought us some time, as creepy as he is. If anyone asks where we went..." I trail off.

"He'll tell them we're off fucking in a closet some-where," Jasper finishes.

I swallow hard. "Exactly."

I have no idea where the hallway leads, but it's quiet and dark enough that we have no problem sneaking away. Jasper checks several closed doors as we move down the dimly lit space. Finding only a closet and another bathroom, we continue until the hallway curves, returning us to the great hall where our evening began. We take in all the possible ways to go and he curses under his breath.

"Where to?"

"It's too big."

I feel his smirk before I see it. "I've heard that a lot. I promise you can take it though."

With a scoff, I peek around the corner. "Doubtful."

"We already have one bet going, should we make it two?"

"Only you would bring attention to your dick size when we're in the middle of a dangerous situation." I force myself to sound serious.

He shrugs. "You baited me and you know it."

"Shut up, dummy. Let's go upstairs. It looks deserted."

He rests his palm on my lower back again. I sidestep to shove him loose. "Shouldn't we be all over each other? You know in case we get spotted snooping around. We can say we were looking for a bedroom."

I hate to admit it, but he kind of has a point. Sighing, I

grab his arm, which is heavier than it looks, and put it over my shoulder. "There."

Luck must be on our side, since we make it upstairs without encountering anyone. It's actually pretty eerie to be in such a large place, knowing the other side of the house is packed with people, yet we're alone. "Let's hope they don't have any cameras up here."

"If they do, I'm sure Leon would have figured it out," he says. We stay to the sides of the wall in the shadows. "Christ, I don't know how Damon does this whole creeping around thing so well."

"What do you mean?"

Jasper hesitates until I tug on his arm. "Nothing. He's just normally our guy when it comes to stealth. Not sure if you noticed, but I tend to stand out in a crowd."

"Wow, big ego much?"

He chuckles. "You could say that."

We peek into a few open doors—all guest bedrooms from the look of them. It doesn't seem like these Fairfax's spend much time living here. The place is like a museum.

We finally reach a bedroom that looks somewhat lived in. A teenager's room, by the looks of it. I close the door. No reason to invade their space unless we have to.

"Let's go back downstairs. We must have missed something," I say. The adrenaline I felt earlier is quickly wearing off.

At the bottom of the staircase, footsteps echo against the marble floors. Shit. Jasper quickly pulls me around a corner and into a coat closet, shutting the door all but an inch.

"I need you to go over last minute details. Everything is in my office." The voice is cold and matter-of-fact. "We can't let there be any mistakes like last year. Not with Whitaker here."

"They're talking about Brennan," I whisper. It's barely audible over my sharp breath.

Jasper puts a finger over my lips and I automatically want to bite it. How dare he shush me? I start to open my mouth when he spreads his fingers, covering my entire mouth with his hand.

"Whitaker? But I thought—" a second voice rings out, timid but just as cold.

"Do I pay you to think, Wayne? Don't answer that. I've already been gone from the party long enough. Just do as I say."

"I will."

"You will, what?" the first man spits.

"I will, sir," Wayne responds, like a dutiful student. What the fuck kind of power trip is that asshole on? I can't say I have sympathy for Wayne. I'm sure he's the worst kind of person.

"Move your hand," I say, my voice muffled.

"Patience," he croons in my ear. Damn him. I'm adding this to the list of things he'll get punished for.

We wait for their footsteps to fade and finally Jasper moves his hand from my mouth, trailing it down the front of my neck. "You mother—"

He interrupts me. "Motherfucker, I know. Kick my ass later. Right now we have to find our new friend Wayne."

"But..." I trail off, trying to come up with a reason to argue his plan. Something other than it's not safe. I knew none of this would be safe, yet I came anyway.

"Did you want to stay in the closet a little longer? I'll admit it's not my first choice, but at least it's cozy."

I can practically feel his self-satisfied grin behind me. "Don't forget I have a knife and I know how to use it."

He makes a suggestive sound. "Now we're really not leaving this closet."

"Jasper!" I say between gritted teeth. He chuckles and peeks through the cracked door.

"Come on, let's have a little talk with Wayne. Then hopefully we can get the hell out of this place and you can show me how you use that switchblade."

"You're unbelievable." I shake my head, hiding the laugh that wants to make its way out. If only he knew how much that idea intrigues me.

CHAPTER THIRTEEN

JASPER

My night just got a hell of a lot better now that we get to have some fun with Wayne. Don't get me wrong—the night's been fantastic already with Falin in that curve-hugging dress, letting me touch her and play with her until she squirms. All that and the promise of her kicking my ass again, it's enough to make me bite back a moan.

Now it's time to do what I do best—Well, other than fucking. Wayne will not be getting fucked by me. I need to make that clear.

We found the office easily, thanks to Fairfax's lackey. I almost wish he gave me more of a challenge, but the night is still young. He's flat on his back on the floor, my foot holding him down, hands tied in front of him with my tie. Oh, and I can't forget the gun that I have pointed at his face.

"Whff duh yuh wahn fruh meh?" Wayne mumbles around the makeshift gag I made from my sweaty dress sock.

"What was that, Wayne? Can't quite understand you." I chuckle. Man, this is fun.

""Ffuhk, whuh duh yuh—" I shift my weight forward and his words are cut off with a groan.

"I think you know the answer. And let me tell you, Wayne. I'm great at getting what I want." My eyes find Falin across the room and linger. She looks up from the computer, like she can feel my gaze.

"Anything?" I ask, ignoring Wayne's grumbles.

"Nothing out of the ordinary, but I'm copying everything onto a drive. Should be done soon." She clicks a few times and straightens out. "It's doing its thing."

"I've got him. Why don't you search around? Fairfax must have been talking about something tangible when he sent his little manservant in here." At that, Wayne tries to thrash around—emphasis on *try*. Poor dude, I almost feel bad for how weak and pathetic he is. I kick him again and smile. *Almost, but not really.*

"Did you see these photos? They look like the perfect suburban family." She glides her finger over a framed family portrait on the wall. It must be our distinguished hosts— nice to see them without the masks—and two kids, a boy and a girl, both elementary school age.

"Just goes to show that looks can be deceiving." I bend down and stuff the sock farther into Wayne's mouth. Hopefully Falin finds some useful information, or I'll have to try and get something out of him the hard way.

"That's the truth," she says as she stares at another family photo of the four of them on a sailboat. "What about your family? Were looks deceiving?"

I grab Wayne by his bound wrists and drag him toward Falin, getting a better look at the photo that's caught her attention. "Before or after Bailey was taken?"

My throat goes dry as I say Bailey's name. It shouldn't be that way. She's my baby sister—talking about her should come as easily as anything else, but after all this time, saying her name out loud brings a visceral reaction.

"I'm sorry. That was a stupid fucking question." Falin sucks in a breath and moves on to the built-in bookshelves, pulling out leather bound volumes and searching the pages.

"No, it's okay. Honestly, it feels good to say her name." I drag Wayne toward the plush armchair near the bookshelves so I can sit while I keep a foot on his torso and my gun trained on his head. "Is it crazy to say that I grew up pretty normal? Little league and Boy Scouts, summer barbeques, fishing and hiking with my dad. Bailey and Mom had always been super close, but we all made it a point to have dinner together most nights. Then when I met Damon, we basically took him in. My parents didn't hesitate. We were never rich by any means, but they did okay enough to send me and Bailey to college with the help of some scholarships and loans."

She looks up from the legal pad she's skimming. "That sounds pretty normal to me." Her small laugh lights up my chest. "Especially for a guy who's currently pointing a gun at someone."

The irony didn't go unnoticed.

"Yeah, well, normal can change in the blink of an eye." I try to hide the sadness in my tone, but it's pretty damn clear. "When Bailey was taken, everything fell apart."

"I can't even imagine the pain you've all gone through. To lose someone like that, not knowing if she's... Shit, here I go again. I'm not the best at these types of conversations."

Dead or alive.

Those were the words she was about to say. She's right, not knowing is the hardest part of all. The guilt that I'll never do enough to find her. It eats me up from the inside like a disease.

"What about you? Did Trouble have a normal childhood with her family of cops?"

She heads back to the desk, opening drawers and digging through them. "You can say that."

The way she bites on her bottom lip and avoids glancing up tells me a different story. "I bet there was lots of bedazzling in your past. Your dad must have loved that," I say, trying to break the tension.

She laughs again, the best fucking sound I've ever heard. "Surprisingly, my crafting hobby didn't start until college. I know, I'm so amazing at it you probably thought I had a lifetime of practice."

"I'm genuinely shocked. Those were not the hot glue gun skills of a novice." She scoffs, her eyes rolling of their own accord. While she keeps up her search, I pull up the last photo I took of Bailey on my phone. It's hard to look at, but I can't not ask Wayne here if he's ever seen her. "She look familiar to you?"

His eyes bulge as he shakes his head no. It was a long shot, but I had to try.

Falin gestures for me. "I think I found something. Bring him over here."

"You hear that? Time to be useful." Wayne struggles against the binding as I drag him to his feet. "What did you find?"

"It's a New York address." She lifts the hastily scribbled note, holding it where I can read it. "Everything else here is just for show. Even those family photos feel carefully curated. The whole office has this artificial perfection, like it's staged by a realtor—pristine, untouched, unlived in. Almost as if it's all just an elaborate decoy."

"You know, now that you say that, I see what you

mean." The rest of the house felt the same way. Is this place even their home? Is the whole thing fake?

I hold the note up for Wayne to see. "What's at this address? Why is it the only thing here even remotely personal?"

He mumbles something through the gag. "I'm going to take the sock out. If you yell, I won't think twice about blowing your brains out all over this expensive rug."

"Won't that attract attention?" Falin asks. She steps aside to finish up whatever she was doing at the computer.

I hold up my gun. "Silencer. It works wonders."

"Smart," she says, a small smile at the corner of her lips. The fact that she has absolutely no issue with me potentially shooting a man is so fucking hot.

"Sometimes I think ahead." I direct my attention back to Wayne. "The address. I'll give you thirty seconds to give us something worth sparing your pathetic life."

I barely pull the saliva-coated sock from his mouth before he's wailing like a little baby. "Please, I don't know anything!"

"Don't lie to me, Wayne. I really hate liars." I tap his forehead with my gun.

"I'm not lying. He doesn't tell me things. He doesn't trust me yet." His words are stifled from deep, sobbing breaths.

"What was that conversation earlier then? Go over the final details? Tell us what he meant, and fast. I'm getting bored."

Falin cuts in. "Almost done here. I'm going to make it look like his computer has a virus."

"I'm getting nowhere with him," I say to Falin. "Might be time to put him out of his misery."

I don't know what kind of reaction to expect from her. Disgust? Anger? Resignation?

"I like that plan. Do it over here. We can leave him under the desk. My gut tells me he's a piece of shit."

Holy fuckballs.

That was so not the reaction I expected.

Is it too early to tell her I love her? Because I think I do. My cock certainly feels strongly.

"You heard the woman," I tell Wayne. My voice bounces off the gleaming wood shelves and luxury wallpaper. "Last chance."

The metallic click of my gun cocking sends him into hysterics. A dark stain spreads across his khakis as piss runs down his leg. "Fuck, fuck, fuck," he sobs, words tumbling out between rapid breaths.

"Now that's just nasty, Wayne." Shaking my head, I eye the growing puddle on the carpet. "They'll never get that stain out." I laugh at my joke, a dark rumble from my belly that almost sounds foreign to my ears. "Any last words?"

His eyes dart to the door, then back to the gun. "Downstairs..."

Now he has my attention. "What's downstairs?"

He rocks back and forth, eyes squeezed shut. "He'll kill me," he mumbles, the words becoming a broken mantra. "He'll kill me. He'll kill me."

"I'm the one with the gun, Wayne. What the fuck is downstairs?"

Falin stands by my side. "Wayne," she says. "Help us out here. Fairfax treats you like shit. Why keep his secrets?"

At the sound of her voice, he opens his eyes. Something shifts in his features as his eyes narrow. "Fucking cunt. Why would I tell you a word?" He shoots a lob of spit from his lips right onto Falin's feet, and I see red.

My jaw clenches hard enough that my teeth could crack. I grip my gun so tight that my knuckles burn. Beside me, Falin goes deadly still—the kind of stillness that comes before a storm. The temperature in the room seems to drop ten degrees.

Wayne's lips curl into a sneer, his earlier terror forgotten in this small act of defiance. He doesn't realize he just made the biggest mistake of his soon to be very short life.

"Do it." Before she can blink an eye, I pull the trigger and put a bullet between Wayne's eyes. As he goes down with a thud, crimson sprays like fireworks across the fancy wallpaper. We don't stay long enough to watch him bleed onto that pretty rug.

I grab Falin's hand and pull her toward the door, making sure the hallway is empty before we leave the study. "Shit." Falin's voice shakes.

"It's okay. We're both wearing gloves. This won't come back on us." Normally I get rid of our bodies, but this is different. Leon and Damon are going to fucking freak. "Let's get the hell out of here."

I start toward the door but Falin plants her feet. "No. We have to see what's downstairs."

I sigh and run my hand through my hair. "Fuck. I don't think that's a good idea. Not without the guys."

"What the hell did we come here for then?" Her words are laced with ice. Of course she's right, but hell, I just killed a man. Everything in me is screaming to get the fuck out of here. "Come on, our bet's not over yet. I still need to save your ass."

"And this is why your name is Trouble," I say with a long exhale. "Lead the way."

CHAPTER FOURTEEN

FALIN

I'm going to have to examine why I'm not freaking the hell out later. Jasper just ended a life in front of me. Blood and brain matter coated the walls. Yet, I'm barely rattled. What the fuck is wrong with me? It may not be the first time I've witnessed a death, but it was definitely the most gruesome.

It doesn't matter, not now. We have other things to worry about, like getting downstairs unseen.

We find the massive kitchen where a dozen caterers move food onto trays.

"Maybe we can ask one of the staff for help?" I suggest. "It's not like they have anything to do with Fairfax. They're just caterers."

Jasper vibrates with energy beside me. "Too risky."

As the words leave his lips, one of the servers turns her head in our direction. I notice her before Jasper, and without thinking, I sling my arms around his neck, pull his face to mine, and whisper. "We've been spotted."

He catches on quickly... almost like he was hoping for this. I shake that thought away, threading my fingers into his hair and silently counting the seconds until the server looks away. His breath hitches against my skin. It would be so easy to kiss him now, but I *can't*. This is all for show. If only my heart hammering against my ribs would get the message.

"I think she moved on," he breathes. "But I'm willing to stay here like this all night."

I back away slowly to double check. "Yeah, she's gone."

"I think I see a door over there, off the kitchen," he says, nodding his chin in the direction of his gaze.

A tap on my shoulder has me jumping out of my skin. "Are you lost?"

Shit.

I spin and find myself eye to eye with Fairfax.

Before I can think of an excuse, Jasper reaches out his hand and places it on Fairfax's shoulder. "Was just having a little private time with the wife. You know how it is, buddy." Every word from his lips is as smooth as melted chocolate.

"Is that right?" Fairfax says, his mouth pulling into a grin.

I press myself against Jasper's side, playing the part of lovesick wife while also using him as a shield from Fairfax's predatory stare.

"She can't keep her hands off of me after a few drinks. Can't blame her though, I am a handsome devil." It's a miracle I keep my eyes from rolling.

"Well, lucky for you two, it's almost midnight. I'm glad I found you. I know with these masks it's all supposed to be anonymous, but Whitaker, I'm shocked you finally showed. Three years in a row you passed up my gala. I'd almost begun to think it was personal."

A weight sinks in my gut. *Brennan's never been here.* This guy has no idea that he's dead. I figured as much when we eavesdropped on his conversation with Wayne, but now there's no doubt.

Jasper lets out a nervous laugh. "You know how it is. Ivan keeps me a busy man."

"Well, I'm sure he'll be happy to know you'll finally be initiated properly." Fairfax's dark stare bores into mine and a chill creeps down my spine. "And you must be Ivan's lovely daughter?" He holds his hand out for me and I reluctantly shake, drawing away as quickly as I can. "You can come with me now, Whitaker. I'm sure Mrs. Fairfax can keep your wife company while us men get to it."

I flash Jasper a look, hoping he'll understand my silent plea. "Actually, I think I'll bring the Mrs. in on this one. She's eager to be initiated too."

Fairfax's eyes widen and he purses his lips. "I'm sure you understand what that means?"

"Of course I do," I say, channeling my inner confidence. "I'm Ivan Orlov's daughter."

Fairfax is quiet for a moment, the outline of his jaw clenches from where it's visible in the mask. When he speaks all pretense of friendliness leaves his voice. "Very well. We're getting off schedule with all this chatter." He turns to walk toward the kitchen but stops to look us over again. "Swear you'll vouch for me with Orlov, no matter what happens."

Jasper's fist tightens on my dress as he nods. We've just sealed our fate. There's no turning back now.

WE FOLLOW Fairfax down a set of stairs, my steps feeling like I'm walking through sludge. Whatever we're about to walk into isn't good. My gut is telling me to leave. I brush my palm across my switchblade and that gives me some relief.

The only light in the darkened space comes from a handful of dimly lit wall sconces and tall pillar candles set up throughout. Once we reach the bottom, the space in front of us opens up to an enormous room. A dais of sorts is set up between two columns at the front of the room and nearly a dozen chairs face it, all filled by masked men. My skin crawls.

What the hell is this initiation? Every type of terrible thought swims in my head. I was never part of a sorority in college but I've heard of all the crazy customs some of them have for initiating newbies. Would this be something similar? I wish I could call Blake and ask her if she heard Brennan talk about anything like this. The answer would probably be no, but it would be worth a shot.

"I won't let anything happen to you," Jasper whispers beside me as he moves his body closer to mine.

"You mean *I* won't let anything happen to *you*," I say with false bravado.

Our entrance into the room is noticed immediately and all heads turn in our direction. A sea of dark eyes in the dim light focus on us. Fairfax motions to the remaining empty chairs. "Take a seat in the front."

We don't argue, there's no reason to. But it feels like the temperature drops the moment I sit down.

Fairfax steps up onto the dais at the front of the room, his voice booming. "Welcome to our most anticipated night of the year." The guests clap and holler. "This has been an honored tradition for a long time now and it's the perfect way to ring in the new year. I'd like to give a special thanks to Mr. Brennan Whitaker." He gestures to Jasper. "If it weren't for your good work, this night would've never been possible."

The men continue to clap while Jasper raises his palm in thanks.

"I know we're all anxious to get started, but first, our new guests need to be properly initiated."

A few men murmur around us, the noise reminds me of buzzing mosquitoes. "But she's a woman!" I turn and see that the outburst came from a man old enough to be my great-grandpa.

"Yes, astute observation," Fairfax chides. "She is Ivan Orlov's daughter."

More murmurs sound out, and I realize my palm is inching toward my weapon strapped to my thigh. If even one person here knows about Brennan's death, then we are so fucked.

"But who will—"

Fairfax slams his fist against the podium, his exposed skin bright red. "Enough questions. I will not have you, of all people, Helsman, questioning my authority." The room turns silent and Fairfax goes on. "Friends, join me up here on the dais." As we make our way over, two younger looking men in full ski masks carry a leather chaise lounge out, placing it on the center of the raised platform.

"What is this?" Jasper's voice stays level, although I catch the slight tension beneath his mask.

"Typically, we provide... arrangements for this part of the ceremony." Fairfax's creepy gaze slides over me with curiosity. "But it seems you've brought your own tribute tonight. Our brotherhood is built on three pillars of power, as you know—wealth, blood, and..." He pauses, letting the words hang heavy in the air.

My eyes flash to Jasper's and somehow he's managed to

stay calm. I know he's reeling on the inside though, just as much as I am.

Money, blood, and what?

Three offerings. Three sacrifices.

My skin crawls imagining what this means for us.

Another man in a ski mask comes from out of nowhere, handing a bag to Fairfax. I stand stock still, my mind trying to process what's happening. Every part of me wants to shirk away from the hard eyes of all these men, staring at me like I'm a piece of meat. But I can't blow our cover.

Fairfax pulls out an ornate dagger. Its blade gleams in the dim light. He holds it above the flickering flame, the metal seeming to absorb his darkness. A low murmur begins in his throat, and within seconds the assembled men join in a haunting chorus. The words slither through the air, some archaic tongue that makes my body tense.

"What the hell?" I grit through closed lips for only Jasper to hear. His fingers find mine in the darkness, gripping tight as Fairfax turns to face us. When he speaks, his voice fills the room with commanding authority.

"This covenant has bound the powerful for generations. World leaders, philanthropists, celebrities. To be chosen is to join the architects of history itself. Brennan Whitaker and Mischa Orlova, do you swear upon your fortunes and futures to honor the brotherhood, to guard its secrets until death claims you, to place your brother's interests above all other loyalties, and above all else, maintain absolute power through lifelong secrecy? Our prosperity depends on the shadows we cast. Should our true faces ever see daylight, should you ever break this chain of silence that binds us, you will lose everything. Your wealth, your influence, your very identity will be erased. Do you accept this covenant?"

Fear spreads throughout my body, stiffening my limbs.

Jasper straightens out beside me, and without hesitation, he nods. "Yes, I do."

Fairfax's eyes are on me now. I know I need to open my mouth but my lips refuse to move. *You can do this.* My gaze meets Jasper's, his eyes holding a promise that it'll be okay. *For Bailey.* "I do."

"The time has come for tribute," Fairfax says, his voice commanding. He holds out a black velvet pouch. I'm mesmerized by what's happening in front of me, the mystery of what's inside the bag seems to suck the air from my lungs. "Place your first offering in the vessel."

Money. My heart stutters. I hadn't thought to bring cash to whatever this was supposed to be.

Jasper's hand finds mine in the darkness and he presses cool metal into my palm. Relief floods through me as I watch him step forward, adding his coin to the pouch. It clinks softly as it drops onto the countless others. I follow, trying to keep my hand steady as I make my own offering to whatever darkness I'm stepping into.

Fairfax inclines his head and hands the pouch to the masked man beside him. "And now, we come to the blood binding." He raises the dagger, its metal catching the fire-light again as he presents it to Jasper, hilt first. "Each initiate must mark the other. Whitaker, you will receive Orlova's offering, and she yours. Your shared blood will forge your bonds to our brotherhood."

Jasper's hands shake as they wrap around the dagger's hilt. This is nothing like how he held the gun against Wayne. That was justice. Ridding the world of evil. But this? I see the struggle in his eyes, and I don't want to make it harder for him. Before he hesitates, I hold out my palm, steeling myself for the bite of pain to come. His eyes meet mine, shadowed with fear and regret as he cradles my palm in his. "I'm with you," I whisper.

He draws a shaky breath, then drags the blade across my palm. A sharp hiss escapes through my teeth as crimson wells up in the blade's wake.

Fairfax takes the dagger, performing some ritual with the pouch as I hold back tears. Once he's done with his creepy shit, he hands me the hilt. I feel sick. I'd imagined too many scenarios where I'd get to draw Jasper's blood, paying him back for his maddening arrogance. But not like this. Nothing about this twisted ceremony is fun. He extends his palm and I make the cut quick and clinical, not wasting time in dragging out his pain.

My hands shake so badly, I almost drop the dagger as I pass it back to Fairfax's waiting hands.

Two offerings down, one to go. Money, blood... What fresh hell could they want from us next?

My eyes find Jasper's and I see my own dread mirrored in his expression.

"Now for the fun part," Fairfax says with cruel delight.

CHAPTER FIFTEEN

JASPER

I know what he wants from us before he even opens his mouth. I can't. I refuse to do that to Falin. Fuck this creepy initiation. I'd rather put a bullet in each of these prick's skulls than take advantage of Falin like that. I don't care if it lands me in a jail cell. It would be worth it. My body stiffens as he begins to speak.

"The final offering—" Fairfax's voice is so damn ominous, it gives me chills. "—is the most intimate. You see Whitaker, secrets bind us, but sharing sins... that binds us tighter. Every initiate must surrender all pretense of virtue. Your wealth has been given..." He gestures to the pouch. "Your blood has been spilled..." His eyes drift to our bloody palms. "And now, you'll prove there's *nothing* you won't sacrifice for our brotherhood. No lines you won't cross. No boundaries you won't break." His lips curl into a sinister smile. "After all, power knows no shame."

Falin's chest heaves while she glances at the lounge behind us. I'm sure she's caught on to what Fairfax wants. I lock eyes with Fairfax, showing him I don't back down.

"And if I refuse," I say, my tone deadly serious.

Fairfax laughs and a few of the men in the crowd join him. "I think you're smart enough to figure out what happens if you refuse."

Fuck.

We know too much already and I'm sure we've barely scratched the surface.

"If you'd prefer to not sully your personal relationships..." His eyes glide over to Falin and he darts his tongue out to moisten his lips. Bastard. I'll fucking rip his eyes out and feed them to him. "We have other arrangements available. Many to suit your specific preferences."

Falin's eyes go wide. We were spot on. There are people here against their will. Could Bailey be here? I'm barely able to contain my anger, but I ball my hands into fists to control their shaking.

"No," Falin says. "My husband and I will do whatever it takes. We're committed to the brotherhood. To making my father proud."

I want to fight her on this, but if I do, our cover is blown. We'll have no chance of helping whoever they have down here.

Fuck.

Stepping in front of her, I incline my head so only she can hear me. "We don't have to do this."

"We do," she says. Her eyes drop to the floor and she continues, her voice almost too quiet to hear. "I know you don't want to... with me. I understand. But I can't see another way."

My chest clenches at how wrong she is. If she only knew that this is killing me because I—

A low chanting begins from the back of the room, startling me. "Let it begin," Fairfax's voice commands.

She reaches for my hand. "Unzip my dress, Jasper."

I dart my eyes around the room at all these mother-fuckers about to lay their eyes on Falin. *My* Falin. Hell no.

I let her hand drop and blow out each of the candles set up on the dais. It helps to dim the space. Fairfax lets out a gruff sound from his spot on the edge, but I pay him no mind.

When I'm back in front of Falin, she turns, asking me silently to unzip her gown. I close my eyes and ground myself—if I'm going to get through this, I need to be there for her. To make sure she's okay and to shield her from their filthy eyes.

Slowly, I unzip her dress, and the fabric falls to the floor, pooling at her feet. She's like my own personal wet dream standing before me in nothing but a black lace thong and strapless bra, her curves silhouetted against the dim light. Her ass—holy fuck—is the perfect heart shape. Good enough to bite.

I hate myself, but there's no helping it. My cock goes rock hard. I've waited to see her like this and it kills me that this is how it's happening. She turns, her face still angled down.

I crowd against her, using my body as a shield from prying eyes. My knuckles instinctively graze her cheek, sliding lower until I reach her jawline. "Are you okay?"

She nods, still not meeting my gaze. I cup her jaw and tip her face up. Her watery eyes kill me. "I've got you."

"I know. Just do it," she says.

She steps toward the lounge and I see her shoulders rise and fall as she takes a deep breath before laying down. I follow her, my body almost on autopilot at this point. She's going to fucking hate me for this.

I've never felt so dirty as I remove my jacket, unbutton my shirt, and slide off my pants. I won't take everything off.

There's no reason for that. Falin's eyes drift to my boxer briefs, widening as she takes me in.

I hover over her. "Can I touch you?"

"You have to touch me," she whispers. "I don't think this works without it."

Such a smart fucking mouth, always.

"You know what I mean," I say.

She rolls her bottom lip between her teeth, and nods again. "Yes."

The chanting gets louder and faster, or maybe that's just my pulse pounding. I situate myself between her legs, doing my best to shield her, and slowly rake my palm down her body from the dip of her throat, over her peaked nipples, to her stomach. The tips of my fingers reach her underwear band, and I hesitate. There's no going back.

"Just—Just take them off," she says, her voice low and breathy. If I take them off, that's allowing everything on display for *them*. There's no way I'm sharing the sight of her perfect pussy with anyone else. The only exceptions are Damon and Leon, only *if* she ever wants that, and *if* it were consensual. But even the thought of them seeing her, touching her, sends a wave of anger through me. I'm not there yet.

I slide my palm over her underwear, dragging my fingers slowly over her clit and between her lips. She's soaked through them. Fuck. She feels so good. My cock throbs from one touch. I want to lean in and kiss her, run my tongue down her body, taste every inch of her, but I won't. I'm saving that. Instead, I'll make this fast.

I repeat the motion, gliding my finger over her clit, adding pressure until she's lifting her hips and reaching for my back. Leaning closer, I bring my lips to her ear. "Don't you dare come, Trouble. Those sounds are for my ears only."

"Fuck, Jasper... Please just do it."

She wants me to fuck her. Get it over with and satisfy these asshole's demands.

I slide her underwear to the side and drag my finger through her soaking wet folds, biting back a moan. I stop at her entrance, barely touching her. I won't. Not here.

A soft whimper leaves her lips, and my eyes flash to hers. "They don't deserve to hear you, baby. Hold it in. Bite me if you need to."

She buries her face against my arm as I slide my boxers down just enough to free my cock. I give myself a quick tug, all the way down to my leaking tip. Even here, like this, I'm gone for her. Her gorgeous gray eyes are on mine as I press myself against her pussy, grab her outer leg and wrap it around my hip to hide most of our bodies from view.

I won't fuck her. But they don't have to know that.

"Fuck, baby. You're so incredible." I whisper for only her to hear as I glide my cock between her lips. "So perfect."

The chanting takes on a different rhythm now. Faster and more haunting. I refuse to look at them. For all I know, they could be beating off to us, and then I'd really have to kill them.

Falin rocks her hips and I almost slip inside her. "Shit," I pant. "I need you to stay nice and still for me."

"What?" she asks, breathless.

"Please, baby. I'm barely holding on." She flashes me a confused look but then buries her face back into my arm as I glide my head over her clit. Her teeth sink into my skin, giving me the perfect pain to focus on. "Yes, do it again."

She bites lower, sucking my skin into her mouth. I shudder, hissing a breath. I up my pace, grinding my cock against her, holding her hips still. "Oh my God," she says, muffled against my skin.

She's going to come on my cock. Holy fuck.

I close my eyes and block out everything around me. The chanting. This sterile room full of weirdos. The fact that we're here on a job—a job that could save lives. The only thing that matters in this moment is her.

I feel it tingling at the base of my spine and shooting through my limbs. I'm going to fucking come. Then she opens her filthy mouth and I know I'm done for.

"Come on me, Jasper. We need to make it real."

Oh, it is real. So fucking real.

Another soft whimper leaves her lips as I rub myself against her clit again and again and... shit. I push up to kneel just as my cock explodes, shooting hot streams across her belly. I'm panting like I ran a marathon and as I look down, she is too.

For that moment it's only the two of us, soaking in what we just shared. Hell, she's more incredible than I ever even imagined.

The room suddenly goes quiet, the abrupt change jolting me back into the here and now. I grab my jacket and lay it over her, then get myself dressed.

"The offerings are complete!" Fairfax booms, making me jump out of my skin. I bend to pick up Falin's dress, once I'm buttoned up, and stand in front of her as she pulls it over her head. "Blood has been spilled, wealth surrendered, and innocence sacrificed. They have proven themselves worthy of our fellowship."

My jaw clenches as he turns to address the masked figures. I so badly want to grab Falin and book it out of here. "Tonight, we welcome two more into our ranks. No longer are they outsiders—they are bound to us by deeds that can never be undone."

Well, he's not wrong. What just happened can never be undone... or forgotten.

He steps forward, raising his hand like he's some kind of twisted reverend. "Rise, brother Whitaker. Rise, sister Orlova. The darkness has embraced you. Welcome to the brotherhood." His eyes gleam with satisfaction. "May your loyalty never waver... for you know the price of betrayal."

Wonderful. Another group that'll want us dead. *Aren't we lucky?*

I carefully zip Falin's dress, letting my fingers trail down her side until I reach her hand. I slide my palm beneath hers, waiting to see how she'll react. The small, unspoken gesture will tell me so much about how she's feeling at this moment. Are we broken or can we get through this? Time stretches on forever, but then I feel her weave her fingers between mine, gripping my hand. I breathe out, knowing that we'll be okay.

A trilling sound begins from the back of the space, and within seconds, more begin. Different noises—clanging, chiming, reverberating through the room. Fairfax chuckles and gestures to one of his masked helpers on the dais. "Ah, just in time. Happy New Year, brothers."

More masked servers come from side doors, carrying trays of champagne and amber liquid, passing them throughout the seated men.

Fairfax gestures for us to take our seats, but I interject. "We need to get cleaned up."

His eyes dart between us before he nods. "Very well. Don't take long. I'd like you here so you can relay details to Ivan personally. After all, it's thanks to your hard work that this is possible."

Fairfax waves us off and I squeeze Falin's hand, leading her toward the stairwell. We press our backs against the cool stone wall, keeping our eyes on the dais. From here we can watch, we can run, we can fight if we have to. The shadows offer us some much-needed cover.

Now that we're able to whisper freely, I lean in, still on alert. "Are you alright?"

She sniffs but inclines her head. "I'm fine. What's the plan?"

My throat turns to sand before I can answer her. A side door opens and Fairfax's masked lap dogs come through, dragging a group of people with black bags covering their faces. They're all dressed in white, slip-looking dresses on the women and cotton pants and undershirts for the few men. Each one has a large number written in ink on their chest. Fifteen—there's more than a dozen of them.

Their feet drag across the floor in an unnatural shuffle. Some stumble, others sway, but none resist. Are they drugged? If they are, whatever they've been given has turned them into puppets. The way they move makes bile rise to my throat. It's too mechanical, too wrong. Like watching shells of living beings take a death march.

"Oh my God," Falin breathes.

As the last of them line up before the crowd like some sick collection of dolls, one thought slams into my mind.

Bailey.

Could my sister be one of them?

CHAPTER SIXTEEN

FALIN

There's no time for me to digest what just happened with Jasper in front of all these horrible people. Or to figure out why the hell it was so hot. I'm quite literally frozen in shock by what's happening before my eyes. These people... Who are they and how are we going to help them all?

"We have to do something," I say. Jasper doesn't respond, so I tug on his arm. "What are we going to do?"

Jasper rakes a hand through his hair, forcing out a breath. "We should go, call the guys, and figure out a way to help them."

That's a solid plan, but what will happen to them while we're gone? What if we get back and they've been moved? Too many different scenarios run through my mind... none of them giving us a positive outcome. Then there's still the matter of Wayne in the study—like a real life game of Clue. Who killed Wayne in the study with a gun? When Fairfax finds him, I'm sure he'll want to investigate and there's no Colonel Mustard here to pin it on.

"And now the moment we've all been waiting for,"

Fairfax booms. "I trust your wallets are ready, gentlemen. As always, a portion of tonight's proceeds will benefit the Children's Hope Foundation."

What a sick joke. My stomach churns as the crowd erupts in excited chatter. "We should go now, while they're occupied," I say, my voice hidden by the noise.

"I can't... I need to see."

He sounds broken and I can hardly blame him. I don't know what we'll do if one of them is Bailey.

I keep my eyes fixed on Jasper's face as they remove the hoods one by one, watching hope and dread war in his expression. When the final woman is revealed, his shoulders sag. "Is she..."

He shakes his head. "No, she's not here."

I can't tell if it's relief or despair in his voice, and there's no time to ask.

"Twenty thousand for number five!" a voice bellows from the crowd.

"Number twelve is mine, boys," another calls out.

The room erupts in a bidding frenzy, numbers and obscene amounts of money flying through the air. I want to be sick. I thought watching Wayne die tonight would be the worst thing possible, but this... This is true horror.

I tug Jasper's hand, getting his attention. "Come on."

We make it upstairs unnoticed, but there's no telling how long that'll last. Servers bustle around the kitchen and it hits me that there's still a normal New Year's party going on in the ballroom. The contrast is absurd. Champagne toasts and canapes right upstairs from some poor soul's worst nightmare. This night is a clusterfuck. Times like these I wish I'd learned more from my dad. He wanted me to go the family route... become an officer like him. It was never in me. Maybe I was meant for this life, living outside the boundaries of the law.

Jasper stops and I almost pile into his back. "Let's find a back way out."

There's a server coming out of the kitchen with a motherly look about her. My heels click on the floor as I rush over to her, doing my best not to startle her as she loads a tray with more canapes. "Hi, sorry. My husband and I have an emergency at home, and well, we need to leave through a back entrance. Where did you all come in from?"

Her eyes widen as she takes in Jasper behind me. He's either freaking her out, or she likes what she sees—either is fine with me, as long as she talks... and fast.

"Please, darling, we have to get home to the kids. The little one is sick with a fever." Jasper sounds smooth as silk as he lays it on thick. Her face tinges pink and she smiles.

"Poor thing. Here, follow me. But please keep this to yourselves. The hosts are very particular." Leaving her tray on the counter, she leads us down a hallway through more closed doors until we reach a back entrance. From the looks of the coats and boxes, this space is used for the help to come and go.

She squeezes Jasper's shoulder, and turns to leave.

"There's one problem," I say through chattering teeth as the cold hits me like a ton of bricks. "The valet has the keys."

And they're all the way at the front of the house.

"Fuck." His eyes widen as he turns to me. "Your coat. Here, take mine."

"I'm fine." He ignores my protests and I let him wrap his coat around me. It may not be the warmest thing, but I sigh in relief anyway.

He takes out his phone from his pocket, waving it above

his head for signal. I try mine as well, and unsurprisingly, we're still in the dead zone. "When we get in the car, we're calling the guys."

The pathway along the side of the estate is pitch black and covered in icy patches. My ankle rolls on a slick patch and I almost bust my ass, but Jasper's hands catch me around the waist just in time. I'd give anything to be wearing my Doc's right now instead of these heels. Pants too—each time the wind blows, it cuts straight through my dress, numbing my legs to the bone.

I follow Jasper around a shadowed corner when he freezes mid-step. "What's wrong?"

"Jas? Falin?" A familiar voice rings through the open air.

Leon and Damon. They're actually here. A wave of relief washes through me so intense I blink back tears.

They rush to meet us, and in seconds Damon has me wrapped in a hug so tight, I can barely breath. "You're okay. We were losing our minds."

"Is Blake alright?" My thoughts instantly go to my best friend on the floor of that restaurant. I'll never lose that image from my mind.

"She's fine. Just worried about you guys." Damon turns to Jasper. "What the fuck happened in there?"

"I was about to ask the same question," Leon adds. He takes one look at me and winces. "You must be freezing. Let's get in the car and you can fill us in." He takes a step forward, switching on his phone's flashlight to illuminate the darkened path.

Jasper and I stay where we are.

"We can't leave yet," I say.

Damon and Leon look at me like I've lost my mind.

"She's right," Jasper adds. "They have men and women in there, drugged and being sold off to the highest bidder."

"You're serious?" Damon says. "We actually found them?"

Jasper paces the path in front of us. "Bailey's not in there, but it's a start. They know about Orlov. It's a long story and we'll fill you in, but we can't just leave them here."

As the guys talk all at once, bickering and brainstorming, a plan starts to take root in my mind. It's going to be crazy and requires a lot of moving parts, but if everything goes well, we can get those people out without anyone else getting hurt tonight.

"No, you can't just go in and start shooting," Leon chides.

"You're not Rambo, brother," Damon adds.

"You didn't see them... I need this. I gotta crush some fucking skulls." And there's the Jasper I know.

"Hey," I interrupt.

Damon puts his hands on Jasper's shoulders, halting his movement. "You can't."

"Just one skull?" Jasper says, pinching his fingers together to show an inch.

"Hey!" I repeat louder. This time all three guys turn to face me. "I think I figured out a plan. Damon, please tell me you still have those smoke bombs?"

Damon's face lights up, his dimples even pop.

Jasper scratches his chin. "Trouble, I like how this is sounding."

THE NEXT THIRTY minutes are a whirlwind of chaos. Within that chaos, I manage to keep a semblance of control, guiding the guys through my plan. We make it far enough away from the estate to get our devices working again, and while I work on unjamming the frequency blocker, Jasper calls someone named Ray for back up.

With precious time ticking down, my pulse feels like a pounding drum. It could already be too late to help any of those victims, but I haven't seen many cars on the road, so I'm holding onto hope.

"We need this to go perfectly," I say to Jasper, harsher than I mean to. We're about to reach the back door. Walking in there again feels all kinds of wrong. It's only my own sheer will and stubbornness that keep my feet moving forward.

"What makes you think I don't know that?" His tone tells me we're right back to our favorite game. Instead of being annoyed, it calms me. I know this—our push and pull.

I exaggerate scratching my head and tapping my chin. "Hmm, I don't know... past impulse control issues, I guess."

He smirks at me. "If I have impulse control issues, then you have control issues."

"I do not."

"Okay..." He chuckles and checks the entrance for anyone we'd need to watch out for.

"I don't like your tone."

He turns quickly just as I'm about to enter the doorway, catching me off guard. His body presses against mine while his hand reaches above my head, resting on the door frame. Heat flows through my previously chilled limbs, settling in my core. "Well, I like yours. Go on, keep being a control freak. It turns me the hell on."

A server hurries nearby and I shove him away. I'm sure my face is red from how flushed I feel, but we don't have time for this. "Keep it in your pants."

"You'll be saying differently soon enough." God, he's so arrogant I wish I could smack the shit out of him.

With things looking exactly how we left them, we head to the ballroom, where the sound of drunk party goers and lively music is even louder than before. "Ready?" I ask.

His eyes are alight with a fire I haven't seen before. This must be the Jasper I'd been missing out on. He pulls a smoke bomb out of the larger bag on my shoulder, a wide grin on his face. "Fuck yeah."

All at once, chaos breaks out and we're the masterminds behind it. We set off smoke bombs in the ballroom while Leon triggers the security and smoke alarms. In the confusion, Jasper and I run downstairs into the auction chamber. It's empty... Not even a flickering candle is left.

"Fuck!" Jasper picks up a candelabra and throws it against the stone wall.

This was the one part of the plan we were unsure of. In the time it took us to figure everything out, they must have moved the victims. We don't have time to sit here and throw a tantrum; we have to act. "Come on. Let's go check down there. That's where they brought them in."

I don't wait for him to catch up. I'm running before I can think, the blaring of alarms making my head spin. My feet pound against the stone floor and I collide with a large figure as soon as I turn the corner into the corridor.

The masked figure faces me, and I recognize him as one of Fairfax's guys. Jasper falls in behind me, but I barely feel his presence. I'm too busy taking in the huge gun in the masked man's hands.

"You can't be down here." He looks us over, Jasper in his tuxedo and me in my dress, looking like party guests who have taken a wrong turn. He clearly doesn't remember us from earlier. Which, weird... I don't think I could forget two people I watched essentially fuck in front of me that quickly. If it were me, I'd never forget.

"Our bad." Jasper wraps his arms around my shoulders, pulling me against his chest. He sounds like he's chatting with a buddy as he asks, "What's going on with the alarms?"

"The party's upstairs," he says. His dark eyes dismiss us as his cell phone rings.

Leon's voice is in my ear at the same time. "I found the blueprints of the house. There's another exit down there."

Jasper flashes me a look. It's quick and I know exactly what he's thinking.

But I beat him to it.

CHAPTER SEVENTEEN

JASPER

IN THE TIME IT TAKES ME TO PULL OUT MY GUN,
Falin's already slammed the guy over the head with hers,
knocked him out, and grabbed his phone. She's panting
hard, her eyes glazed over as she passes it to me. "Here, you
answer."

"What in the fuck just happened?"

"Take the call. It must be Fairfax or one of the others."
She kicks the prick for good measure before peeling off his
mask.

Shaking my head, I answer the call, putting on a false
voice. "Yeah."

"Where the fuck are you? Number two ran off and
fifteen is missing. We gotta find them and get the hell out of
here before the fire department shows up."

Footsteps pound overhead as my mind whirls, but this is
a perfect opportunity to get what I can from this guy. "And
the boss? He made it out?"

"You fucking stupid? You were with me when we got
him out. Lay off the powder, man."

Falin fishes through the slumped guy's pockets,

recoiling when she pulls out a pair of panties. I bet I know where they came from. While Fairfax and his group of freaks were busy chanting and watching us, his hired guys were busy themselves.

Anger bubbles up from my chest. We need to find them all and end them.

"Where are you?" I drop the fake voice, each syllable coming out through gritted teeth.

"Waiting out back. Do another sweep for fifteen and meet me up here. Both our asses are on the line if she's lost." The line goes dead before I can ask another question.

I stuff the phone in my pocket. Maybe Leon can get some info from it later. Falin pushes up to stand, tossing the guy's wallet on the floor next to him and gives him a hard kick in the side. I can't help the smile that lifts the corner of my lips.

"Having fun over there?" I ask, watching her face go from curiously inquisitive to playfully annoyed.

"Since you asked, yes. He's lucky I only knocked him out."

That's my girl.

"There's still time to finish him," I say, folding my arms across my chest while she considers. "But make it quick. They're missing two of the victims. They think one of them is still down here."

While she takes a moment to consider my suggestion, I patch Leon and Damon in. "There's a runner. Only info I got is that they call them number two—gender unknown. Get one of Ray's guys on it. Oh, and D, there's a van waiting up there."

Falin starts moving down the corridor before the guys respond. She must have heard what I said about the missing victims. I hurry after her.

"On it," Leon answers.

Damon's voice comes in less clear. "Got it. Meet you out back. Be quick, there's a shit ton of people leaving all at once."

"Slow down, Trouble. We don't know who's down here." I hold my gun at the ready while she flies through the dark hallway. I'm honestly impressed by how fast she can go in those heels. I'd fall on my ass in two seconds flat.

She pokes her head through an open doorway, only briefly stopping before stepping inside. "For fuck's sake. Let me check the space first," I pant, freezing as I see what she sees.

Mattresses on the floor. Discarded used needles. Restraints.

My blood turns cold.

I take a few steps toward Falin and pull her against my chest. "We're going to help them."

I force hope into my voice, trying to mask the rage burning beneath.

She leans into me. "There's still one missing. We need to find her."

"Let's keep looking." We don't have long. Who knows when our knocked out friend will come to or when the cops will show up?

"I saw her face." Falin's voice trails off. "Fifteen. She was terrified. So young too."

Movement from the corner of my eye sets my senses on alert. "Shh," I whisper to Falin as I point in the direction of the disturbance. Then I hear it—a shuffling across the room.

"We won't hurt you." I raise my voice over the still trilling alarms. I wish I had her name. It kills me to have to call her by a number those animals gave her. "The bad people are gone."

"Please come out," Falin adds. "I promise we'll get you home."

A mattress against the wall shifts a few inches and like an optical illusion, a girl looking no older than sixteen pulls herself from beneath it. Somehow she wedged herself under the mattress, using the corner of the room to hide. So fucking smart.

Falin rushes to her as she stumbles on her slippered feet, catching her in her arms before she falls. "I've got you." The young woman clutches Falin, sobbing and mumbling incoherently. "It's okay. We're here to help."

All at once the alarms stop and the contrasting silence is menacing. Falin and I lock eyes, and I scoop up the young woman in my arms. "We gotta go."

"Wait," Falin says. She takes off my tux jacket that I gave her earlier and drapes it over the frightened girl's chilled, bare arms.

We take off running, but instead of going back toward the chamber, I lead the way further down the unexplored corridor. It's brisk as hell down here, the stone walls and floor not helping the situation. I know there's a goddamn door somewhere. It must be some Nancy Drew secret hidden door bullshit because this place is built like a maze. I'm about to get Leon on the com when Falin stops.

"Wait. I feel a draft." She jogs over to the last door we passed, which ends up being another study, much less decorated and furnished than the one upstairs. This one is clinical, more like a cubicle someone would occupy for a week while temping at an office. "In here."

I feel it too. This room is colder than the others, like it's only an extension of the outdoors. The sobbing girl has calmed some, but she clutches at my neck for dear life, almost choking me out. "Hey, it's alright. What's your name?" I ask gently.

"Kay—la," she barely manages. "Please... I can't."

Falin crosses the room, shoving a rolling desk chair so hard it topples over. With strength that's equal parts terrifying and arousing, she pushes the utility desk, letting loose a groan that I may or may not ask her to recreate at a later time. With it moved enough for her, she turns on her side, squeezes between it and the wall and pushes hard. A fucking door opens. These pricks set up a secret door in the wall and blocked it with a desk. Smart... but mostly evil.

"Come on, Kayla, let's get the hell out of here," I say, hoisting the poor thing up higher. We climb a set of crude stairs, the cold leeching into my bones with each step, until we reach a cellar door. Falin shoves it open, the wind immediately blowing her hair in her face.

"Leon? Damon? We're out back. No time to find Ray's van. We'll meet you at the car."

As soon as my head peeks out the door, I see what made her say that. Two firefighters are coming forward, with an unmasked Harrison Fairfax.

Our eyes lock—Fairfax's shine with malice. A promise in them that he knows who we are, and he'll hunt us down.

We don't linger, this may be our only chance of getting Kayla out of here. With a final glance at Fairfax, I follow Falin into the night, toward safety.

Frozen and exhausted, we meet up with Ray and the others about a half mile away. Ray's van sits in a dark driveway; he mentions the homeowners are away for the holidays. I don't ask how he knows that, there's far more important shit on my mind.

I carry Kayla to the warm van, easing her onto the seat. "We're taking you to get checked out. You're safe now."

Leaving her with Falin, I update the guys and Ray. I give them a shortened version of how the night went. They let me know that despite searching for the runner and the other victims, they came up empty. The consensus is that the victims were moved somewhere else while we were busy figuring out a plan. I wish I could punch something… or better yet, someone. As we take a moment to digest how everything went down, Leon breaks the silence.

"I'll come with you to bring Kayla to get looked at," he says to Ray. "It's the least I can do to help."

I shoot Leon a grateful look. Ray's not the type of guy I'd want to leave alone with a woman in my care. Not that I think he, or his team of medics would harm her, but he's not exactly the most empathetic guy either.

"Yeah, alright. We should head out. I'll call you with updates." Ray pulls a cigarette from a pack in his pocket and lights up. He looks as dejected as I feel.

A keening wail comes from the van, snapping our attention towards it. "No, please! I can't!"

I rush over to find Kayla clinging to Falin, both dissolved in tears while Ray's medic stands there, eyes wide.

"All I did was say it's time to go," he says with a shrug.

I ease into the van beside Falin. Kayla flinches at my touch but relaxes when she recognizes me. "Hey," I croon. "What's wrong?"

"She's terrified," Falin says, wiping her own tears away. "When he said it was time to go, she just broke down."

Kayla pulls Falin closer, her body rocking in the seat. "Can you give her something?" I ask the medic.

"Absolutely not," Falin cuts in. "She's already been stripped of every shred of dignity, drugged, and God knows what else. Drug her again and she'll never trust us."

I sigh as Leon speaks up behind me. "Falin's right. Jas, let me in. I've got her."

At the sound of Leon's calming voice, Kayla's sobs slow. She looks at him with swollen eyes as Falin smooths her tangled hair. "This is Leon," Falin murmurs. "He's family. He'll take care of you."

She unwraps her arms from Falin's torso and inches away from Leon. Understandable after what she's been through. As they speak to her in gentle tones, I step away to collect myself.

My hands shake as a craving hits me hard. Maybe the adrenaline is wearing off, maybe it's their sobs that echo through my mind. Either way, if that medic offered me something to knock me out, I'd gladly accept. Numb would be perfect right now.

But as I glance back at Falin's silhouette through the smudged window, I know I'm full of shit. She needs me here. Really here. Not floating in some doped up haze. I jam my hands into my pockets and draw in a breath, the realization hitting me: I want to be her rock. I'll take it all—the pain, the regret, the shame—because caring about her is worth feeling everything.

Falin climbs out of the van, wiping her eyes with the back of her hand. My feet carry me toward her without a thought, and when I open my arms, she falls into them silently. No fight, no bratty remark. She takes the comfort that I so desperately need to give.

We stay like that until Ray's van drives away and Damon taps me on the back.

"I didn't want to interrupt, but I'm freezing my nuts off and it's late as fuck." He hands me the keys to his car. "I'll take Leon's bike home."

This is big for him. "Thank you. I wasn't even thinking about how we'd all get home."

Damon squeezes my shoulder, eyeing Falin in my arms. "I think you had a few other things to worry about."

"It's a long drive. You want to hop in the car? We can leave the bike somewhere safe and grab it tomorrow."

"Yeah, and get murdered by Leon? I'm good." He stretches his arms above his head. "It'll be good to clear my mind anyway. Just check on Blake if you get home before me."

He walks off toward Leon's bike. Falin starts to pull away, but I hold her close for one more moment, savoring the feel of her soft curves and warmth. When she finally eases back, I brush my knuckle down her cheek, tipping her chin up. Our eyes meet and I give her a lopsided smile. "I don't know about you, but I could demolish a double cheeseburger and a huge ass piece of apple pie. Saw a twenty-four hour diner on the drive in. You up for it?"

She lets out a surprised laugh, and her tear-stained face brightens. My chest loosens at the sound. "Only you would be thinking about food right now." But she squeezes my hand. "And yes. Yes to all of that."

CHAPTER EIGHTEEN

FALIN

"I think that may have been the best cheeseburger I've ever had in my twenty-four years of life." I sink back in the vinyl booth and lift my mug of steaming coffee to my lips for a sip. "And the best coffee." Jasper polishes off his last bite of apple pie and before I can second guess myself, I lean across the booth and dab a few stray crumbs from the corner of his lip, then pop my finger into my mouth.

His eyes follow my finger, lingering on my lips. They're dark and intense, like he can see underneath my skin. He adjusts slightly in the booth, and I clear my throat to break the tension. "Saving those crumbs for later? A little early morning snack?"

"I'd much rather have a different snack."

I shake my head. I guess I had that coming after what I just did. He reaches over and takes my cup of coffee. "Hey... I'm still drinking that."

"Just a sip. Sharing is caring." He gives me another one of those dumb yet adorable grins. Our waitress comes by with the check as he hands me back my mug with nothing but a drip left in it. I scowl at him.

"You two close to home?" our waitress asks as she tidies our empty plates.

"Not too bad," Jasper answers for us.

"Oh good, it's really starting to come down now. I'm off at five. Hope I can get out of this dang parking lot."

We turn at the same time to look out the window into the dark. I can't see much in their limited lighting.

"It's snowing out there?" Jasper asks.

"Oh yeah... my husband said we're looking at around six inches. Might be a couple on the roads already."

Well, isn't that just wonderful.

Jasper pays while I use the restroom, and when I head back over to him, he holds out an article of clothing. "What's this?" I lift it up and laugh. It's a brown hoodie with a picture of a smiling apple pie. I read the slogan. "Life's short, eat dessert first."

"I fully agree with that statement," he says with a wink. "You need something warmer to wear."

I slide it over my head, refusing to argue with that logic. It's cozy and soft on the inside, even if it's cheesy as hell. "Thank you, that was really nice."

"Maybe you can bedazzle it when we get back home." He smirks again and this time I give his arm a light punch.

"Or maybe I'll bedazzle you some more. I had fun with the glue gun."

We head outside and I'm immediately assaulted by a blast of snowflakes to the face. It feels like the temperature dropped a few degrees while we sat inside eating. There's a light layer of snow over Damon's Chevy, and covering the parking lot from what I can see in the dim lighting.

Jasper wraps his arm around my waist as I almost slide on the slick ground. "Damn heels."

"I got you."

He opens the car door for me before hurrying around the front to the driver's side. I pull the sleeves over my hands and rub them together. "Heat, please."

Man, I'm really missing California right about now. Jasper starts the engine and turns the dial to blast the heater. I steal a glance at him, warmth spreading through my chest as I picture us cruising down the Pacific Coast Highway. Salty air would whip through the open windows while he drives with one hand on the wheel and the other resting possessively on my thigh, our favorite music blasting through the speakers, louder than the crashing waves.

The little daydream almost warms my frozen limbs. "Can you check the GPS while I dust off the windshields? I know we're about halfway, but I want to make sure there's no road closures."

He uses the back of his shirt sleeve to clear the windows while I check. He's right, we're about halfway to the city. Once he's back in the car, I let him know. "No closures, but I doubt they've got the plows out yet."

The car fishtails as he backs out, making me lunge for the *oh shit* handle, white-knuckling that thing. His low laugh fills the car at my reaction as he straightens the wheel. Only then does my chest loosen enough to take a breath. "I've had enough adrenaline for one night. Wiping out in a snowstorm is so not on my winter bucket list."

"Don't worry, Trouble. I can drive in the snow."

IF ONLY I recorded him twenty minutes ago. *"Don't worry, Trouble. I can drive in the snow."* Right. That's why I'm staring at a utility pole halfway down a ditch.

"That pole literally has a smiley face spray painted on it," I say. "How ironic."

He slides back in the car after assessing the damage. "I'm going to push the car to a safer spot. We should be able to run it for heat, but driving's out until they plow and salt." He roughly pulls a hand through his long hair, grimacing. "Fuck, Damon's going to kick my ass."

"Should I call him?" I offer, trying to redirect him from his self-loathing.

"Nah, he's probably still riding."

"What about a tow truck?"

"Not necessary. I got it."

I huff, clicking my phone off to save battery. "You're seriously planning to push this massive hunk of metal back onto the road by yourself? I know you're built, but you're not exactly The Hulk."

"All I heard was, *I'm built.*"

How is it that he can make me go from wanting to kiss him to wanting to throttle him in less than three seconds?

"Jasper, I'm serious. I'm not turning into a human popsicle because you're too stubborn to admit you need help."

"A Falin flavored popsicle... I could eat that," he teases in that low voice. I scowl and cross my arms. "I'm kidding! Alright, I'll head out there again and if I can't get it up the hill, you can call a tow."

Satisfied with that compromise, I nod. "I'll climb in the driver's seat and put it in neutral."

"Mmm, I like a woman who knows her way around a stick shift."

As he heads back into the storm, I call after him, "Don't slip on ice and break your neck."

Sliding into the driver's seat, I mutter under my breath, "Freaking stubborn ass infuriating man. There's no way he can actually—What the hell?"

The car rocks beneath me as it lurches backward. My jaw drops. Is he seriously managing to push this entire car by himself? It rocks again, and this time I definitely feel it moving.

What feels like inches at a time, he manages to push the car up the ditch and back onto the road. Once we're on flat ground, I shift the car into drive and straighten it out as best as I can, moving us to a safe spot along the shoulder.

Jasper comes around the driver's side and I slide back over. He's panting, red-faced and hair wet from snow. God, he's never looked hotter.

"I can't believe you did that." There's genuine shock in my voice.

"Told you," he says, partially out of breath.

"I stand corrected." I adjust the vent so that it's blowing toward him. "So what now? There's gotta be at least four inches out there." He chuckles, and I immediately know why. Exasperated, I sigh. "Just say it."

"Hell of a lot more than four inches in *here.*"

"You're a child," I say, holding back a smile. He rolls up his damp sleeves, showing off his tattooed forearm, so perfectly muscular that I have to look away. "Really though. What now?"

"Heat's running, we have a mostly full tank of gas. We should try and get some sleep until they clear the roads or the sun's up, whatever comes first." Without waiting for my response, he reclines the seat almost fully. So many thoughts run through my mind but mainly how easy it would be for me to straddle him in that position. Also to strangle him. *A straddle, strangle combo.*

"We should at least text Blake and the guys so they don't worry," I say, forcing myself to be logical.

"Go ahead. Check up on Kayla while you're at it." My heart lurches at the reminder. Poor thing. I hope she's okay. I type out a quick message to our group chat and put my phone on the dashboard.

Moonlight shines through the sparse branches overhead, illuminating the falling snow. It's pretty fucking peaceful now that I've slowed down enough to notice. The kind of peaceful that almost makes me forget everything else exists in that moment.

"It's beautiful," I whisper, exhaustion and awe in my voice.

"Yes, it is." The warmth in his voice has me turn to face him. He's not looking at the moonlit snow. His eyes are fixed on me.

Heat creeps up my neck, to my face. "You're supposed to be looking out the window," I manage, hoping I sound unaffected by his intensity.

"I like this view better," he says softly.

Suddenly, the car feels too small, too hot. My limbs are heavy with fatigue but my pulse is racing, the charged air between us making it impossible to look away from him. Images from earlier flood my mind—Jasper's weight hovering over me, the delicious friction as he rocked against me, the wet slide of his hard length through my soaking pussy, how he could barely hold it together, his restraint shattering with each movement.

Knowing his cum is still painted on my skin, like a branding mark, drives me wild. He was so close to pressing into me. And I wanted it, even there, like that in front of all those terrible people. If he sunk inside me, I would have welcomed him with open arms.

He reaches out and drags his knuckles down my cheek, cupping my chin with his calloused fingers. A ragged breath leaves my lips as every ounce of resolve snaps like a broken rubber band. I don't care what happened months ago. Right now, we're here, stuck in this car, and I can't deny what I want.

"Come over here," he breathes. "Please."

I shift onto my knees, the leather seat creaking beneath me as I gather my dress higher on my thighs. With one fluid motion, I turn and settle onto his lap, my knees bracketing his hips. My pulse pounds with anticipation as I stare down at his perfect face. I arch my brow and slowly roll my hips, deliberately teasing him. "I'm here. What are you going to do about it?"

"You're going to ruin me, Trouble," he whispers hoarsely. I hear the plea in his voice, the desperate need. "No doubt in my mind." He cradles my face gently, his hooded eyes begging me to break down every wall he's ever built.

"We shouldn't," I say, as my fingers trail down his shirt, working his buttons open one at a time. His chest heaves beneath my palm when I finally reach his warm skin. "But I need you too much."

He pulls the side lever, angling the seat up so we're chest to chest, inches between our lips. I raise my arms, and he pulls the hoodie up and over my head, leaving me in just my sleeveless dress. His hands scorch my skin, sliding over me, down the slope of my neck, over my arms, and back up burying into my hair. It's like he's trying to memorize the feel of my skin beneath his palms. He pulls me closer, ghosting his lips over mine, but freezes as I close the distance.

I pull back and look at him.

"Don't kiss me again unless this is real," he says, breathless. I blink, my head foggy with want and need. I breathe out and lean against his neck, sucking his warm skin between my lips until he hisses.

I work to open his shirt, and he pushes up, helping me. In seconds, his shirt and my dress are off. Our hands are all over each other, ripping off my bra, undoing his pants. I don't kiss his lips. I can't promise him what he needs. He's not ready for that and neither am I.

He cups my tits, rubbing his thumb over my peaked nipples. "Fucking hell, these tits are a work of art."

I'm so needy, I grab his head, arch my back and shove my tit into his face. "Suck them. Please... I need—oh God." The warm heat of his mouth envelops my nipple, sucking and nibbling until I cry out. I wrap my fingers into his hair and hold him in place, greedily grinding my pussy against his fabric-covered length. "That feels so good."

He lifts me slightly, not breaking his hold on my tit, and slides my thong to the side. As soon as his fingers glide between my lips, he breaks away from my tit with a *pop*. "Goddamn, baby. You're soaking wet for me."

"Yes," I breathe. "You like that?"

"Do I like that?" We groan as he slips a thick finger inside me. "Sweetheart, *like* doesn't begin to cover what you do to me."

He works his finger in and out while teasing my clit, driving me to the brink of coming. When I can't take another second, I run my nails down his tattooed chest, until I reach the waistband of his boxers. "Please tell me you have a condom."

He's sucking my neck, my collarbone, my tit. So busy driving me to the edge, I almost wonder if he didn't hear me. When I adjust myself and pull his cock out, he finally groans a response. "I don't know."

"You don't know?" I repeat, each word punctuated by a moan as he goes back to sucking my neck.

I slide my fist up and down his length, spreading his dripping pre-cum. He's so big and thick, I'm not even sure he could fit inside me.

"Shit, baby... I'm gonna come if you do that." He's desperate and breathless, exactly how I like him. "Check the glove box for a condom... please."

I slide off his lap and scoot toward the glove box. Before I can open it, he leans over me, kissing my stomach, holding me in place. My heart races to the point of dizziness as his stubbled chin grazes the top of my pussy. "God, Jasper."

"The things I'd do to this pussy if we had more space." He leans in as far as he can but he's just too big for the front seat.

I check the glove box, finding nothing but a gun and some paperwork. *Fucking perfect.* "No condom."

"That's okay. Get in the backseat." He slides the driver's seat up all the way and climbs back there. It would be almost comical to watch, if I wasn't too busy eyeing his cock like my next meal. Whatever he has in mind, I'm one hundred percent there for it.

As gracefully as I can, I climb over the seat, but he doesn't wait until I get situated before his palms slide against my ass. I fall onto the seat on my back, laughing at the absurdity of this. Scrambling to a sitting position, I reach for his cock again, but he grabs my hand, pinning it above me. "Move back and wrap your leg around me."

I scoot as far back as I can, my back pressing against the

side panel. Jasper kneels on the floor of the car, his chest leaning against the edge of the seat. He spreads my thighs wide enough to squeeze his body in, one leg over the front seat and the other wrapped around him. "Please."

"Please, what?" he asks, ghosting his lips over my pussy.

Arching toward him, I grab his head and guide him where I want him, my answer a moan as he sucks my clit between his lips. "Oh fuck, yes."

CHAPTER NINETEEN

JASPER

I'm fucking gone for her. Feral. Past my breaking point. I breathe her in, inhaling long and deep. She smells like heaven, tastes like nirvana. I've never felt like this before. This all consuming need. So desperate that I can't get enough.

I spread her legs as wide as I can, nuzzling my face into her pussy so her scent will be embedded in my skin. My cock throbs, dripping from the tip, almost painful at this point.

"Jas," she hisses as I fuck my tongue into her cunt. I do it again, wrapping my hand around her waist, helping her grind into me. It's so fucking hot how she takes what she wants. I'd expect nothing less.

I take long strokes, savoring every drop that she gives me. Flicking her clit when she cries out. She's so perfect. So fucking delicious.

Her body shakes, her pussy spasming, as she lifts her hips. I pull back, smiling while she desperately curses my name. "Jas, fuck. Why'd you stop?"

"Because I can, Trouble. I've dreamed of having you this desperate." She wraps her fingers in my hair and pulls me down. My scalp's on fire but I fucking love that I'm getting to her. "So needy. We've got time. I'll stay down here until the fucking sun comes up."

"Just shut up," she pants. "And fucking lick my clit."

I chuckle against her skin, savoring her needy moans. "So bossy—" She bucks against my face, and I can't wait any longer either. I spread her lips wide, and flick her clit with my tongue, pressing in and matching the rhythm of her hips.

She's close. I feel her orgasm building. "Fuck, yes. Right there. Don't you dare stop."

As her body tenses, I slide two fingers inside her, curling them against her G-spot. Her entire body shudders, and her fingers tighten in my hair to the point of pain. I keep my tongue pressed firmly against her clit as she grinds, riding out her release. Fuck, she's perfect. Her pussy grips my fingers like a vise. She's going to feel amazing choking my cock.

I lap up her cum, savoring every last drop. When I pull back, I rise up on my knees and hover over her panting lips. "Open up. Taste how fucking delicious you are."

Her eyes search mine, heavy with want and hesitation. When I don't back away, she parts her lips and holds her tongue out. It takes everything in me to not kiss her like I want to. Suck her tongue into my mouth. Instead I spit, and watch her swallow down her cum like my perfect slut.

As moisture seeps from the side of her lips, my cock twitches. I'm so goddamn unhinged right now. I don't think I could stop her if she wanted to fuck me bare. Hell, I'd give anything to sink inside her. That line between doing what I want and what's right fights dangerously in my mind.

My hands shake as I adjust my dick and climb back to the front seat. The effort it takes to move away from her tests every fiber of my being. Her voice cuts through my thoughts. "Where are you going?"

"We don't have a condom." The words come out rough in my throat. I can't bring myself to meet her eyes. She's too hard to resist, and my control is already hanging by a thread.

It's quiet for a moment, the only sound coming from the heating vents and our rasped breaths. I'm giving her the control. She knows if she were to climb up here and sit on my cock, there's no way I'd stop her. But I won't be the one to make that decision.

"Can you hand me my clothes?" My heart sinks, but I don't show it. I gather her dress and hoodie, passing them back to her. "Thanks."

She silently dresses while I will my cock to go down. It's not behaving. Can't blame the guy.

Giving myself something to do instead of watching her get dressed through the rearview, I grab my phone. Leon answered Falin's text from earlier.

> Leon: Do you need a tow? I can call someone. I already found your location.

> Leon: Kayla is doing alright. Ray's team has her resting with fluids.

"Leon answered. Kayla's doing okay. Ray's team is taking good care of her. I'll tell him we don't need a tow truck."

"Sounds good," she says. I don't like how quiet she's gone. It's not like her. "I'm glad Kayla's okay."

"Me too."

"I'm going to spread out back here and get some sleep. We probably have a few hours until dawn."

"Yeah, good idea," I say, my voice thick.

<hr>

SHE TOSSES and turns against the leather seat for a long time. I'm conscious of her every breath, her every move. I force my eyes closed, knowing she's right. We should get some rest. There will be so much to unpack when we get home, I doubt we'll get much rest then. But behind my closed lids the events of the night replay like a twisted movie reel. I force myself to think of Falin, but then my cock starts to get hard again, which is also not what I need.

"Fuck," I huff, scrubbing my palm over my face. "I'm not going to get any sleep in here."

"Same," she says. The car rocks as she climbs back into the front seat. "Damon should really think about a more comfortable car."

I laugh. "That'll never happen. This is his baby." I blink, realizing that I just had Falin spread out like a buffet in Damon's car. I don't know if he'd kill me or pat me on the back if he found out.

"So..." Her voice trails off.

"I think you owe me an answer," I say.

She turns and arches a brow. "What?"

"Our bet. I definitely saved your ass."

She scoffs. "No way. *I* saved *your* ass."

"Oh, really? Where's your evidence?" I ask.

Rolling her lip between her teeth, she thinks for a second. "That guy in the hallway. I knocked him out."

Laughing, I say, "That was not saving my ass. That was you having a good time."

She shrugs. "Still, I knocked him out, which led to us finding Kayla and getting out of there."

"Okay, well, what about when I killed Wayne? Who knows what damage he would have done if we let him live?" I exude smugness as I cross my arms over my chest.

"You killed Wayne because he spit on me."

"That too... *but* I was also saving our ass." I reach out and adjust a stray hair in front of her face. "What about with Fairfax?"

Her eyes widen. "What about it?"

I can tell she's thinking about what we did up on that dais. It runs rampant through my mind too. "Nevermind. How about this? We each have to answer a question?" I offer.

"Fine, but you go first."

Shit. I want to make this good, but I haven't thought ahead. There's so much I want to learn about her. *Everything*. I'll keep it fairly light though, considering what we went through tonight and the vibe in the air. "How did you get into hacking?"

Her brows raise, and she tilts her head. "That's really what you want to ask?"

"I'm genuinely curious." I flash a smile, the kind that I know lovingly annoys her.

"It's kind of a long story," she starts, and takes a breath. "I'm adopted. I won't get into the whole thing of how and when, but basically when I was about fourteen, I got really into trying to find my birth parents." She drums her fingers on the dash, collecting her thoughts. "At first, it was just normal stuff—searching adoption records, birth certificates, all that. But everything was sealed tight. The more doors that closed in my face, the more determined I got."

Now I'm even more curious. "Could your parents help you? Your adopted ones, I mean?"

"I tried to get information from my dad, but he was always super vague. My mom passed when I was nine, and my dad wasn't much of a talker. He told me where he found me, how they ended up adopting me. So I started spending lunches in my school's computer lab, or using friend's computers so my dad wouldn't get suspicious. I taught myself how to dig deeper."

"Did you ever find them?"

She shakes her head. "Not then. But I found this whole world of puzzles and barriers that were just waiting to be solved. Each new skill I learned opened up ten more possibilities. Before I knew it, I was spending more time learning about network protocols than actually searching adoption records. It became less about finding my birth parents and more about proving I could get past any obstacle. Every secured system was like a personal challenge. Taunting me, telling me I can't. And well..." She grins. "I've never been good at taking no for an answer."

Hearing that story connects the pieces I already know, forming a clearer picture. Those gray eyes light up when she talks about her skills and I can't blame her. She's worked hard for everything she's learned and done it all through sheer determination. I'm even more intrigued.

"You said you didn't find them then. Does that mean you ended up finding your parents later?" I ask.

Wagging her fingers, she says with a smirk, "The deal was one question, cheater."

"Can't help myself. You're so very mysterious."

"I'm really not, but I'll let you think I am," she says. Her eyes stray toward the window.

"Thinking about your question?" I wonder out loud.

"You could say that." She gets quiet again, drawing shapes in the window's condensation, little swirls and stars.

I want her to ask me things—about my life, about what makes me who I am. Something real... beyond the surface. I can't force her to want to know me though, and maybe that's for the best. It's safer if she just sees Jasper the jokester, the charmer who can get out of anything. If she looks too closely, asks too many questions, she'll see how broken I really am. How I failed Bailey and how it fucking kills me everyday. How I'm barely holding it together most of the time.

No one wants to know *me*. Who I wanted to be before everything fell apart... Who I am now. Maybe we're all as lost as I feel, but it doesn't hurt any less knowing the woman breaking down all my walls has nothing personal to ask me.

"Look, I—"

A flash of blinding lights in the rearview cut off my words. We turn, shielding our eyes, and are greeted by the roar of a snow plow.

"Thank fucking God," Falin says. "I know we're in bumblefuck but I really didn't think they'd take this long to plow."

She's excited to get home... to get space from me. Understandably. Can't help the lump in my throat from forming anyway.

Once the truck passes us, I pull out and follow a few car lengths behind. The ride back is silent except for the squeaking of Damon's wipers and the low melodic tune of my mellow playlist.

Dawn breaks as we pull off the parkway, early light glinting off the Hudson to our right. As the skyline comes into view, it almost makes it easier to pretend the past twenty-four hours weren't real. That Falin and I could go back to how we were before the gala. She taps her fingers on the car door to the beat of the music and that small gesture has me smiling. There's no going back for me. The walls are crumbling, and Falin's the only one I want to let in.

CHAPTER TWENTY

ALEXANDER

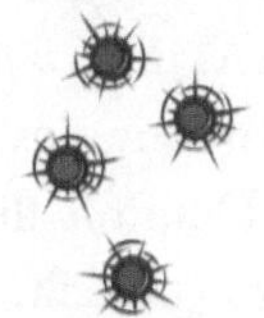

THE MOMENT I SAW HER FACE ON THAT NEWS CLIP, everything clicked into place. Blake Hyland. The girl who fucked up my life has been right under our noses the whole time. And there beside her, that platinum blonde I'm sure helped ruin everything we'd built right along with her friend.

I'm grateful that I happened to be scrolling the news that night. I'd never have put two and two together. Never would've spotted her.

Here she is again, being nothing but a thorn in my side.

I drum my fingers against my polished mahogany desk as I study her features on the screen. The security footage Fairfax provided may not be high definition, but it's clear enough that I recognize her. Dolled up in a barely there dress, tits hanging out like one of my whores. She may be masked, but I know it's her. The friend. *Falin Sinclair.* And next to her, I'm sure I've seen him before.

"Pause it," I command. Bruce fumbles with the remote, almost dropping it before freezing the image.

Those two cost us millions. Our most valuable clients closed their wallets tight after their auction got disrupted. Months of careful planning and relationship building, destroyed in minutes. Multiple assets lost. Fairfax will never trust me again.

I rise from my chair, circling my desk to get closer to the screen. "What do you know?" I ask my two useless lapdogs.

"We tracked them to Manhattan. They're living in a—"

I bang my fists against my desk, successfully silencing him. He grimaces while Dominic flinches a foot backwards. "Keep that information to yourself. If it gets out too soon, it could ruin us." My lips turn up as I imagine presenting this gift to my uncle. Ivan has been breathing down my neck since Brennan's unfortunate demise, demanding answers, results. This intel could change all that. Blake Hyland and her boyfriends—the cause of Brennan's death, the reason for the collapse of our businesses in Willowbrook.

"What do you want us to do?" Dominic asks quietly, hiding partially behind Bruce. The bruises from our last conversation are still visible on his face. *Good.* He needs the reminder of what happens when he fucks up.

"Watch them. Learn it all. Take pictures, videos. I want to know everything. Where they shop, eat, fuck. Who they talk to." I turn back to my desk, grabbing my straw and leaning over to do another line. "But do not engage them. If they catch on, I'll make last time feel like your first blowjob."

They're eyes widen but they quickly adjust, nodding. "Got it."

"And find out everything you can about the rest of them. The big one with the blonde hair and that quiet one. Background checks, known associates, everything." I tap out more powder, forming it into a tight line. Realizing they're still standing there with their heads up their asses, I yell, "Get out!"

Once they've finally left, I pace my office. After weeks of obstacles and failures, finally something is going my way. I replay the security footage from the gala, watching again as chaos erupts in the ballroom. Months of work destroyed because these dogs couldn't keep their noses out of my business.

My phone buzzes from my desk, Ivan's name lighting up the screen. I let it ring twice before answering.

"Uncle."

"Tell me you have something." His voice carries that edge I've grown to hate.

"Actually, I do." I stand in front of my floor to ceiling window, watching the ants below go about their pathetic lives. "How would you like to hear some very good news about the people who disrupted our New Year's celebration?"

The line goes quiet for a moment. "I'm listening."

"I've found them. All of them. And I think you'll be very interested in what I've discovered." I pause for effect.

"Who did you find?" He asks, impatience in his tone.

"Blake Hyland and her boyfriends. There's so much more." He's quiet on his end of the line so I quickly add, "Let's meet in one week. Same place. I'll have it all then."

My hands shake as I hit the end button before he can respond. He'll be angry, but I can tell him we were cut off. Soon, something as trivial as hanging up on him won't matter. I'll have everything I need to restore his trust. To prove I'm more valuable than Brennan ever was.

I pull up the frozen image of Blake's blond friends as

they snuck out a back entrance and study their details. "You should have stayed away from New York," I murmur, heading over to my bar cart and pouring a shot of vodka. "But I'm so glad you didn't."

CHAPTER TWENTY-ONE

FALIN

As if it isn't already messy enough in the apartment, now we can add a busted pipe and water leak to the mix. In *my* bedroom—because of course the universe would punish me that way. "What did I do to deserve this? And don't bring up that time in Cabo... that was an accident."

And now I'm having a conversation with myself.

Blake hurries in with another plastic bin. "This should be big enough to get everything off the floor and out of maintenance's way."

"My entire life is being relegated to a Hefty bin. Tell me again, who picked this living arrangement?"

She hesitates as she picks up one of my wet T-shirts from the floor. "I honestly don't know. Leon, probably."

"Speak of the devil," I say, as Leon taps on the outside of my door frame.

"I spoke with the building manager and maintenance is getting a plumber here first thing tomorrow."

"So what does that mean for tonight?" Blake asks, almost as if she pulled the question straight from my mind.

"Well, they're shutting the water off for the floor in the meantime." He looks around at the soggy mess. "And I guess you'll want to sleep somewhere else."

I hold in the massive groan that's dying to escape my lips. "When do Kayla's parents get here again?"

"Two days. They're driving in from Texas." He must see the look in my eyes. "I know it's been tough having another person in the mix the past week, but I couldn't just leave her with Ray."

"I know. It's not Kayla—I'm glad she's been here and that we've been able to keep her safe until she gets home." I bend to grab another soggy item of clothing... my sleep shorts.

"I think what Falin's trying to say is that this situation is not ideal," Blake says. "She's been working nonstop since the new year and I'm sure she's just tired." She stands beside me and gives me a side hug.

"We're all tired, but tonight will make it all worthwhile." A rare Leon smile lifts the corner of his lips, brightening his eyes.

"Are you sure you're ready?" Blake asks. I've been wondering the same thing. It took us days to work out the encrypted files from Fairfax's hard drive and days more to track the money moved to random offshore banking institutions. The only thing of any use so far is the address we got off Wayne. That scumbag was good for something, at least.

The guys have been surveilling the address—a run down house in the Bronx—for days and finally saw some movement yesterday. A couple of guys going in and out, but that wasn't what's got Leon smiling. Jasper recognized one of the auctioned girls from Fairfax's gala with them. It was a quick sighting, but he swears it was number two, the runner.

It took everything in him to not blow their cover and bust down the door then and there.

"Need any more help?" Jasper asks, peeking inside the room.

I flash him a polite smile. "No, we've got it."

"We were just talking about the sleeping arrangements," Leon says with a smirk. "Any input, Jas?"

"You can take my bed," Jasper says without hesitation.

I toss a waterlogged paperback book into the bin and stand up straight. "Where will you sleep?"

He shrugs, and pulls his hand through his hair. My breath catches... I don't know what it is, but that movement does it for me. "The floor."

"Attaboy," Leon says, patting him on the shoulder. "So chivalrous."

"No. I won't take your bed," I argue, knowing it won't matter.

Damon stops behind Jasper. "Whose bed?"

It's like a line of hot tattooed men coming into my bedroom. If I wasn't so aggravated, I'd laugh.

"Nothing," I say. "Don't we have to leave soon?" The guys exchange looks. "What is it?"

"We think it's best if you two stay here with Kayla," Damon says carefully. "We have no idea who or what we'll find in there and we can't risk either of you getting hurt."

I open my mouth to argue, but Blake beats me to it. "But it's okay for you three to risk your lives?"

"I—" Damon starts.

"Absolutely not." She crosses her arms over her chest. "If you're going, so are we."

"But—" Jasper cuts in. I glare at him and he shuts his mouth tight.

"So, when are we leaving?" Blake asks.

WE CLIMB out of Ray's borrowed van as night blankets the street in darkness. Only one dim street light flickers from a few houses down, almost like the residents of the neighborhood know nothing after dark needs to be seen.

Old cars line the sidewalk—rust-damaged and missing paint. A few bicycles lean against brick siding. But what I focus on is the rundown house we're headed to. It looms ahead, three stories of crumbling yellow stucco and peeling red trim. I watch my step on the cracked sidewalk—one slip on ice and I'd be down for the count. From what I can see, the house could have been beautiful a long time ago. Possibly some original owner's pride and joy. But now, the sunroom windows are nothing but broken glass, jagged like a jack o' lantern's teeth, and the porch made of sagging rotten wood.

I shiver through my heavy jacket, a loaner from Jasper. After the other night, I wasn't getting caught outside in nothing but a dress. We've gone over the plan so many times, I could recite it in my sleep, but something feels off.

Strong hands grasp my shoulders and I freeze. I know it's Jasper before I turn. "I need you to stay back here... just for now."

I flip around and try to make myself tall, although that's laughable considering I come up to his chest. "I want to help." I know I sound like a petulant child, but there's no avoiding it.

"Please, Falin." He says my name with the kind of desperation you'd hear from a man begging for his life. It takes me aback.

I glance over at Blake, who's most likely getting the same talk from Damon, judging by her body language. If something were to happen to my best friend because of my stubbornness, I'd never forgive myself. I nod, my shoulders sagging in defeat. "Fine, but I swear you better get us on the comms if anything goes wrong."

He's relieved. It's difficult to tell in the dark, but I see how his chest loosens like he's finally taking his first full breath of the night. "I promise, I will. We'll need you to keep an eye out here. Let us know if anything at all looks off."

I wrap my arms around my chest and take a few steps back toward the van. Blake must have given in as well. Her eyes meet mine and she jogs over to join me. "Watch out for black ice," I warn.

"I know, I know." Man, I must be extra on edge tonight if even Blake is sassing me.

Jasper turns back, pulling on his mask with a smirk—his ridiculously sparkly mask. Even in this fucked up situation, I can't help but smile.

Blake and I climb into the warm van, squeezing close so we can watch from the side window. "I can't believe he's wearing that mask," Blake says.

I laugh. "You know, if it were anyone other than Jasper, I'd agree with you."

She shoulder bumps me. "So, you and Jas have been getting pretty close."

I knew this conversation would come. I'm honestly surprised it hasn't happened sooner. "Not any closer than all of us in the house."

"Hmm, if you say so." She does that twirling her necklace thing that she always does when she's thinking. I tap my ear, and she understands what I'm asking. We turn off our comms.

"I mean... I don't know. There's an energy with us. He

makes me laugh even when we're driving each other crazy. And yeah, he's hot. Of course he is. But I know there's more to him." I cut my rambling off when I realize Blake's totally smirking at me.

"I knew it! You like him. I've never seen you get flustered over a guy. Actually, I've barely ever seen you get flustered, period."

"I'm not flustered!" I say as I raise my voice to prove my point. *Wow*. "Fine, you got me. I might be just a tad bit flustered, but to be fair that man is the definition of irritating."

Blake laughs again. "You're not wrong, but he's a giant teddy bear. He'd be good for you, Fal."

I blow out a long groaning sigh. "It's complicated. Some things have... transpired," I choose my words carefully, "and I'm not sure either of us wants anything serious." Focusing my gaze out the window, I add, "And really, with all of this going on, it's not good timing anyway."

"You're probably right. If Damon wasn't so... Damon, I doubt things would have moved so quickly for us."

A plastic shopping bag blows across the street, catching my eye. I follow its path until it vanishes over the hill. Time stretches. Each minute since the guys walked toward that house could have been an hour. My hands ache from the cold, and I curse myself over and over for not grabbing the van keys from Leon.

"Should we check in?" I ask, my finger messing with my comm.

Blake's already tapping her phone screen. "It's only been ten minutes. They're fine. Right, guys? What's happening in there?"

The silence feels wrong in my chest. "Weird. Jasper never shuts up on these things."

Blake takes hers out and jabs the buttons. "Maybe they're not working."

My skin prickles, that ominous feeling washing through me for the second time tonight. A shadow flickers on the hill—or does it? I narrow my eyes to take a closer look, but before I can focus, gunshots shatter the night.

"Shit!" My body moves before my brain catches up, legs carrying me out of the van and toward danger. Blake's footsteps pound behind me, her medical bag thumping against her side. "What the fuck is happening? Jasper, answer me!"

I knew we shouldn't have let them go alone. Why didn't I trust my instincts?

I tear through the yard, my boots crunching in the packed snow, my heart pounding. Through the darkness, a shadowed figure appears from behind the house—Jasper, mask rolled up on his head, face grim. There's something in his arms—

"Falin," he calls out. "Here, come take her."

I move on autopilot. A child is placed in my arms, her cries are distant, like we're underwater. Blake moves beside me with outstretched arms, so I pass the child over and catch up to Jasper.

As I round the corner, Leon emerges, blood smeared on his face, dripping onto the pure white snow where it spreads like watercolor paint. Two young women wearing nothing but thin T-shirts stumble after him, frantically clutching each other. "This way," I hear myself yell.

Leon tosses me the keys to the van, and understanding clicks into place. I nod, and sprint back, pulling it as close to the house as I can. My hand's on the door handle when Leon ushers the girls inside. "No, stay. I'll need you to drive."

My fingers tremble against the steering wheel. "Where's

Damon?" Blake's voice cracks, barely audible over the wails of the child.

Where is he? Where's Jasper? Whose blood? Was Leon shot? Questions spin but won't form words.

I open my lips to speak, but the words get lost in my throat. Jasper emerges from the shadows again, carrying another child. This one looks smaller than the first. My heart cracks in two. As he steps in front of the headlights, I see the dark stains coating his clothes, wet like spilled ink.

Damon appears last, a woman by his side. She moves differently than the others, standing straight and confident, wearing loose jeans that hang from her hips and an oversize flannel. As she gets closer I see the pain in her expression. There's something familiar—

"Oh my God!" Blake's voice cracks as she drops a roll of gauze. "Mischa?"

CHAPTER TWENTY-TWO

JASPER

I place the child into the van as gently as my shaking limbs allow and she shuffles across the seat into the arms of one of the older victims. "Bella, come here." It's number two, the young woman with more strength than I could ever muster. She's holding them all together by a thread. I tried not to spill blood in front of them, but it was impossible.

"Jasper?" Falin's voice cracks. She's behind the wheel, eyes wide, taking in the chaos unfolding.

"I'm okay," I smear the blood on my hoodie. "It's not mine."

She visibly shudders and her gaze moves to Mischa Orlova. I'm still in shock myself. Blake's asking the questions we're all wondering.

"Are you hurt?"

Mischa holds her head higher, but I see the mask she wears. "I'm fine."

"Why are you here?" Blake asks.

"Listen," Damon interrupts. "We're running out of time. Angel, I need you to go with Leon and Falin to meet up with Ray's team. I'll meet you back home soon." He blocks Mischa's body, not so gently moving her out of his way to get to Blake. She falls into his arms, speaking softly so only he can hear.

My eyes stray back to Falin and I have the same urge to hold her. I don't know if it's reassurance that we'll come out the end of this unscathed. Or maybe I simply need to feel her against my skin. I should say something to break this thread of tension between us. "I'll get him back to her in one piece."

"You better," she says.

Blake climbs into the van, attention focused on the girls again. Leon pats my shoulder. "You know what you have to do?"

"Yes." At this point it's not about what I *have* to do. It's about what I *want* to do. I'll take pleasure in ending his life. My eyes stray back to Falin, who's nervously tapping the steering wheel, her lips moving.

"I've got them," Leon says. "Don't worry, brother."

"And what are we doing with her?" Damon asks, his words like venom. Mischa wraps her arms around her chest and I barely notice her begin to sway on her feet.

"Grab her!" I yell.

Damon holds her by the shoulders right as she's about to go down. "Fuck. She's not right. She should go with you guys, if we keep her here with us, she'll be a liability," he says.

Leon nods. "Let's search her for weapons or anything she can use to communicate with King or her father. Be quick."

Mischa's high-pitched laughter breaks through Leon's words. "You think I'd try to reach him? He couldn't care less if I was found rotting in a ditch."

The three of us exchange baffled looks. We don't have time to discuss any of that at the moment. Damon gives Mischa a quick pat down and ushers her into the van with the others. He pats the top of the van and stares at Blake like a lovesick puppy again. These two really need to read the room. "I love you," he tells her.

"She loves you. They love you. We love you. There's love all around," I joke. "Let's get going."

As soon as he slides the van door shut, his posture changes. The Damon that I need slips back into place. I take one last look at Falin through the foggy window and tell myself she'll be safe with Leon. For this, I need a clear head.

We check the surroundings once the van is safely down the street. With all the commotion, we could have woken neighbors or busybody late night pedestrians. I point to the hill across the street. "Should we check up there?"

Damon thinks for a moment. "Eh, there's nothing up there but dead trees and snow."

I shrug. It would only take a few extra minutes to jog up there and check it out, but that's usually Damon's thing. Plus, like Leon said, this needs to be fast. "We should finish this."

I slide my gloves on, not that it'll matter if we leave prints once we're done. This place is a dump. I wouldn't want my worst enemy to live here. Okay, maybe that's not true... but plain and simple, it's fucking nasty. Crumbling walls stained with ash and tobacco, the stench of piss in the air, rotting food and beer cans strewn around the filthy floor.

I try not to imagine what's crunching under my boots with each step. "And you thought I was a slob?"

Damon shakes his head. "There's slob and then there's *this*. I wish we had fucking hazmat suits."

We step over a body—the big guy I shot earlier. I kick him with the toe of my boot. Damon notices and flashes me a confused look. "What? I want to make sure the fucker's dead."

"I think the bullet through his skull is telling enough."

He would think, but I've heard some wild stories about people surviving gunshots to the head. "You never know."

Something moves in my peripheral and I twist, aiming my gun. "Is that a fucking rat?"

"Probably. I'm sure that's not the worst of what's living in this place." He moves toward the stairwell, stepping over an ancient-looking pizza box. "Remind me to have Leon or Falin find out who holds the deed to this place."

"Yeah, okay." I'll try to remember. Kinda difficult when there's one main focus in my brain right now.

"I'm going to check the rest of the house, make sure we didn't leave anyone behind. I'll see if there's any useful information in this hovel. Meet you upstairs." He doesn't wait for me to nod before he's stomping into one of the bedrooms, gun aimed forward.

Each stair groans under my weight as I climb, my heart racing with anticipation. How will I find the scummy bastard that I hog-tied earlier? Will he be broken? Crying and pissing his pants? Or maybe the arrogant streak that I quickly witnessed still runs through him, forcing me to pry every word from his filthy mouth. I hope for the latter. It's much more fun.

I steel myself as I step into the bedroom. The smell is almost too much to bear. The way these victims were kept... I have no words. Dirty mattresses along the floor, a large dog cage in the corner. Restraints everywhere... ropes, chains, handcuffs. The worst of it isn't in this room though. It's in the second bedroom, the one with the cameras.

There he is, face down on the filthy mattress. His ankles bound tight to his wrists, forcing his legs to bow backward. He squirms as he hears me enter, mumbling incoherently. He's afraid. Fuck yes. That's what I was hoping for. I know the fear he's feeling isn't a fraction of what those girls felt, but it's something to fuel me. I crouch beside him, keeping my voice casual. "Having fun?"

He lifts his head as much as he's able. "I'll kill you. Motherfuc—"

"Hey, hey, no need to bring my mother into this." I press my boot against the small of his back, giving him my weight. "If you stay nice and still, I'll untie you. We need to have a little talk."

"I'm not telling you shit." At least that's what I think he says. Hard to tell with his face smashed against the mattress.

Man, what I wouldn't give to blow off some steam and really take my time with him. I'm so tense, and as vile as this house is, it's the perfect place to have a little fun with a monster. But first I need to turn him over so I can see the light leave his eyes.

"Suit yourself. I was going to let you up the nice way." I yank his bindings, dragging him from the mattress over the splintered wooden floor. Using all my strength, I swing my arm, tossing him against the wall with a loud thud. His head makes contact with the ancient plaster shooting dust into the air. I'm with Damon, we need fucking hazmat suits or gas masks in this damn place. The way his body settles has me chuckling. "You ever do yoga? Pretty sure you're doing a pose."

He doesn't find me hilarious, which I guess I understand, but seriously, I can't stop laughing. Not until the floor creaks behind me, letting me know that Damon's come to join the party.

"Umm, I think you've officially lost your mind," he says.

I point, ignoring our floor friend's threats and curses, and say with a laugh, "He's doing yoga."

Damon tilts his head, letting loose a dry laugh of his own. "You know, you're right. Bet we can put him in a better pose though."

"Corpse pose?" I offer. Damn, I'm clever.

"I knew you did yoga in Florida. You lying ass," Damon accuses. "How else would you know pose names?"

"Let me go. You're dead men. Both of you."

Damon drops into a crouch, jabbing a finger in my direction. "You better spill the truth later. Those yoga pants I found in the dryer—definitely yours."

I flash him my innocent smile, the one that women fall over themselves for. Well, most women. Falin's been immune to its charms. Wait, is it weird that I'm giving my best friend my sexy look? Eh, question for later. "Let's get his name."

There's no need to waste our time asking when we know he won't tell us. Damon moves him every which way, using his binds for leverage. "I see something in his pocket. A bulge. Maybe it's his wallet. Grab it while I hold him."

"I don't want to feel around this fucker's bulge. I'll hold him and you do it. And can we gag him while we're at it? I'm sick of listening to him, he's so unoriginal."

Damon shoots me a look that says I'll be the next one tied up with rope if I don't do as he says. *Kinky.* Too bad I don't swing that way, even for someone as dreamy as Damon.

"Fine. Just hold him still." I kneel beside them, shove a dirty rag from the floor into his mouth, and reach into his pocket. "Yup, it's a wallet." Thank God, that's *all* I felt.

Damon gestures his head toward it. I'm already on it. I flip the black leather open and find his ID. "Yuri Kozlov. There's a Jersey address listed." I rifle through the rest of the shit in there —a bank card, a gym membership, a photo of a young woman with light hair. "Who's this, Yuri? She's too pretty for you."

He mumbles through the gag, his face red in the dim light.

"What was that? Can't seem to hear you," Damon taunts.

I pocket his ID and bank card, tossing the rest onto the floor. I bend again so I'm closer to his eye level. Keeping my voice calm, I ask, "What is this place, Yuri?"

Silly me, I forgot the gag. I yank it out and he wastes no time spitting in my face. That's just nasty. He better not be carrying any diseases. Wiping my face with my sleeve, I grab my blade and bring it to his throat. "You forget that we killed all your friends without breaking a sweat. Now, I'll ask again. What is this place?"

"Ask the whore. I'm sure she'll tell you whatever you want while she spreads her legs." Damon and I share a look. We know who he's talking about. *Mischa*.

Now it's Damon with murder in his eyes. "What did you do to her? To all of them?"

I inch my blade closer, smiling as blood beads from a sliver of his skin. "Answer him," I seethe.

"You think *I'm* the one who touched them?" He laughs, a harsh sound that settles in my skull. "He'd kill me if I so much as grazed a titty."

I press harder. "Who would kill you?"

His eyes dart between us, a smirk playing on his lips. "If you don't know already, you will soon enough. There's no hiding from him. No escaping. He'll kill everyone you've ever loved." As his voice trails off, his gaze lands on the discarded picture on the floor.

"That room next door," I say, growing more and more impatient by the second. "What went on in there?"

For a second, I almost think a flash of pain crosses his face. It's too late—I have no pity, not for a man like him.

Honestly, maybe we're better off not hearing the play by play. I'm already filled with more rage than I know what to do with.

Damon lets out a frustrated groan and I move my hand from Yuri's throat. "He's useless." Which means it's time to end him. "I'll go prep the house."

Damon lets the rope loose and Yuri sags like one of these old mattresses. I stand and toy with the locking mechanism on my blade, retracting it and releasing it with soft clicks.

"What are you going to do to me?" His voice is calm, matter-of-fact. He knows the end has come for him.

Do I believe that he never touched those girls? Does that make him less evil than the men who did?

"Give me something, Yuri, and I'll make this quick."

His eyes flick to the picture again and he sighs. "Orlov... he's the one you want."

I crouch, and meet his pained expression with my own hard one. "Something I don't know."

His eyes widen but he doesn't ask how I know about Orlov. "Get it over with, then. I'm a dead man already."

I stand, release my blade, and slice across his throat in one fluid motion. No need to drag it out. Yuri stopped being fun ten minutes ago.

He sputters for a moment, his body twitching while blood drains from his neck. I'm already out of that cesspool of a bedroom before he takes his final breath.

I find Damon in the kitchen holding two bottles of vodka. "Having a party without me?"

"Is he dead?"

I grab a third bottle from the top of the filthy refrigerator. "Yeah, he wouldn't give me shit. Said we need to find Orlov."

Damon shrugs. "We'll have to see what we can get out of Orlova."

He walks through the lower floor, pouring vodka onto pizza boxes, the couch, the dead man's body. I follow suit—pouring extra over the splintered wooden staircase. "I'm out," I yell across the house. He tosses me his lighter, and I let it spark to life, watching as the staircase erupts, orange flames dancing up the splintered rails.

I make my way to the front door, where Damon waits admiring his handiwork. "Nice job," I say as we exchange dark smiles. Heat presses against our backs as we leave, and I can't resist murmuring, "Burn, baby, burn."

CHAPTER TWENTY-THREE

FALIN

WE CLIMB THE STEPS TO THE APARTMENT AS DAWN begins to break. I've never been more exhausted in my life, and that includes the time I went on a three day long bender in Thailand.

Those girls, their faces and cries, will haunt me for the rest of my life. But I can sleep easy knowing they're safe. Ray has them getting medical attention and then his contacts will transfer them to a safe house while they locate the families.

All except for one, who refused medical treatment. Mischa. I wanted to toss her ass out on the street, but Blake wouldn't have it. How she can still have an ounce of care in her body for that woman is beyond me. So now instead of one extra person in the house, we'll have two. At least it's only temporary.

Kayla greets us with a look of relief. "How did it go?"

I muster a smile that probably looks more like a grimace. "We got four out. They're safe."

Her body sags and she swipes tears from her cheek. "Thank God."

Blake hugs me goodnight before heading to her bedroom, where Damon waits. Leon settles on the couch next to Kayla, scooping the kittens into his lap and updating her about where they took the girls and sharing details from the night. When the bathroom door opens, my attention shifts. Jasper emerges wearing gym shorts and a white sleeveless undershirt. Even exhausted, he's still the most gorgeous man I've ever seen.

My gaze trails over his muscled shoulders and down his tattooed arms. His undershirt clings to his damp chest, showing every dip and curve of his pec and ab muscles. And his thighs, holy fuck, they're thick. The fabric from his shorts can barely contain him. My skin heats as I remember how his body felt between my legs.

His fingers work through his tangled hair as my gaze fixes on his face. A day's worth of stubble lines his jaw, making him look extra rugged. I'd love to rub my cheek against it. Even with dark circles shadowing his eyes, those bright blue irises and thick black lashes still make my lungs squeeze.

They darken the moment he catches me staring. His lips turn up in a flirty smirk as he steps closer. "You okay, Trouble? Looking a bit flustered."

I swallow the lump in my throat and raise a brow. Too tired to think of a witty comeback, I mutter, "I'm fine."

Mischa picks that moment to emerge from Jasper and Leon's bedroom. Her eyes brighten when she notices him, a small smile lighting her tired face. All at once, jealousy engulfs me, scorching my body in flames as she crosses her arms over her chest and moves toward Jasper.

"I hope you don't mind me taking your bed. Your friend said I should," she says. She tries to make her high-pitched voice sound sultry but the result sounds like the kittens' wails when they're hungry.

Jasper turns and offers her a small smile. "It's no problem. You should get some rest. You've been through a lot."

Leon and Kayla stop talking as we all watch Mischa run a finger down Jasper's bicep. "Why don't you join me? For old time's sake."

I push up from the couch and storm past them to the bathroom, cursing myself for being so obviously jealous. But hell, I can't help it. I'm too tired to mask. Too exhausted to play games. If he wants to fuck Mischa, like he's apparently already done, then he can go ahead. I won't stop him. It doesn't mean I want to sit and watch it unfold.

After using the bathroom, I clean up with the lukewarm water bottle Blake left behind, taking time to wipe and moisturize my face. As I step out, two realizations hit me. I'm supposed to sleep in Jasper's bed tonight, and maintenance arrives in a few hours to fix the broken pipe in my room.

Either I take my friendship with Kayla to a new level and cuddle on the couch or I pack my shit and head to the nearest hotel. Honestly, that sounds amazing. A big fluffy bed, clean and quiet and all to myself. But I think of leaving Jasper here with Mischa and dig my heels in. As much as it'll hurt, I need to know where that goes.

Maybe I'll curl up on my damp mattress with a throw blanket. At the very least, I can sleep for an hour. Set on my decision, I head back to the main area of the apartment, freezing when I find Jasper, shirtless and sitting on the couch in his boxers, his arms casually resting along the top of the cushions and his legs wide. He looks me up and down and that warmth returns to my skin. "What are you doing out here?"

"Waiting to see if you want to be the big spoon or the little spoon," he says with a smirk.

"But I thought—"

He pats the couch cushion beside him. "Come here. Let's get some sleep while we can."

How can he be so casual about this? Did he just turn Mischa down... for me?

"Where will Kayla sleep?"

He shifts, and I get a peek of what's hiding under those boxers. My cheeks flame. "She's in Leon's bed, Mischa's in mine, and Leon went for a ride to clear his head."

I nod, all of this making sense, except for Jasper turning down Mischa's offer. Thinking about it, I guess he wouldn't sleep with her after knowing she's Orlov's daughter, and she's obviously been through some shit. He's loyal to the guys, and they'd kick his ass if he went down that path.

My body feels so weighed down, each step I take toward the couch is like a mile. I should argue, tell him to take the floor, but as he reclines onto his side and opens his arms, I can't help but fall into his chest. He wraps me tight against him, leaving no space between us, then covers us with his blanket. I breathe him in. Although neither of us have showered, he still smells like clean cotton. I love that he grabbed his comforter for us. Mischa doesn't need to be wrapped in his scent the way I am.

As we settle in, I let out an unconscious murmur. His chest shakes with a low laugh, but I don't have the energy to sass him. Especially not as Havoc and Mayhem jump onto our legs, their little paws digging in as they find their own cozy spots in the dip where our hips meet.

"Come to Daddy," he whispers, scooping one of them to nuzzle.

I laugh, unable to hold it in. "You're ridiculous."

"What? I was talking to the cats. Wait, did you think I was talking to you?" There he goes with that flirty tone again.

"I *know* you were talking to the cats. If you think I'd call you daddy, you've got another thing coming."

He plops the kitten back with her sister and splays his palm over my waist. His touch is electric. And damn, his hard length is already pressing against my ass. "How about good boy?"

"You'd have to *be* a good boy first." I wait for his response, clocking the way his chest rises and falls faster.

"I've been very good." His fingertip grazes the underside of my breast and I bite my lip to keep from moaning. "Some might say, I've been an angel."

Closing my eyes, I focus on the sensation of his calloused fingertips trailing higher, so slow it's agonizing. I want to push and grind against him, give us the friction we desperately crave, but edging him is so much more fun.

"Some might say?" I rasp as his thumb glides over my nipple.

His voice brushes my ear, trembling with need. "Yes. But you're the only one who matters."

I should be soaking in his words. They're exactly what I want to hear. But frustration burns through me instead. I've been with a lot of men who would say anything when their hard cock was pressed this close to getting what it wanted. Hell, a strong wind is all we need and he'd be inside me. I can't give in.

His hand trails lower, over the curve of my belly, sliding under the band of my sleep shorts. I'm taking back my power here. I shift, pushing his shoulders until he's on his back, and swing my leg over him. The kittens scatter, protesting loudly at my audacity. "You want to be a good boy, Jasper?"

His face is the picture of desperation. I bask in it. "Fuck yes. I'll be so good for you."

I rake my nails down his bare chest, over the light dusting of hair, until I reach his stomach. His abs contract as he sucks in a breath. I repeat the motion, this time stopping just above his boxers.

He moans, wrapping his hands around my waist. I pull them by his wrists, putting them firmly back by his side. "No touching."

"Fuck, baby, whatever you say."

Everything in me wants to ride him senseless until we're screaming our releases. I'm exhausted and drained but there's something magnetic between us, something that makes me feel more awake with every passing moment. I need to take out my frustrations on him the only way I can right now.

I slide down so I'm resting on the tops of his firm thighs. He's so hard, his cock is practically splitting his boxers in half. Wetness seeps into the fabric. Under my gaze, he juts his hips. It's a slight movement but I catch it.

Lazily, almost painfully so, I drag his boxers down, freeing his cock. It's perfect. Of course, it is. He's watching my every move with reverence. I raise a brow and lean in, letting my T-shirt graze his cock. He fists the blanket and groans. "Oh fuck."

"Does that feel good?" I do it again, this time purposely brushing over his head.

"Yes... anything, please."

He's already begging and I've barely touched him.

"Do not come. I don't allow it." As the words slip from

my tongue, a heady wave of control washes over me, and I savor the sensation. It feels better than I could imagine to hold his resolve in the palm of my hand, knowing I'll do everything I can to break it.

His answering groan is desperate as he struggles to keep his hips still. I toy with his inked torso, scratching along the sides of his body until I reach his hip bones. Stroking every inch of skin around his cock with the lightest touch as he curses under his breath.

I'm soaking wet, and more turned on than I think I've ever been. Knowing what kind of man Jasper is—that he's taken a life with his own hands, yet I have him under my control like a whimpering dog, that power is intoxicating.

"So hard for me," I tease. "That looks painful." Trailing my finger from the base of his cock to the tip with feather-light pressure, I watch him struggle to maintain control, his jaw clenched tight. "Imagine how good it would feel to have my mouth on you," I whisper, my touch teasing as I gather his pre-cum between my fingertips. I bring one to my lips slowly and moan, tasting his salty moisture.

"Jesus fucking—" His words end in a hoarse groan as I grip him. I glide up and down, just once, before going back to dancing my fingertips along his shaft, barely touching.

"Do you want more?" I whisper.

"Please," he begs, his voice thick. I pull off my shirt, not caring that at any moment someone could walk in and see us. It only heightens my need. "Christ, baby."

He reaches for me, but thinks better of it, resting his hands beside my thighs, fingers twitching with the need to touch. I sit back, drinking in how he trembles, memorizing every inch of his features like this.

"Remember, you're not allowed to come." I finally touch

him again, agonizingly slow. Each light stroke takes him closer and closer to the edge before I stop. Over and over, I pause just before he breaks, until his eyes shine with frustrated tears. "Look at you," I murmur. "So desperate, so obedient." I hover over him, letting my tits brush against his face. He lets out a choked whimper. "You'd do anything I ask right now, wouldn't you?"

"Anything... anything you want. Fuck." He nods frantically, burying his face between my tits. I let him suck and lick my breasts between his panting and whimpering for more.

"Oh God." The words tumble out of me as my control breaks apart. He sucks harder, nibbling, until I hiss a breath.

"Please," he pants. "Please let me eat your pussy, baby." I pull back, my mind clouded with want. This was about my control. About seeing how far I could take him. "Please, I'll be so good for you."

I trail my fingers down his chest, feeling his muscles jump beneath my touch. My mind is at war. Either I give in to what we both desperately want, or keep going with this delicious torture. I'm so hot, so needy. Just the thought of his mouth on my pussy almost sends me over the edge.

Those blue eyes lock onto mine, crazed with need, but still waiting for permission.

"Tell me again," I whisper. "Tell me how good you'll be."

In one fluid motion, he lifts me and pins me against the couch, pressing my back into the cushions. He tears my underwear down my legs before spreading them wide. My head dangles off the armrest, but I'm past caring. Nothing else exists but this moment. He settles between my thighs, dragging his face along the sensitive skin there, making these deep, primal sounds that pull a whimper from my throat.

"You're so wet, Falin. You love tormenting me, don't you?" Before I can answer he glides his tongue through my slit, slowly, like he's savoring every second. "So fucking sweet."

"Please." I arch against him. My mind has whiplash from how fast our positions changed.

"Make a mess of my face, sweetheart. I want to be drenched in you." There's nothing slow or teasing about the way he eats my pussy. His whole fucking face grinds against my clit, his tongue flicking in a punishing rhythm. He's whimpering and groaning, trembling between my slick thighs, grinding into the couch.

"Oh fuck, Jas," I hiss. He grips my thighs, sucking my clit hard as his whole body spasms. I lose myself to the feel of him as my climax slams into me so hard I have to bite my arm to keep from screaming. I lock my legs around him, trembling as waves of pleasure roll through me.

Puffs of air hit my sensitive skin when he raises his head to meet my gaze. I know the answer before I even ask, but I ask anyway. "Did you just come all over the couch?"

An exhausted laugh escapes his lips. "Yeah, I did." I don't know why, but that makes me feel incredible. "But I'm not the only one."

"I'm useless right now," I mumble. "That couch is your problem." He laughs softly, standing to pull up his boxers before helping me into my shirt. Once we're halfway decent, he slides in behind me.

"Sleep, Trouble."

I melt against his warm chest, already drifting. "Why Trouble?"

The silence stretches so long I'm almost asleep when his

voice rumbles against my ear. "Because you're everything I told myself I couldn't have."

"Mmm. My good boy," I mumble, feeling so light and content that what we went through hours ago is almost unbelievable.

His chest shakes with silent laughter as I drift off.

CHAPTER TWENTY-FOUR

ALEXANDER

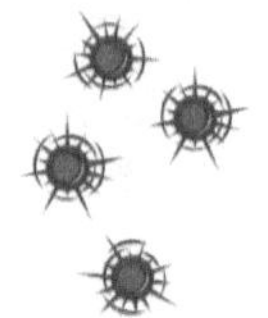

The vodka burns my throat. Three shots and it's
still not enough to dull the rage rolling through my veins,
twisting my gut until I want to scream. Dominic's body lies
in a heap at my feet, his blood mixed with amber whiskey
pooling on my imported Persian rug. The decanter I used to
bash his head in is discarded by his side. Bruce trembles in
the corner, tears streaming down his pathetic face. I glance
back at Dominic's body, disgusted by its presence.

"Clean this up." When Bruce stays put, I launch my
glass against the wall next to his head. "Now!" He scrambles to his feet, slipping in his brother's blood. "Get me a
towel first."

"Yes, sir." Pathetic. His blubbering is making me crazy.
He drops a fresh towel from my bathroom onto my desk,
and I wipe the blood off my shaking hands.

Everything's falling apart. The house, Yuri, Mischa—all
gone in one night. And these incompetent fucks just
watched it happen. Didn't do a goddamn thing!

My phone buzzes. NYPD lights up my screen. I let it

ring while I scroll through the preliminary report. It helps to have friends in high places.

The fire destroyed most of the evidence, but they found traces of accelerant. Two bodies. The property records on that dump lead straight to MechExpress.

Fuck.

I need this taken care of before Ivan finds out. Before he realizes how I've let everything turn to shit. The thought of his disappointment, his rage, makes me want to bash Bruce's head in too. I dial Fairfax's number, pacing as it rings.

"What?" His tone is a complete one-eighty from how we greeted each other weeks ago.

"The investigation. Handle it."

"And why would I do that? After what your people cost me on New Year's—"

"Because if I go down, you go down with me." I imbue my voice with all the rage I feel. "Every dirty deal, every charitable donation. I have records, Harrison."

The line goes quiet. Finally, he sighs. "I'll make some calls. But Orlov? We're done after this. You won't see a dollar from me."

I hit "end." Done? He thinks he can just walk away? No one fucks with me.

A harsh laugh escapes my lips as I sit back down in front of my computer. Bruce hoists his brother's body, dragging him toward the door, leaving a crimson trail in his wake. What a mess. Yet another problem I'll have to deal with because of his incompetence.

"Get rid of him properly," I say. "Or you'll join him."

I go over the details I was able to get out of Dominic. My mind keeps returning to thoughts of the blonde. The pretty one with the sense of defiance. Bruce was smart enough to get a few blurry shots of her that night. About all he got. Useless, I swear.

My hands steady as I type *Falin Sinclair* into the search bar. Images fill my screen. A news article, professional head-shots, snippets of her life before she met Blake Hyland. Ah, she has a cop daddy. How interesting.

This Sinclair girl. She helped destroy everything I've built.

I zoom in on a photo of her at some tech conference. Her hair is different, darker and falling over one shoulder as she speaks into a microphone, but it's her. Such confidence. Such control.

I'll enjoy breaking her while her boyfriend watches.

They think they're so clever, playing hero and saving those worthless girls. But they have no idea what's coming. I don't need Fairfax or my uncle's resources. I'll handle this myself.

I click through more photos, committing every detail to memory. Soon enough, I'll fuck that self-assured smile off her face. I'll kill all her friends, saving Blake Hyland for last.

Then I'll give her to Ivan as a gift. He always had a thing for blondes. I'll show him that I'm still worthy. Still his most valuable asset.

"Sir?" Bruce's shaking voice interrupts my thoughts. "It's done. May I go and—and..."

"Get out. I'm done with you." I wave him away without looking up. My eyes widen as I scroll through a particularly interesting article from a small Ohio newspaper.

I shoot down the rest of my vodka, enjoying the burn. "Now this is exactly what I needed to find."

CHAPTER TWENTY-FIVE

JASPER

BANG, BANG, BANG.

Somebody's trying to break in. I jump up, disorientated, my heart hammering from the sudden intrusion. Falin stirs beside me, mumbling in her sleep, and I remember how we defiled the couch in the most delicious way.

"Maintenance!" a deep voice sounds. Before I'm able to get my bearings, Leon strides to the door, pulling it open and greeting whichever bastard had the nerve to jolt me from dreamland.

I watch through groggy eyes as two guys lugging a ladder and a tool kit hurry into the room, getting directions from Leon. The first one stops, his eyes lingering on Falin's bare leg stretched out over the blanket. "If you'd like to keep your eyes, you better get moving," I say. He darts his gaze away, muttering an apology. I flash a grin to show I'm only kidding, but honestly, I'd do much worse than take his eyes.

Climbing over Falin, I go to take a piss, struggling with my insane morning wood. I'm so distracted, I almost forget that we can't flush. As I set up my toothbrush, uncapping the bottled water someone left in here, I roll my lip between my teeth, still tasting Falin. I wish I didn't have to brush my fucking teeth or wash up. She was drenched for me, soaking my face like it was her job. I want to remember that every time I wet my lips, but I can't go around with rancid breath.

By the time I leave the bathroom, the two workers are walking out the door. "Where the hell are they going?" I ask Leon, who's locking up behind them.

He shrugs and lets loose a tired sigh. "They need to order parts, apparently."

"They were here for thirty seconds. How could they know that?" I glance over at Falin, feeling awful that she's still out of a bedroom. Although we seem to have claimed the couch as our own, literally and figuratively.

"I'd fix it myself if I knew a damn thing about plumbing," he said.

I notice the shadows under his eyes and the way his shoulders sag. "Did you get any sleep yet?"

"A wink or two." He won't meet my eyes, so I'm guessing that's a lie. "My father called this morning while I was out. He's in town and wants to have some 'father-son bonding time.'"

I stop halfway into the kitchen. "He's in New York?"

"That would be what I meant by in town."

I'd give him shit for being a know-it-all if he wasn't so miserable. His father could win an award for biggest prick in England. "I'm sorry, man. Can you blow him off?"

I grab what I need to brew a pot of coffee while listening. "I wish, but unless we want to get cut off, I need to keep kissing his ass."

The coffee machine's hiss is like sweet music to my ears. "How long will you be gone?" Last time he had to meet up with his father for "dinner" he was gone for three days, paraded around to every colleague like a prized horse. Nothing could be further from reality though. Leon will never be good enough for his father. The man will always pick him apart, and who knows what else, until Leon can shut him out for good.

"I won't let him manipulate me this time. Just dinner, that's it. We have too much happening." I pour his coffee first, grab the creamer from the fridge and slide both across to him.

"If you need backup, I'll be there in a second."

He nods, watching the steam rise from his mug. "I know."

The apartment comes alive from the smell of coffee, I guess. Blake and Damon emerge from their room, looking fresh and rested. Minutes later, Kayla and Mischa's door opens, which is perfect timing. I slip in to grab a T-shirt and some sweatpants, coming back to find Falin sitting up on the couch, the blanket covering her lap.

Our eyes lock, and I take in the way her breath catches. I'm so gone for her, it's wild. I busted Damon's balls for being obsessed with Blake not two months ago, and here I am, googly eyed from one look.

"We need to talk." We both turn toward Blake's voice to see her standing in front of Mischa. She's clearly upset, but she's standing her ground. I'm proud of her. "There was so much going on last night, and you were clearly dehydrated, and well... What the hell were you doing there, Mischa? Tell us everything."

With the eyes of everyone in the apartment on her, Mischa's face turns red. I can see her facade start to crumble, and in seconds she runs to the bathroom, shutting the door.

"Fuck," Damon says, pulling his hand through his hair.

He squeezes Blake's shoulder and heads for the front door. "I need a smoke. I'll be right back."

"I can understand her not wanting to talk," Kayla says, surprising me. She's been pretty quiet since that first night. Some of her confidence must be returning. "I don't know her, but if she came from the same situation I did, she'll need time."

Blake nods, collapsing on the couch next to Falin. "I understand that, but it's different with her. She's more involved."

"Plus, we need to get whatever information we can from her, as fast as possible," Falin adds.

"Maybe she'll talk to me," I offer. Falin pins me with a hard gaze. "People tell me things. I don't know, I guess it's my charm." At that, Falin and Blake both snort. "It's worth a shot."

"Go ahead," Blake says. "You're doing me a favor, because I can barely stand to look at her. Brennan..." She trails off, her voice faint. Falin pulls her into a hug.

"Go," Leon says. "See if you can get her to talk."

I grab a cold bottle of water from the fridge and head to the bathroom, knocking gently. "Hey, it's Jasper. Can I come in?"

No answer.

I wait for a moment. I know it's not the same, but I remember how I felt when my parents told me about Bailey's abduction. I didn't know how to talk to people about it. Every thought was a tangled mess of fear, fury, and grief. I'm not sure what Mischa knows about her father. She could be just as innocent in all of this as we are. For some reason, I want to give her the benefit of the doubt.

I knock again. "I'm not upset with you. I just want to talk."

She finally cracks the door enough to let me see her tear-stained face. I gently push it open and squeeze inside.

"I didn't know," she cries. "I swear, I had no idea."

Her head hangs as she quietly sobs. "What did they do to you?" It's the one thing I ask that I almost don't want the answer to.

She keeps her gaze trained on the tile floor. "Nothing nearly as bad as what they've done to others. He kept me safe."

I tilt my head, wondering who she means. "Who did?"

"It doesn't matter. He's gone now, they both are." Frustrated, I tip her chin so she's forced to look at me. I haven't slept nearly enough to deal with cryptic half answers.

"Did your father make you stay there?"

She shakes her head. "No, it was my cousin. My father too, possibly, but I don't know."

Okay, now I'm getting somewhere. "Alexander?"

"Yes. That son of a bitch killed Brennan." Her lip quivers as she holds back a sob.

"He did, and he tried to kill Blake too," I add. "We know he was upset with you for talking to me. He thought you were sharing information. Why would he think that?"

"Like I know? He's a psychopath. I knew my father's business wasn't exactly on the up and up, but I had no idea what he and Brennan were doing. How evil they were."

I study her face. I'm not as good as Damon and Leon at telling when a person is lying, but she seems genuine. "Can you give us anything on them? We think he may know something about my missing sister." Her eyes widen. I grab my phone from my pocket and swipe to a photo of Bailey. "Have you ever seen her?"

She scans the photo, fidgeting with a loose string on her shirt. "No, she wasn't one of the girls at the house." A mix of relief and disappointment washes over me. "But there's a way you could check if my father has her."

I almost drop my phone. "What did you say?"

She smiles for the first time since I met her months ago, and a glimpse of her beauty shines through. "I hope you have a shovel."

WE'RE all gathered around the couch eating pizza and catching up after an eventful day. Except Leon. Poor guy was miserable when he left to meet his father for dinner.

Earlier, Falin and I brought Kayla to the train station, where she shared a tearful reunion with her parents. Watching that moment, I couldn't help but feel hopeful that someday soon we'd have the same experience when we find Bailey. Even though I know Kayla has years of healing ahead and her life won't return to normal any time soon, seeing her safe because of our help fills me with a feeling of pride I haven't felt in a long time.

Breaking down doors and confronting bad guys is one thing, but witnessing someone like Kayla get their life back, seeing it through to the end, that's something else entirely.

"How'd it go with Mischa?" Falin asks. "When you texted me, you didn't say much." I've been thinking the same thing since we sat down, but didn't want to be the one to ask.

"It went fine." Blake takes a small bite of her gluten-free pizza.

"Okay," Falin says, drawing out the word. "So what happened?"

Damon hasn't touched his pizza. I glance his way with

questioning eyes, but he doesn't notice. He's too busy watching Blake.

"We dropped her at the airport, just like we planned," Blake answers.

Silence falls while we chew our food. They don't ask about Kayla, which isn't like them. I take a sip of my beer, and catch Falin watching my throat.

Finally, Damon breaks the silence, his voice laced with anger. "I still can't believe you gave her your money."

Blake drops her plate on the table. "It's my money to do what I want with."

"But you deserve that money. You'll need it for school."

Falin and I lock eyes across the coffee table, both feeling the tension thicken.

"Who knows when I'll go back... if I can even get into another med school."

"That's bullshit, of course you will. You're fucking brilliant."

"If I'm so brilliant, then why can't you respect my decision?"

In a fucked up way, I'm enjoying this. Makes the dream couple seem as normal as the rest of us. I swallow another mouthful of beer, leaning back on the couch while they volley back and forth. I can see Falin's expression morph, like a dormant volcano ready to burst. She can't *not* rush to Blake's aid. It's impossible for her.

"She didn't deserve your help. Not after how she treated you. Look who her father is!"

"What I do is my business! If you don't like it then—"

"For the love of baby Jesus in the manger! Will you two stop for two fucking seconds?" Falin yells. They both go quiet. She takes a deep breath—which I know she'll need to hand deliver their asses to them. Man, I wish I had a bowl of popcorn. But I'll settle for finishing off my beer. "Damon, Blake is an adult and you're not her keeper. If she wanted to help that raging she-devil then none of us can stop her. Blake, of course your smart ass will get into med school. Don't you dare put yourself down! And for fuck's sake, just tell us what happened!"

Falin's chest heaves in the hottest way as she stops talking. I break the silence with a well-placed slow clap. It earns me three sets of glaring eyes, but if there was ever a time for a slow clap, it was right then.

"Where's my knife?" Blake mutters, her glare turning into the cutest scowl.

"In the bedroom. Want me to get it?" Damon answers. He's back to having big love eyes for her, his hand on her thigh.

I hold up my hands in surrender. "No need to get stabby, just loosening the tension."

Falin sighs, rolling her eyes and shaking her head. "I'm waiting. Before you guys left with her she casually mentioned digging up a body. You can't leave us hanging here."

Blake finally relents. "I pulled a bunch of cash for her and told her to never come back to New York. To start over somewhere new. I hate her, of course I do. But some part of Brennan loved her. I know he did. And from what little she told me, she hasn't had it easy the past few months."

"And the whole, 'I have information that'll lead to Bailey' thing?" I ask. "She wouldn't tell me specifics, not until we delivered on our promise to get her to the airport safely."

Damon wipes a drip of beer with the back of his hand, a slow smile spreading across his face. "We should have led with this. I was just too pissed. So apparently Orlova had a boyfriend at the house. One of her cousin's guys."

"She has a type," Falin mutters. Blake shoots daggers at her. "Sorry."

"Anyway, this guy, she wouldn't tell us his name, was helping her. Making a plan to get away from her cousin, run off together. He stole a flash drive, something to blackmail Orlov with. She didn't know exactly what's on there, but she thinks it has information on all the victims. That guy Yuri figured out what was going on and killed him. Buried him across the street on that hill. She swears he was buried with that flash drive."

We sit quietly, absorbing this information. Falin's the first one to speak. "So, you're saying we have to dig up a body, in the freezing cold, with no exact location, to maybe, possibly, get a flash drive that may or may not exist?"

Damon shrugs. "Yup, that sums it up."

Falin swallows a sip of beer, and grins. "Sign me the fuck up."

CHAPTER TWENTY-SIX

FALIN

THE NEXT DAY, WE SPEND THE AFTERNOON PREPPING. Who knew tracking down shovels in Manhattan would be such an ordeal? With Leon still stuck with his father, it'll be the four of us trekking back to the Bronx on a mission to find a dead guy.

"The looks I got lugging these shovels from the store," Jasper says. "Like everyone assumed I was about to bury someone."

I smirk while finishing with my boots. "I mean, they're not wrong."

"I'm unburying a body. There's a difference." When I stand from the couch, his eyes rake over me. "You sure you'll be warm enough in that?"

That being my black buckle skirt, tights, and leg warmers. "I'll be fine, Dad."

Shit. The word slipped out before I could catch it.

"Dad?" He raises a brow, closing the space between us. "Or... Daddy?"

I hate when he uses his sexy voice. It always turns me on and I swear he knows it.

"Definitely Dad." I rise on my tiptoes until I'm barely an inch from his lips, trailing my finger from his temple to his jaw. "Daddy needs to be earned." He pulls me against him with his free hand, and I fight back a gasp.

"Keep being a brat and I'll show you what happens," he says, voice thick.

"Am I interrupting something?" Damon snickers from the doorway.

I try to step back but Jasper's grip stays firm on my waist, his eyes locked on mine with an intensity that catches me off guard. Like he's done playing games and knows exactly what he wants.

Blake follows Damon in, focused on her phone. "Hope I dressed warm enough. Glad you found those HotHands things though." She stops short. "Oh."

I dart my tongue out to moisten my lip, noticing how Jasper tracks the movement. It's hot... so fucking hot. "We need to go," I finally manage. He releases me slowly, and when he steps away, the absence of his body against mine leaves an ache.

"Fal, you're gonna freeze in that. Where's your pants?" Blake asks, always being a caretaker.

I shrug, purposely looking at Jasper and adding innuendo to my voice. "Dirty." I swear his eyes darken.

Blake grabs a shovel, shaking her head. "Wish Lee was here. Feels wrong without him."

"His fucking father," Damon says. "I knew he'd be gone awhile. Always happens."

"He texted earlier," Blake says. "Said he's okay, and has something to tell us when he gets back."

"He texted you, but not me?" Jasper says. "Rude."

Blake grins, knowing full well she has us all wrapped

around her finger. "He wished us luck. Said to message him if we find anything."

"Metal detector in the car?" I ask Jasper.

He nods. "All set. Let's go find our Russian popsicle."

I swear to God.

THE SUN PAINTS the sky in shades of gold by the time we park near the hill. I had no idea about the fire Jasper and Damon set the other night. If I knew, I may have thought better of coming back here. This whole thing is a huge gamble anyway. I don't trust Mischa for a second. I could see her drinking champagne on some first class flight to Paris, laughing away at how she sent us on a wild goose chase. Or more aptly, a dead goose chase.

But on the off chance she's telling the truth, it's worth a night of numb fingertips and cold feet.

The damage to the house is worse than I imagined. What little structure it was holding onto is gone, replaced by the charred bones of a home. Good riddance. I hope the memory of what happened in there burned along with it.

"I'll go with Blake to search," I offer. "We can use the metal detector."

Damon and Jasper laugh in unison like a pair of cartoon villains. It's honestly weird as hell. Damon turns to look at us in the backseat. "Abso-fucking-lutely not."

Blake squeezes my hand. "I have to agree with him, Fal. Not that I wouldn't love some girl time, but we kinda need the guys to do the digging."

I scoff. "We're strong. We can dig ourselves."

"Yeah, have fun with that," she says, sliding out of the backseat. The same backseat where Jasper had me bent like a pretzel. My cheeks heat despite the chill that blows into the car from the open door.

Jasper flips the seat so I can climb out from the passenger side, smirking as I stand up. "I'll just enjoy the moonlight and fresh air while you do all the manual labor. Better stretch first."

"Thanks for the reminder. I'll make sure to dig you a grave with a nice view," I say.

He cages me between his chest and the car door, lowering his head so only I hear him. "Careful, Trouble, the last time you threatened to put me six feet under, I had you coming apart on my tongue."

I stand tall, working my fingers from his cheeks down the slope of his neck. His breath hitches and pupils grow like the shadows stretching around us. Once I reach his throat, my hand forms a collar, squeezing lightly. "Funny, I remember you being the desperate one." His pulse jumps against my palm as I give his body a firm shove.

Jasper's stare scorches my skin as I grab a shovel and flashlight from the trunk. I love having the last word and he knows it.

Once we reach the top of the hill, I'm even less optimistic that we'll find something. The area spans the entire block—over a thousand feet for sure. There's rocks, trees, and dead branches scattered everywhere. It looks as if the only living thing to come through here are deer or squirrels. The ground is going to be frozen solid.

Damon and Blake don't seem too put out. "We'll take this side," Damon says pointing to the right. "Do you want the metal detector first?"

Blake's holding onto it like a kid with a new toy. There's no way I'm taking it from her. "No, it's fine. We'll just look for places where someone's been digging."

"Okay, call us if you find anything." He reaches for Blake's hand and they start heading in the opposite direction.

Jasper stretches his arms above his head, groaning suggestively. "Lead the way. I'll hang back a step and enjoy the view." I rest my free hand on my hip and glare at him. "I meant the stars... my God, woman, who's the cocky one now?"

"Keep your eyes on the ground, not my ass," I say as I almost immediately trip over a rock.

Jasper's hand shoots out, catching me around the waist. "You should take your own advice."

I don't have a comeback for that one.

We walk, and walk, and walk some more. Shining my flashlight on the ground, I pay extra attention to anything that looks out of place, but really, I only manage to scare the shit out of a raccoon.

"Should we call them and see if they've picked up on anything with the metal detector?" I ask. I'm getting frustrated and cold and Jasper's gone irritatingly quiet. He's not even humming anymore.

"I'm sure they'll call us if they find something." He pokes a pile of sticks with the end of the shovel, sighing when there's nothing but frost-covered earth beneath them.

"What are you thinking about over there?" I stop and lean against a tree, dropping my shovel to rub my cold hands together.

He smooths a mound of dirty snow haphazardly. "Stuff, nothing important."

Of course he's going to make me dig for more. Who knew I'd be metaphorically digging as well as physically digging tonight. "How have your cravings been?"

He lets out a dry laugh. "Loads of fun."

"I bet." I soften my voice. "I'm proud of you."

His eyes drift up to meet mine, blue irises sparkling in the moonlight. "I have you to thank, Trouble. I've traded one addiction for another."

I'm caught off guard and my pulse speeds up. "What do you mean?" His feet crunch against dried branches and dead leaves as he closes the distance between us. Once again, I'm trapped against his hard body, his delicious warmth soaking into my skin.

Gently, like I'm made of glass, he trails his knuckles down my cheek, cupping my jaw. "Your rose scent. That smart mouth. The kindness you try to hide. Your fierceness." His voice wavers and he wraps his palms around my waist. "And God, your body. I won't pretend I don't love the way you look. You're beautiful, every damn inch. I can't get enough. You're even in my dreams, and it terrifies me." His eyes find mine again, wide with vulnerability. "So yeah, Trouble, I'm addicted to you—even though I know I'll probably mess this up like everything else."

"Jasper." His name catches in my throat. I want to understand every thought in his mind, to fight against his self-doubt and show him he's more than what people give him credit for. But right now, words aren't enough. I hold his face and rise on my tiptoes, slowly pressing my lips to his.

When our lips meet, it's like the first crack of lightning in a storm—electric and blazing. Our hands can't get enough, mine fisted in his hair, his cradling my face. His taste is intoxicating. Wintergreen and spice. When I press my tongue to the seam of his lips, he lets out a desperate curse, opening for me. Our tongues brush, gently at first, until I hum into his mouth and he deepens the kiss. He lifts me, and I wrap my legs around him as his body pins me against the tree. His hard cock is pressed so deliciously into my core. Everything in me wants to reach down and pull it out so he can fuck me shamelessly against this tree.

I yank on his hair, eliciting the hottest whimper. "Fuck, baby, you taste so goddamn good."

He squeezes my ass while I kiss his jaw and say, "So do you."

"Been waiting so long for this," he manages between breaths.

I capture his lips again, and this time our kiss is slower, deeper. Memorizing every part of each other. His hands spread me wider, fingers roaming closer to my core. I nibble his bottom lip, loving the way he moans my name.

"Christ," he breathes against my mouth, his forehead resting against mine. "You're going to be the death of me, Trouble."

"I'll dig the grave." I let out a breathy laugh, resting my head against the tree. He leans in again, peppering kisses along the slope of my neck, pressing his hard length into me.

"I'd die a happy man." I wrap my fingers in his hair and his eyes meet mine. They're dark but softer than before, like he means every word he's said.

The way he looks right now has me questioning everything. But before I can pull him back to me, a branch cracks in the darkness. We freeze, reality crashing in. *Fuck.*

The woods. The shovels. The dead guy.

My body screams but I motion for him to put me back on my feet. "We should..." I gesture to the shovels.

He releases a long exhale, running a hand through his hair. "Yeah, you're right."

I watch as he not so subtly adjusts his boner, clenching my thighs together.

Ah, fuck it.

"Hey." He turns and I reach for his face, kissing him softly. "Let's find this body, then maybe we can finish what we started."

His answering smile is pure joy. "Sweetheart, I'll dig faster than I've ever dug in my life."

After a few hours of nothing, Blake calls, telling us she's done for the night. Jasper and I exchange looks, silently asking if either of us wants to keep up the search. I won't be the one to admit I'm also frozen and dying of hunger, but I'm not too proud to beg with my eyes.

"Tell her we'll meet them by the car," he says.

I know he wanted to find something. We all did. Trying to cheer him up, I force optimism into my voice. "I'll come back with you tomorrow. This area is huge, it'll take a few days to search it."

"You will?"

Why does he sound so surprised? A flutter of nerves hits me out of nowhere, but I fight through the cursed feeling. I reach for his hand, entwining my fingers in his. "Of course, and maybe we can get dinner beforehand?"

Holy shit, did I just ask Jasper Shea out on a date? An actual *date*, date?

He squeezes my hand, and answers, his voice so smooth it makes my freezing legs weak. "Dinner then digging up a body. How romantic."

As we head back home, it hits me. I've never asked a guy out before. Hook-ups, yeah. I've initiated plenty of those. But this feels different, and I can't figure out why.

We've already crossed so many lines together. Made each other come. Killed a man. We've even fallen asleep in each other's arms, for fuck's sake. So why does the thought of sitting across from him at a restaurant make my stomach go all berserk? Like somehow dinner is what makes this thing between us real.

I'll have to talk to Blake and let her diagnose me with the help of her psych textbooks. But right now, with Jasper's hungry eyes meeting mine in the car's visor mirror, I can't think of anything I want more than him.

CHAPTER TWENTY-SEVEN

JASPER

I REPEAT MY NEW MANTRA THE ENTIRE WAY HOME. *Don't fucking overthink this.* Falin knows how I feel about her. Finally expressing those feelings felt incredible. Incredible and terrifying all at once. Memories of that first night flash through my mind. Her more vulnerable than I've ever seen, telling me she's been hurt too many times before. That she sees me as one of the good ones.

Hell, I still don't know if I can be that for her. I'm not good... even if I've been trying so hard for her. I've never not fucked someone when the opportunity was there.

Never.

With Falin, feeling her come for me has been more than enough. I still can't wrap my brain around that. But for the first time since Bailey was taken, maybe even the first time in my life, I feel like I deserve something good. Something real. *Her.*

And fuck, even if I don't deserve her, it's too late now.

I meant every word that I said.

She's my new goddamn addiction.

Unless she flat out tells me to fuck right off, I'm holding on tight to whatever I can.

Do not overthink.

WE STOP for some mediocre burgers, all four of us trying not to let the disappointment over our failed plans get us down. I can tell Blake's taking it harder than all of us. She wants so badly to see the best in people, even Mischa. Life's thrown her enough to break even the strongest person, yet she still holds onto hope.

When we reach the apartment, Blake and Damon say goodnight and head right to their room, leaving Falin and me standing there, waiting for one of us to say something.

"I—"

"Want to?"

We speak at the same time. "You go first," she says, her lips curving into a small smile.

The kittens take that moment to weave between our legs, yowling for food. I laugh and scoop them up. "Lemme just feed these wiggling furballs."

"I wish I could take a hot shower." She wraps her arms around her chest. "I'm still cold."

"They better fix that shit tomorrow, or it's going to start smelling really fucking bad in here," I say.

"Thank God for deodorant. Anyway, I'm going to go change. Want to watch a movie? Get warm under a blanket?"

I wrangle the girls into the kitchen and open a can of food, grateful for the distraction while I try to play it cool. A movie, nothing serious about that. No overthinking required. "Yeah, sure."

She smiles and heads into her room. I secretly hope all

her pajamas are still dirty, because her in that tiny fucking skirt does things to my sanity.

The girls make happy little chirps as they eat, and I lean against the counter, my mind spiraling.

She's going to come out here looking hot as hell.

We are definitely going to fuck.

Finally going to fuck.

But should I?

Goddamn.

She wants this. Has wanted this. I want this.

What the fuck is wrong with me?

Jasper, stop being a little bitch. You've done this a hundred times. Dick in pussy. Simple.

I'm so caught up in my head that I don't hear Leon come through the front door until he says my name.

"Why do you look like you're having an aneurysm? Should I get Blake?"

"Lee? I didn't think you'd be back tonight."

He kicks off his shoes and drops his bag by the door, sighing like he hasn't released a breath in days, which is probably accurate. "Not happy to see me?"

Well...

Falin comes into the room, her face surprised to see Leon standing there. "Hey, we didn't think you'd be home tonight."

"I feel so welcome," Leon says flatly.

Falin hurries to hug him. "Stop, you know that's not what I mean."

"It's fine, I'm just absolutely done in." He scratches the kitten's heads on his way to the fridge and grabs a beer. "Fill me in on everything I missed."

Falin and I share a look, but she says, "Yeah, alright. Grab me one too while you're in there."

I shake my head at the absurdity of yet another night getting cockblocked by someone or something in this apartment. "Me too."

BY SOME DIVINE MIRACLE, I manage to get Falin alone the next day. Leon's working on some program to track a money trail and Blake woke up feeling sick. Damon, being Damon, wants to stay by her side.

Fine with me.

What's not fine though, is the fact that my balls are so blue I think they may fall off, and Falin came prancing out of her room dressed in another little skirt.

Fuck me.

She actually lives to drive me to the brink of insanity. I'm calling those world record people to let them know they have a new entry. Me, for eye fucking.

"Ready to go?" She pulls her hair off her neck into a messy bun. I actually fucking lick my lips like a dog.

"Yeah." My voice cracks. "You want my coat?" I grab it from the arm of the couch.

"I'm good. It's almost sixty out today. Isn't that nuts?" I nod, barely hearing her words. I'm too busy staring at the swell of her tits popping out of her black sweater.

"Nut. Yeah, totally." Fuck, I sound like a robot. She bends over to grab her boots, her skirt barely covering her round ass. Is she wearing panties? Holy hell, my cock is going to explode.

"Nut?" She laughs. "Someone has a dirty mind."

"We should go," I manage to say. *Before I bend you over this couch and fuck the life out of that sweet ass.*

"Almost done. I just need to tie my boots."

I rush over before she has the chance to bend over again and sink to my knees. "I've got it."

"Oh." I lift her foot, one at a time, tying her boots with trembling hands. I could lift her skirt from here. Devour her pussy until she screams. My breaths come in quick shallow bursts, until I hear her voice. "Jasper? Did you hear me?"

Blinking, I clear my throat. "What?"

She laughs again. "Nevermind. Let's go."

On the drive over, I turn the music all the way up to drown out my racing thoughts. What I'd give for something to take the edge off. Something like a healthy dose of bull tranquilizer should do the trick.

Since it's still early and neither of us are hungry, we decide to go straight to the hill. I'm about to start digging like a goddamn groundhog just to let out some pent up energy.

I park on the same street, but closer to our area, and hop out to open Falin's door. She gives me a sideways glance, like she's trying to figure out who replaced me with a pod person. "What's going on with you? You've barely said two words all morning."

I nod, but it ends up looking mechanical and forced, like I'm an NPC in The Sims. "Let's just grab the shovels."

Since it's broad daylight this time, I scout the area, making sure no one's lurking around. It's oddly quiet for a sunny winter day. Nothing but some kids playing in a back-yard in the distance and barking dogs.

We reach the spot we marked the night before, and I get to work right away, using my shovel to poke around.

"This is much easier in the daytime." I turn to see where she's digging to find her bent over again, moving some rocks. *Fucking hell.*

She hums a Pierce The Veil song that I had on in the

car, acting completely unaware that I'm five seconds from my breaking point. I take a deep breath, and walk a few steps away, staring up at a puffy cloud that just so happens to look like a dick. Freud would definitely have something to say to me right about now.

"Christ," I mutter under my breath. I need to focus. Find a spot and dig away.

"Jas?" I jump, not realizing Falin followed me over here. She trails her hand down my back, stopping right above my ass. "Find something over here?"

"Uh, yeah. I don't know. Maybe."

I keep circling the area, but Falin shadows my every move—touching me constantly. Her fingers glide down my back, dance across my arm, brush against my hand. Each touch pushes me closer to the edge. "You're so stiff, Jas."

Ha! If she only knew.

She slides behind me, rising to her toes to work my shoulders. Her fingertips graze my hair, and a groan escapes me. I squeeze my eyes shut, counting backward from ten when she leans in, her breath warm against my ear. "Relax."

And that's it.

I throw the shovel on the ground and spin to face her. With my chest heaving, I growl, "Get on your hands and knees right fucking now."

A slow smile spreads across her face, like this is exactly what she's been waiting for. With unhurried deliberate movements, she turns and bends at the waist, giving me the perfect view of the globes of her ass. I'm already unbuttoning my pants with hands that don't even feel like my own. She's on her hands and knees, arching her back like a cat. "Like this?" she asks, her voice full of practiced innocence.

"Just like that. Don't you fucking move, Trouble." I pull

out my cock, running my hand down my shaft. My God, I've never wanted anything more than I want her. This time, I came prepared. Rolling on a condom, I get on my knees behind her. "Look at you, on your hands and knees for me like a good little slut."

I lift her skirt and find that she isn't wearing anything underneath. I fucking knew it. "Please, Jasper."

"You better be ready for my cock." I slide my fingers through her cunt, groaning at how wet and ready she is. "You wanted this, didn't you? So fucking wet for me."

She turns to look at me, her breath catching when her eyes lower to my length. "Yes, fuck me, please."

Without another second, I grab her hips roughly and slam into her. I have to say a silent prayer because fuck, she feels incredible.

A saint. An angel. A fucking goddess.

"Oh my God. Fuck... You feel so good," she moans, and I'm done. There's no amount of restraint left inside me. My knees sink into the melting snow as I brace myself, gripping her ass so hard I know I'll leave marks. I pull all the way out, groaning at the loss of her wet heat, before filling her inch by sweet inch.

"You take me so well, baby." Pumping in and out at a punishing pace, she strangles my cock. I know I make noises—whimpers, groans, curses under my breath. Fucking tears coat the corner of my eyes. "Your cunt is perfect. Everything I've ever fucking imagined. I never want to leave."

Words spill from my lips, like prayers, as her answering moans fill the open air around us.

I pull out again, and spank her ass with a full palm, thrusting in again when a red mark appears. "Tortured me for days with this ass, didn't you? I'll fuck you here soon."

"Yes, please... yes." She backs into me, taking every last thrust, moaning her pleasure for anyone to hear.

I know I'm close. That tingle comes from my spine, shooting down into my balls. Wrapping one hand around her neck, I pull her onto her knees and sit her on my cock. I give her a gentle squeeze, loving the control. She's tormented me for so long, this is exactly what I need. "Rub your clit, baby. Come for me."

One hand on her neck, and the other around her waist, guiding her to bounce up and down on my cock, I thrust into her while she fucks her fingers. "That's it. Harder, baby. I'm so close." Her pussy clamps around me as her body trembles. "Oh fuck, Falin." I groan against her ear as my entire body spasms. I come so hard, I almost black out. "Holy fuck. Christ Jesus, baby."

Smoothing my palm down her throat and chest, she collapses back against me, both of our breathing ragged. I kiss her neck, her answering hum of satisfaction is the best sound I've ever heard.

"I'm a changed man," I manage through heavy breaths. "You and those tiny fucking skirts will be the death of me. I hope you're ready for me to fill every single fucking hole in your body, Trouble, because you're stuck with me."

She laughs, it's low and raspy. "Nah, I think I'm good now."

I pick her up, my cock slipping out, and toss her over my shoulder. "Oh, yeah?" I say, swatting her ass. "Too late now. If you think I'm spending another day without being inside you, you're more than wrong." She smacks my back, squirming against my shoulder, but I take my time, loving the way she feels in my arms. When I finally set her down, I stop to drink her in. Her flushed cheeks, those wild smokey eyes, the way her chest rises in quick breaths. Everything about her is perfect. I press her back against the rough bark, pinning her there with my body. "Come here."

She smiles and my chest tightens. I kiss her like it's our first time. Like her lips hold the antidote to every poison coursing through my veins. I kiss her like I'm starving for her. And God, I am. She's breathed life back into my soul, and I'll never get my fill.

I inch away, knowing if I don't stop, I'll need to be inside her again. "That was..." she manages while fixing her skirt.

"Incredible." I finish.

While Falin fixes her hair, I grab the shovels. I'm about to suggest that we come back later. A cheeseburger and a beer sound perfect. But my eyes stray to a spot a few feet in front of me. A dark patch that stands out like a bruise on pale skin.

She must notice it at the same time. "Holy shit, is that—"

"Only one way to find out."

CHAPTER TWENTY-EIGHT

FALIN

"Holy fuck!" Jasper's shovel hits something solid and we both freeze. My shoulder muscles burn from digging, but adrenaline takes over as we drop to our knees.

I scramble back, climbing away from the hole before I vomit. There he is. Mischa's boyfriend, body preserved by the cold earth. I try not to look at his blank face as Jasper quickly searches the pockets of his tattered jeans. When he raises his hand, holding a small flash drive, we let out shocked curses.

"She wasn't lying," I breathe, dropping to my knees.

"She wasn't fucking lying." Jasper steps away from the body, frozen, staring at the drive in his hand.

The emotion hits us both at once. Relief and surprise so sharp, I can hardly believe it.

One moment he's staring at the drive, the next he's pinning me down, his mouth on mine, kissing me with desperate intensity.

I end up on my back, my legs wrapped around his waist as he grinds into me. He sucks my tongue into his mouth as I rake my nails down his back. We're wild and primal, too caught up in the moment to care about the cold or the dirt or the body we just unearthed.

"We fucking did it, baby," Jasper murmurs against my throat. He sucks my neck before capturing my lips again.

I don't care if we just fucked or that it's the middle of the day. I reach for him with frenzied hands, ripping his pants down. We're giddy and unhinged like two possessed souls.

"God, you're so hot right now." I squeeze his cock until he groans my name. "I need you." Tightening my legs around him, I grab his ass, rough and hard, arching until his slippery cock notches my pussy.

I don't stop for a condom. It's reckless but I don't care. This feeling is too raw. Too exhilarating. "I'm on birth control," I manage, whimpering as his cock slides between my folds. "Fuck me, baby. Please."

His answering thrust is exactly what I need. He groans my name, pumping into me, fucking me with a punishing pace against the cold ground. Frantic and uninhibited. "Fucking hell, Trouble."

"Yes! Oh, God. Harder." I lift my hips, meeting him thrust for thrust. My nails dig points into his skin.

"You're so perfect." Our slapping skin and cries mix with the sound of distant traffic from the road below. Knowing we're out here in the open like this has me dripping. I devour his mouth, showing him my desperation and need.

He moves faster as pressure builds inside me. "I'm coming. Don't stop."

We tense and shudder, our bodies trembling into the frozen ground as he pulses inside me. Waves and waves of pleasure roll through me so good I cling to him, never wanting to let go.

My breathing slowly evens out as he shifts to the side, almost tumbling back into the hole. "Shit, I almost forgot about the poor bastard," he says.

I sit up and adjust my skirt, already feeling his warm fluid leaking down my thighs. I blink, like I've just been shaken awake from an insane dream. "We should cover him up."

Jasper zips his pants and sighs. "You're probably right."

I CAN HARDLY BELIEVE IT. Mischa was right. A flash drive in the pocket of that unfortunate soul's jeans. I'm dirty, freezing, and aching but I can't stop smiling. This could be the break we need to find Bailey. If I'm this pumped, I can only imagine how Jasper feels.

The whole way back to the apartment, his warm palm rests on my thigh, his thumb tracing circles on my bare skin. I knew I was playing a dangerous game, tormenting him like I did. But I got what I so desperately wanted. And God, it was hotter than I could have imagined.

I glance at him, remembering the way he fucked me in the dirt, desperate and hungry. My thighs press together in a futile attempt to ease the lingering ache.

More than the physical connection—something deeper —shifted between us out there on the hill. I know we're both scared shitless of whatever this is becoming, but if there's anyone worth facing those fears for, it's him.

We open the apartment door to the sound of banging and the smell of solder. Finally, they must be fixing the broken pipe. The timing couldn't be better. We're both filthy, in more ways than one. Everyone rushes us as soon as we step inside, the kittens included, hugging us and asking rapid-fire questions.

"Give us a second to breathe," Jasper says with a laugh.

"Lee, grab your computer," I say as soon as I can get a word in. "Damon, call Ray and give him these coordinates." I text Damon the exact location where we found the body. "We covered him back up, loosely. Hopefully Ray will know what to do."

"You're filthy," Blake says, stepping back to take me in. She eyes me suspiciously. "And your hair is all over the place."

Yeah, she knows. I have a freshly fucked expression... always have. My best friend has been witness to it more times than I'd like to admit. And the way Jasper fucked me twice—there's no hiding the evidence on my face.

"We didn't have a spa day, Blakey. We dug up a body." I realize the plumbers are probably listening and lower my voice. "How did you expect me to look?"

"Got it," Leon interrupts at the perfect time. He opens his laptop on the kitchen counter and we all crowd around it. "Give it a few minutes to load."

My body vibrates with anticipation. I remember feeling this way every time I'd search for my birth parents. Excitement for the possibilities, dread knowing my search would probably amount to nothing.

I used to imagine their photos appearing on my screen. Happy, normal looking people whose smiles would mirror my own when they realized I'd *found* them. Their address would be right there, leading to some picture perfect suburban street with white picket fences and kids playing hopscotch. The childhood I dreamed of, just waiting for me to claim it.

I squeeze Jasper's hand, while Leon clicks open a file. Blake speaks first. "Oh my God. There's so many."

My eyes scan the document. It's like an inventory listing. "This reminds me of what we had to fill out stocking shelves at the craft store I worked at in high school," I say.

"Except these are real people with real lives that were stolen from them," Leon says, his voice dripping with anger.

The numbered spreadsheet has me sick to my stomach —columns for names, most of which are blank, then age, price, and some kind of coded word at the end. Bile rises in my throat.

"How are we going to know which one of these is Bailey?" Jasper asks, his enthusiasm fading.

"I don't know," Leon answers, sounding despondent.

"Can I take a look at it?" I gently squeeze Leon's shoulder, trying to convey that I know how he feels. He nods and moves over.

"I'll make a pot of coffee," Damon says. He must know hovering won't get the job done any faster. They all give me some space, except Jasper, who pulls up a chair next to me.

"If there's something on here, I'll find it," I tell him. His answering look cracks my heart in two. It's full of hope and trust—in me. We didn't dig up a dead guy in the freezing cold just to come back empty-handed.

I write up some quick code to help me sort the list by age. That'll narrow it down quickly. While it's doing its thing, I search the drive for other useful information.

The first file I open is empty. The next has another coded list. And this one—I tap the screen. "This has header info that matches what we found in Brennan's container manifest."

"Can you cross-reference them?" Leon asks, leaning over my shoulder.

I nod, already writing a script to compare the two files. "Give me a sec."

The apartment fills with the gentle clicking of keys and soft purring as Havoc settles into Jasper's lap. He pets her blankly, his eyes never leaving the screen.

"This file here," I say, frowning at a particularly stubborn bit of code. "It's encrypted differently than the others. Triple layer at least, maybe more."

Leon leans in closer. "Let me see." He scans the mess on the screen. "That's not your standard encryption. Look at the pattern in the header."

I squint, following his finger. "RSA with... Wait, is that—"

"A custom key," we say together.

Jasper shifts forward in his seat. "What does that mean?"

"It means whoever the fuckwad was that encrypted this really didn't want anyone getting in," I tell him, already pulling up my decryption tools. "But they probably didn't expect someone like me to find their shit."

My fingers fly across the keyboard as I work through the layers. First the outer shell. Basic stuff, almost too easy. The second layer puts up more of a fight, but I've seen worse. It's the final layer that has me cursing under my breath.

"Need help?" Leon offers.

I shake my head, completely in the zone now. "I've got it. Just need to..." I trail off, focusing entirely on the pattern emerging in the code. There's always a weakness, always a way in. I just have to think like the person who locked it up.

"There!" I say as the final piece clicks into place. The encrypted text transforms into clear files before our eyes.

The first thing we see are photos. Dozens of them. Young women and girls, a few boys too. Some obviously drugged, others looking terrified. Each labeled with only a number.

"Oh, God," Blake whispers from behind me.

I feel Jasper go completely still. His hand reaches for mine, squeezing tight enough to hurt. Because there, labeled simply as #521, is a photo of a young woman with his same ocean blue eyes.

"Bailey," he breathes.

CHAPTER TWENTY-NINE

JASPER

I've stared at Bailey's haunted face on the screen for days now, pacing the floors, waiting on something tangible to do. The photo is my sister, no doubt about it, but she looks nothing like the girl I hugged over a year ago as she went off to college. She's paler, thinner, her wide eyes making her look years younger than nineteen.

Behind her empty expression, traces of her show through, and that's enough to keep me going. She's still in there. The little sister who switched my shampoo for toothpaste and hid rubber snakes in my bed. Who camped out in my closet for hours just to embarrass me when my girlfriend came over, jumping out and yelling boo. The Bailey who wanted to travel the world, teaching kids how to read.

Falin and Leon have been working nonstop. Barely taking breaks to eat or sleep. It's not only Bailey's life on the line, but countless others, and we have no idea where they are. We're out of our league here. I'm pretty sure none of us expected this thing to be so huge, and fuck, I feel so helpless.

Falin's at her desk, bleary-eyed after another sleepless

night. I come up behind her, moving her hair aside to kiss her neck. She hums contentedly, continuing to tap away at her keyboard. "You're distracting me."

That's the last thing I want to do, but I can't help it. "I'm bored and you're irresistible."

She leans her head back to meet my gaze, and I kiss her plump lips. "The waiting is hard. Trust me, I get it. I'll have something for us soon." I kiss her again, pressing my tongue against the seam of her lips. When we break apart, her chest rises and falls rapidly. "You should go take a walk. Get some air. If you keep distracting me, I'm going to have to punish you."

"Is that supposed to make me want to leave?" I tease. She raises her brow, setting her lips in a straight line. Falin's way of saying get lost. "I'll go grab sandwiches from the deli. Turkey and spicy mustard?"

"Yes, please. Spicy chips too. Do you need cash?" I shake my head, too proud to admit that funds are tight.

"I'll be back soon."

I make my way onto the busy sidewalk, dodging a woman pushing a stroller, and shimmying past a pair of tourists. It's another unseasonably warm afternoon, and people are taking advantage of it.

I breathe in the scent of the city. Spices from the food cart around the corner, heavy perfume trailing from the person behind me, a subtle hint of smoke in the air. It's a bummer that we haven't had much time to enjoy being here. The endless possibilities of sights and experiences feels almost overwhelming. I picture Falin and me walking hand in hand, doing typical couple shit. Catching a show, grabbing dinner. Getting handsy in the back of a taxi. Hopping out in the village to drink at some tiny dive bar.

The scene is so vivid, I can reach out and touch us. Lost

in thought, I bump into a guy on the corner. "Hey, watch where you're walking! Putz!"

"Sorry, man." I raise a hand in a show of goodwill, but he's already crossing the street. Ah, gotta love New Yorkers.

I continue ahead, my body thrumming with pent up energy. If this street were clear I'd fucking sprint my way to the deli just to blow off some steam.

I need to take the edge off. To fuck or fight or—

My phone buzzes from my pocket. I grab it, answering without looking at the number. "Hello?"

"I heard you were looking for some pinks?" An unknown voice makes me stop short. I move out of the way, looking at my phone. Shit. I grabbed my burner instead of my normal one.

"How'd you get this number?"

"Listen, do you want them or not?"

Saliva floods my mouth, as an ache hits me square in the gut. I close my eyes and flashes of using play through my mind. A full body shiver rolls through me. I swallow hard, yanking my hand through my hair. "Fuck, I—"

"Texting you the spot. Be there in less than an hour."

The line goes dead before I can respond.

When the text comes all I can do is stare at it. I stare so long that my eyes water and the words blur into a jumble of nonsense. The screen darkens and a flash of my reflection stares back at me. By then, I've already made my choice.

I WAKE to the setting sun burning my eyes, and my hand pressed against gritty, trash strewn sand. "What the hell?"

The sound of waves lapping against the shore mixes with distant voices and squawking seagulls. They circle overhead, drawn to the scattered remains of fast food and snack bags surrounding me. Dizziness hits as I push myself to a sitting position, broken glass crunching beneath my palms.

A fitting place to wake up after what I've done.

A few feet away, a dude higher than I've ever been nods off, barefoot in tattered clothes.

Is that what I'll become?

Maybe it's what I deserve. I sure as hell don't deserve to go back home to Falin.

How long have I been here?

The baggie feels like an iron weight in my pocket. Every last dollar I had, wasted and for what? I feel like shit.

I pull out my phone and stare at the black screen. She shouldn't have this number, but somehow she got it. Rows of missed calls fill the screen. Texts too.

Waiting on that sandwich... you get lost?

Okay, for real. You good?

JASPER SHEA CALL ME BACK

Guilt gnaws away at my gut. Why am I like this? A loser. Fuck up. Junkie. She deserves better.

The water calls to me. Cold and calm. I could walk right into its depths, clench my eyes shut and sink to the bottom. It would be so easy. So much easier than living like this.

The phone vibrates in my hand, her number flashing across the screen. For a second, I have this urge to chuck the thing into the river, but I stop myself. I can't do that to her. My reflection in the glass shows a stranger—pale, bloodshot eyes, hollow. Ugly.

"Fuck!"

I pound my fist into the sand.

"Fuck! Fuck! FUCK!"

My chest heaves as thick crimson drips between my fingers. The sting barely registers through everything else I'm feeling.

I deserve every bit of this pain.

My phone vibrates again and I finally answer, a plan in my mind.

"Baby," I rasp, throat full of gravel. "Punish me."

The words hang there, a plea and a prayer. I need her to give me what I deserve. What I'm too much of a coward to give myself.

She finally answers, her voice thick with emotion. "What did you do?"

I used.

I can't admit it. If I say the words out loud, they become real. No more dreamland. My own guilt is more than I can take.

"Please," I beg.

A siren wails in the distance, and I'm grateful for the noise. Maybe she can't hear the choked sob that escapes my lips.

I stand, glancing at my blood dripping onto the sand. Her voice is my salvation. My judgement. "Get home."

"I will—I—"

"Now." Her tone promises I'm going to get exactly what I deserve.

Getting home was difficult in more ways than one. My *borrowed* credit card declined so I had to panhandle for cash to ride the subway back. I have no fucking clue how I'd gotten so far south to begin with. After I met with that plug, everything was a blur. The whispers and stares as I begged commuters will play in my head for days to come. The little kid asking his mom, "Why does that man need our money? Doesn't he have a job?" cut deeper than the glass did.

I curled into a ball the entire ride home, trying to become invisible. My insides feeling as filthy as I must look. My clothes stained with seagull shit and blood, reeking like the river.

Falin's waiting for me outside the apartment. She doesn't see me yet, and I'm happy I get to prolong that moment. Her hair is tied up in a knot above her head, and she's thrown on a pair of my sweats that hang off her much smaller frame. She's still the most beautiful thing I've ever seen.

She's reading her phone, brows furrowed, shoulders almost touching her ears. I wonder what she's looking at. When she sees me, her expression won't change for the better and I hate myself for that.

Our gazes meet when I'm a few feet away, hers wide and questioning, mine vacant and ashamed. Her lips move as she says something too low for me to hear. *What the fuck?* I think.

In that moment something about her posture shifts. She stands up straight, arms crossed. Her brows narrow and mouth becomes a straight line.

"I'm sorry," I say once I reach her. And I mean it. I really fucking do. Everything feels awkward. I don't know what to do with my hands. Should I reach for her? Hold her?

"Jasper, what the hell?" There's a hint of warmth in her gaze but as her eyes scrutinize me, it turns to flames licking skin. *She knows what I need.* "Save the excuses."

Head hung low, I follow her upstairs. She all but shoves me into the shower, silent the entire time. I don't deserve her kindness anyway.

Once I'm washed, she walks me into her bedroom,

locking the door behind her. The apartment is quiet, but I don't ask questions.

"You were bad, weren't you?" I nod, unable to meet her gaze. "You want to be punished? To pay for your mistakes?"

"Please. Punish me. Make it hurt." I barely recognize my pleading tone. "I fucked up bad, baby."

"I'm not your baby," she says. "Bend over the bed."

I'm already hard as a steel rod. What the fuck is wrong with me?

I obey, bending at the waist until my torso rests flat on the soft bed. Anticipation sends a rush through my veins, sparking the tiniest bit of hope through me. "Tell me your safe word."

My head swims, but I mutter out the first thing I think of. "Banana." A hint of a smile grazes her lips before she schools them back into a line. She pushes me into the bed, standing behind me.

I've barely taken a breath before her palm connects with my ass. "Fuck," I groan into the blanket. She does it again and again, spanking me with all her strength, alternating sides until tears leak from my eyes and my cock throbs. I bite my lip to keep from crying out.

"You fucked up and now you'll pay." She grabs something from the side of the bed, and I feel a different sensation. Sharper. More painful against my raw skin. A flogger, maybe? She whacks my thighs, outside and inside, before dragging the leather up and through my crack. "You like that, don't you?"

I should lie. Tell her no. But it's obvious that I love every second she hurts me. "Yes." She flogs me again until I suck air between my teeth, hissing every curse I know. "Please."

"Don't beg. You deserve this, so take every second." Each time she strikes, I rock into the bed, so close to coming all over her clean linen. She hurls insults and I soak them in, needing this. Loving her putting me in my place.

"You scum." *Paddle.* "You waste of space." *Smack.* "This ass deserves to get fucked raw."

"Oh God, please, baby," I plead. I cry. I'm fucking gone for her. "Please fuck my ass."

"Get on the bed." I push up to stand and almost collapse on my shaking legs. When I glance back at her, my mouth waters. She's wearing nothing but a harness that holds a huge flesh-colored dildo. Fucking hell, she's hot. I can't tell which one of us loves this more. I've never had my ass fucked. Never had more than a finger in there while getting my dick sucked. But I'd let her tear me open with a smile on my face. "Hands and knees, you filthy slut."

With another spanking, she positions herself behind me. Cool liquid leaks down my ass and onto the bed. I groan as I feel pressure against my hole, stretching me. There's no pain. Shocked, I glance back and see that she's holding something—a small toy. I arch as it slides in, her name spilling from my lips.

"I'm getting this hole nice and ready for my cock." She pumps it in and out, and it takes every ounce of restraint in me not to fist my dick.

"Please," I beg. "Make it hurt."

She freezes behind me, but only for a moment before pulling the toy out. I hear the bottle uncapping and feel more liquid run between my spread cheeks. Then she's there, lined up with my hole. I'm so hard, I could burst. I want this. I want her to hurt me so bad that I won't be able to sit for days.

In one swift thrust, she fucks into me and the burn is the most painful thing I've ever felt. Even with the lube, I'm stretched and stuffed beyond what I'd ever thought imagin-able. "Oh, fuck!"

I groan.

I scream.

I curse her name.

"Take it," she says roughly. "You dirty little whore." She punctuates with another hard spank.

She moans with me as she fucks me, and I just know her cunt is sopping wet. My body accommodates her, and we pick up a rhythm. "Harder," I groan.

"Fuck!" she screams, slamming into me, balls deep. "Get on your back."

I'm panting and crying, saliva leaking down my chin, but I obey like her good little slut, turning over and holding my legs to my chest. She takes a second to rake me over with heady eyes, before squeezing more lube over my hole.

"I want to see your face when I finally let you come on my cock." She pushes into me to the hilt. Pounding me with fury in her eyes.

"So full, baby. Fuck, you feel so good." Our skin slaps together, the sound mixing with our shared moans. "I don't deserve you. I'll never deserve you."

"Jasper," she cries. Her tone softening. "Shut up and fuck your fist."

As soon as my hand wraps around my dick, that's it. Her cock destroys me while my hand strokes, and that's all it takes for me to erupt like a goddamn volcano. "Slap my face, baby," I beg. Hot ropes of cum paint my stomach. "Punch me."

With her cock still buried deep, she open-palm slaps my face. "Never ever use again, you hear me?"

"Harder," I cry. She makes a fist and punches me in the

fucking nose. I hear the crunch before a blinding pain has me roaring out. "Again."

"Fuck, Jasper!" She punches me again, leaning in so her cock hits me deep. I can barely take the fullness and the pain. It's terrible. It's exquisite.

I feel hot liquid slide down my face and lick my lips, tasting copper. "Yes, baby. Come here."

She pulls out and I immediately miss the way she fills me up. I wrap her in my arms, kissing her, blood smearing across our faces, in our mouths, mixing with our salty tears.

"I'm sorry," she cries, peppering kisses across my jawline.

I hold her face, staring into her gorgeous eyes. "No. You have nothing to be sorry about. You're incredible. I don't deserve you. I'll never deserve you."

I kiss her with every last ounce of strength I have left, holding her tight against my chest, until our breathing stills and heartbeats sync.

CHAPTER THIRTY

FALIN

Days have gone by and Jasper's still not himself. I'm angry at him, of course. But my anger pales in comparison to the anger and self loathing he carries. That night was... intense. I never wanted to actually make him hurt, but when he begged for it, something broke loose inside me. My soft side hid in a dark corner of my mind and I let my animal instincts take over. It was freeing to turn off my thoughts and surrender to raw impulse. Weirdly, I think it brought us closer together too.

Jasper's asleep on his side, the tension in his jaw now gone. He's hugging my pillow to his chest, tangled up in the blanket. I slid out of bed a few minutes ago, unable to sleep for the third night in a row. Ever since we found Bailey on that drive, I can't get my birth parents out of my head. Knowing we're a step closer to finding her gives me some hope after years of dead ends. They've always been just out of reach.

The closest I got was the summer I turned eighteen. I remember feeling extra frustrated at my father for some reason that escapes me now, so I decided to break into his office at the station. Getting in turned out to be way easier than I expected. Just took some flirty lies to the cop on duty and I was inside. The problem came when I couldn't get into his filing cabinet. That thing had this heavy duty lock. I tried to pick it with a paperclip but got interrupted when the pervy cop came in to "check on me." That ended in the most unenthusiastic blowjob of my life.

I went home and watched everything I could find about lock picking. Practiced on a bunch of locks I found at thrift shops in town, everything ranging from doorknobs to bike locks. When I finally felt like I gained some skill, I figured out that cop's schedule and went back on his night shift, pretending like I was there to see him.

Another blowjob later, and I was in. I scanned file after file, all past cases of particular interest to my dad. I didn't have much time until my *friend* would be back from checking the front. Something in my gut made me stop when my fingers touched a file without a label. It was the only unmarked one. I grabbed it and stuffed it in my backpack, getting out of there before he could try asking me on a real date.

Back in my bedroom, I opened the file with trembling hands, telling myself it's probably nothing.

I was wrong.

It was everything he had from that night. Everything he had on *me.*

How they responded to an anonymous tip.

How it was a run-down trailer, isolated in the middle of nowhere.

How needles littered the floor, mixed in with garbage and filth.

How I was there in the center of it all. Five years old.

Filthy and starving. Drawing with a broken crayon on the back of an envelope. Completely alone.

There was a note. *Please save her. She's all I have.*

No signature. No identification for me. The trailer belonged to some worthless parasite who rented to addicts and criminals for cash. From what the file held, my birth parents may as well have been ghosts.

I always knew my dad had connections with the town politicians, but I never realized the judge expedited my adoption papers. New documents were filed, and my previous life vanished. I became Falin Sinclair. Deputy's daughter. When he got promoted to sheriff a few years later, shortly after my mom died, there was no discussing my past. There were barely any discussions at all. The home grew cold. He turned to whiskey. And I got lost in lines of code, teaching myself to crack passwords like I'd learned to pick locks.

Since then, I've never fucked around with drugs. Knowing addiction is in my blood makes me terrified to turn out the way my birth parents did. I feel for Jasper, and I know how strong the pull to use is. I'll do everything I can to help him.

He rolls onto his back, murmuring in his sleep. He's so damn cute like this, I'm tempted to crawl back beside him. Too bad I can't turn off my brain. When I open a new tab, the bright screen must wake him.

"What time is it?" His voice is thick from sleep.

"Around three," I say with a sigh. When did it get that late? Last I looked, it was midnight.

"Damn. No sleep again?" He rubs his eyes and sits up. "Do you need anything?"

"No, but you're sweet to ask."

He nods, fixing my pillow. "What are you doing?"

Do I tell him I'm obsessively going over my DNA result websites and handmade possible family trees? Or that I'm messaging a random woman in Virginia who shares three percent DNA with me?

"Just stuff, nothing important." I shut my laptop and climb into bed beside him. My wild thoughts settle into a cohesive one—how good it feels to be up against Jasper's warm body. He settles his palm on my low back and I snuggle in, resting my head below his chin.

"Were you looking for them?" His fingertips trace circles over my shirt. "Your birth parents?"

I tip my head to look into his eyes. "How'd you know?"

"Easy enough to peek at the web browser when you're not paying attention." He kisses my surprised scowl. "Any luck?"

"No, but new people join those ancestry sites everyday." I'm suddenly too exhausted to keep my eyes open. "I'll find them. I'll find Bailey too."

"I know you will." From the certainty in his voice, I know he means it.

I'm not sure what pulls my mind back there. It could be all these thoughts of my parents making me feel vulnerable. Maybe it's the way he holds me, or the softness of his words, but the question escapes before I can stop it, the words muffled against his neck. "On Blake's birthday, why didn't you want me?"

His hands find my burning cheeks, tilting my face until our eyes meet. "Is that what you think? That I didn't want you?"

Moisture wells in my eyes. Hell, I hate this. I try to pull back, to bury my face again, but he holds me steady. "We were having fun and then you just left and... I don't know, I figured you just forgot."

"Sweetheart, I didn't leave. I wanted you, so fucking badly." His eyes search mine, his tongue darting across his lower lip. "I was scared. I'm still scared. You told me I was good that night. That you've been hurt so much and fuck, I didn't want to be another one to hurt you."

"I did?" I don't remember any of that. Oh, God. Mortification burns its way down my skin.

He nods. "I figured you hated me after I ruined your night and I'll admit, I tried to stay away. But I wanted you too badly. The way I want you is selfish and if this ends with me sleeping alone with nothing but the smell of you in my bed, I may never recover, but I'm willing to put it all out there for a chance to be with you."

I don't know what to say. His words shatter every wrong assumption I've held since I met him. How he feels, what he wants... I want it all too. Desperately.

"I want that. Every bit of it. Sleepless nights like these where we talk and laugh until dawn peeks through the windows. I want to feel your heart beating against mine. To breathe you in and hold you there until I'm drowning. If it's selfish to want that, then fine. I want to be selfish with you."

For someone who fills door frames and makes furniture look like dollhouse pieces, when he claims my lips, he's devastatingly gentle. Savoring me, brushing his lips against mine so softly that I forget how to breathe.

Our clothes come off and bodies intertwine, hands fisting hair, lips dragging along skin. Slow but just as desperate as every other time we've fucked. He moves between my legs, spreading me wide, and licking my clit until I come with his name on my lips. He climbs up my body, sucking my tongue into his mouth so I can taste myself on him.

"Baby, I'm done holding back." He lines his cock up

with my entrance, his eyes burning into mine. "You won't ever doubt how much I want you."

He thrusts into me, stretching me so good. I cry out, moaning his name. I clutch his back, holding him inside me as deep as he can go.

"You and me." He pulls out and pumps back in. "No more fighting this."

"Yes, oh God, yes," I whimper into his neck.

"Every fucking day." Our lips meet and I swallow his words, holding them inside like sustenance. "You're mine. My woman."

Tears spring in my eyes as another orgasm builds inside me. I whisper against his lips. Everything he wants to hear and more. "Yes, fuck, Jasper."

He fucks me faster, the sound of skin on skin drowns out my thoughts. I'm so close, I arch into him, chasing my release. Grinding my clit against his pelvis.

"These lips are mine." He claims my mouth as I tremble beneath him, my muscles tightening around his cock. "This pussy is mine."

"Don't stop. Don't ever stop."

His answering growl in my ear is enough to send me over the edge, my moans muffled into his neck.

"Goddamn, baby, you're so fucking good," he manages to groan as he stills, almost collapsing on top of me as he comes. I love how he fills me. How his twitching cock, buried deep, paints my insides. Claiming me as his.

I've never been everything to someone. I've barely been a thought in their mind. Everyone leaves, especially the people who were supposed to love me most. I've spent my whole life learning to be okay with that, but maybe with him, I don't have to be.

We hold each other until our breathing syncs. As I drift

off, images of what we could be play through my mind like a movie and for the first time, it doesn't scare me.

For the first time, I'm not alone.

"I THINK WE ALL DESERVE A BREAK," I say as the five of us sit around the living area in pajamas, drinking coffee. "We're in New York City for fuck's sake, and we haven't left the house in days."

Leon barely looks up from his laptop as he mutters, "What do you have in mind?"

"I thought the whole point was laying low?" Damon adds. "You and Blake were all over the news, all over socials. We fucked over Fairfax, we burned Orlov's place to the ground. Don't you think going out for brunch and a movie is a little too risky?"

Blake snuggles against him, her wide eyes meeting mine. "He's probably right." She groans. "As much as it kills me to admit that."

"Hey," Damon says, tilting her face so she's looking up at him. "Don't make me fuck that smart mouth."

"Umm, excuse me! Best friend sitting right here. Not that I don't love a good mouth fucking," Jasper chokes on a sip of coffee, "but I don't need that visual at 10 AM."

"Holy fuck, I was not expecting that," Jasper manages as he wipes drips of coffee from his mouth.

"So... I've noticed the two of you have been practically inseparable lately," Blake says with a knowing smirk. "Are you guys finally going to admit you're together?"

All eyes drift in my direction and I feel my face flush. Jasper brings his palm to my thigh, squeezing with gentle possessiveness. I can't hide my grin. "You could say that."

"I fucking knew it," Damon says. "Pay up, Lee."

"Bloody hell, not another couple," he grumbles, but there's no hiding the smile that tugs at his lips. "At least now you can move your junk into Falin's room and I can finally get that king bed."

"I'm happy for you." Blake grins, warming my chest from the inside. "And I knew I heard something the other night."

"What can I say?" Jasper waggles his brows. "Some of us are just naturally gifted in the penis department. Can't help but keep her up all night... and all morning... and afternoon."

"You're insufferable," I say, shaking my head.

"I second that," Leon says.

"Third," Damon says, laughing under his breath.

"You know what I'm packing," Jasper boasts. "I'm allowed to be insufferable."

"For fuck's sake," I groan, dropping my head into my hands.

"Don't worry, sweetheart," Jasper says with a smirk, "They're just jealous they don't get to experience my magnificence. That ship has sailed."

"And on that note," Leon stands, "I'm going to go bleach my brain."

"If we can't do brunch," I say. "Can we at least have some fun today? It'll be good for us to take a break."

Me most of all. Between searching for Bailey during the day, and my parents at night, among other... activities, I'm drained, mentally and physically.

"You're right," Blake says. "A break is much-needed. We're all exhausted."

"She's been running herself ragged," Jasper adds, his hand moving to massage the back of my neck. The playfulness from moments ago has faded from his voice. "I guess I can blame myself for some of that."

"Let's get drunk and play games," I say. "Just for today. Tomorrow we can go back to business as usual."

Jasper slings his arm over my shoulder. "I'm in."

Blake laughs. "Me too."

"This is peer pressure," Damon groans. "But fine, as long as we get some good booze. None of that cheap ass vodka."

"Done," I say. "Leon? You in?"

He rubs his eyes, shutting his laptop screen. "I do need a break from staring at this thing. When you say games, what do you have in mind?"

"I have an idea," Jasper says, his eyes twinkling.

I know I'll either regret bringing up a game day, or end up learning things about these people that'll haunt me forever. Knowing Jasper, probably both.

CHAPTER THIRTY-ONE

JASPER

"Tell us this game idea again?" Falin asks from her spot beside me on the couch. I can smell her rose perfume even over the scent of booze permeating the area. We're one bottle and multiple beers in, and everyone's feeling much more relaxed. Computers are put away, phones are on silent, and we're ready to let our hair down. I grab a chip from the bowl in front of me, purposely taking my time chewing, just to get Falin to give me that adorable fucking scowl.

I reach under my shirt for my gun, remembering I'd grabbed it earlier, and remove the magazine, pulling back the slide to clear the chamber before setting it on the coffee table. "Truth or death." When everyone stares at me like I have five heads, I add, "Relax, it's empty."

"Truth or death?" Leon asks. "What the fuck, man?"

"It's easy. Spin it, spill your darkest secret. No bullshit allowed." I grin, showing a lot of bravado for a guy with skeletons living permanently in his closet.

"That's fucked up," Damon says, but he's already leaning forward.

"You scared?" Falin teases. That smart tone gives me a semi.

He narrows his eyes. "Nope, bring it on."

"So, it's basically spin the bottle but with a gun?" Leon asks, stating the obvious.

I shrug, and Blake answers for me. "It's like truth or dare, spin the bottle, and Russian Roulette combined? Except no bullets, of course."

"I hadn't thought of spin the bottle," I say, smirking. "Does that mean we get to smooch?" I plant a wet one on Falin's cheek and she laughs, pushing me away.

Blakes eyes light up. "I'll never say no to a little show."

Leon points his finger between me and Damon. "Those two need to scrub their mouths with disinfectant before I'd go near them."

"Hey!" Falin says, tossing a pillow at him. "He kisses me."

Leon laughs, a rare sound. "My point exactly."

"Rules?" Blake asks, ever the student.

I lean in, trailing my finger over the sleek black handle of my gun. "The secret has to be real. Something that makes you sick just thinking about saying it out loud."

"Christ," Damon groans. "Way to kill my buzz."

"I'll spin," I say. This game could be the biggest mistake I've ever made, or could be a fun night. The thrill makes my semi grow to fully hard.

"Wait." Falin grabs my hand as I reach for the gun. "What if someone doesn't want to share?"

"They have to do a dare instead," Blake suggests. "Something equally messed up."

I eye the gun, already feeling my pulse speed up. "Fine by me. Ready?" Without waiting for an answer, I spin. The barrel whirs against the coffee table before slowing to point at Leon.

"Fuck me," he mutters.

"Come on, mate." I lean back, wrapping my arm around Falin. "Show us what's in that dark British soul of yours."

He holds his beer, peeling the moist label into little pieces, his gaze trained at a spot on the wall. "I went to school with my half brother for years. He never knew who I was. Sometimes I'd follow him home, just to see what a real family looked like. I'd watch my father kick the football around the garden, patting his back, and smiling..." He trails off, eyes coming back into focus as he takes a long sip of beer. "Fuck, that was deep."

I reach across Falin to squeeze his arm. "Screw them both. We're your brothers for life."

"Don't ever forget it," Damon adds.

Leon nods, clearing his throat. "Let me give this a go." He spins hard, the gun rattling against the wood. It lands on Blake.

She twists her hands in her lap. "One time a few years ago, I found something on Brennan's phone. Photos. I didn't know what to do or say. I convinced myself they weren't real. That he wasn't a monster." She shakes her head. "He was all I had and I... Maybe if I acted, some of those girls..."

"Don't." Damon pulls her close. "You can't think like that. We'd never be able to make it through one fucking day if we got stuck on the maybes and what ifs."

She nods, inhaling a deep breath. "He's right, Bee," Falin says, her voice laced with care. "You couldn't have known. He fooled a lot of people."

My heart cracks in two for her and everything she's gone through. Seeing her brother die in front of her... Damn. I don't think I'd survive that.

The barrel spins again, finding me. Fuck. The secrets pile up in the back of my throat—the truth about the pills, the darkness that lives inside me, how scared I am of corrupting Falin with it all, of hurting her. But what comes out shocks me. "Sometimes I dream about Bailey being dead. And in those dreams, I feel relieved." My voice cracks. "Because at least then I'd know."

Falin wraps her hand in mine, squeezing gently. Everyone's quiet, and I know I fucked up. How could I say that about my own sister? I truly am a monster.

Blake is the first one to break the silence. "I completely understand. It's the not knowing that's the hardest part."

The silence sits like a viscous fog in the room until Falin snags the gun, spinning it hard enough to make the table creak. The barrel lands on Damon. This should be interesting.

"Alright," he says, taking a swig of beer. He picks up the gun and messes with the barrel as he thinks. "I killed one of my mom's junkie boyfriend's when I was ten years old." He drops the gun on the table, and drags a hand down his face.

When he doesn't elaborate, I speak up. "That's all you're going to tell us? Bro, you can't leave us hanging like that."

He shrugs, and finishes off his beer. "Don't feel like turning this into a therapy session." Before anyone can ask him more questions, he spins and the gun lands on Falin.

With her knees to her chest, she chews her bottom lip for a moment. "I dated this guy in San Francisco. I think I told you about him, Bee?"

Blake nods. "That guy with the tech startup? Alden or something?"

"Yup, Mr. My Shit Doesn't Stink." She straightens her legs and a look of pure hatred flickers in her eyes. "He tried to *help* me." Her voice is bitter with every word. "Called my dad, told him his daughter needed professional help. That I had control issues. All it took was three little clicks of my keyboard to destroy everything he built. His career, his golden reputation, gone." Her eyes meet mine. "And I didn't do it because he cheated. I didn't give a shit about that. I was pretty much done with him and his tiny dick, anyway. I did it because nobody gets to control me. *Ever.*"

"Remind me never to piss you off," I say, even though my cock is rock hard. Twisted is my type.

"Too late," she smiles, lifting a brow. Holy hell, I'm going to fuck the shit out of that mouth later.

"Alright, Satan," Damon says, making Blake slap his arm. "Your turn to spin."

Falin gives the gun her best spin, but it doesn't go very far, stopping on Leon. His jaw clenches. "I already went."

"Come on," I say. "I know there's some dark secrets hiding in that head. Or if you want you can spin and kiss someone," I add, purposely trying to egg him on. With my eyes scrunched shut, I cross my fingers. "Please land on Damon, please land on Damon."

Everyone laughs but him. "Nothing left worth telling. I'm an open book." He reaches for the gun, but Damon's hand shoots out, stopping him.

"Really?" Damon stops to take a sip from the cup in front of him. "Because I can think of one. About a certain girl you met last sum—"

"Don't." Leon's voice could slice skin.

The room goes silent except for the hum of the refrigerator, and the quiet snores from the kittens in their tower. I look between Leon and Damon, clocking something in Leon's expression I've never seen before. Raw panic.

"Okay, what the hell is happening?" Falin asks.

"Nothing," Leon and Damon say in unison.

"I call bullshit," I say. "Someone better spill."

Leon pushes up from the couch, grabbing his beer bottle. "I need a smoke."

"Lee—" Damon starts.

"Drop it." The words are a harsh warning that make my balls shrivel up into my body. He grabs his jacket and heads for the door.

We all watch him go, except Damon, who's clearly looking anywhere else. The weight of unspoken words lingers in the room.

"Well, that wasn't suspicious at all," Falin mutters.

Blake stands, stretching her arms above her head. "I need something stronger than beer after that."

"Same!" Falin says, jumping up from the couch. "Anyone up for Mario Kart?"

Damon and I exchange loaded glances. I've known him long enough to know when not to push for information, and right now is one of those times. Instead, I turn my attention to Falin, smiling like we didn't just scratch the surface of something way deeper. "Only if you're ready to get your ass kicked, Trouble."

"Not possible." She grabs two controllers from the table, tossing one my way. "I'm ruthless with a red shell."

"Want to bet?" I move over on the couch, giving her just enough room to sit next to me again.

She plops down, and her body against mine is enough to lighten my mood. I grab her chin, turning her head for a kiss. "Hell yeah, I do. I love a bet."

I lean in so only she can hear me, and picture those tequila-scented lips wrapped around my cock. "Winner gets to come first."

Her eyes gleam with mischief. "Deal."

Blake sets up the game, cursing as she plugs in the wrong cord. When I glance at Damon, he's still staring at the door, lost in thought.

"Got it," Blake says. Then Mario Kart music breaks through whatever it is he's dwelling on. As soon as Blake curls into his lap with her controller, he seems to shake it off entirely, his cocky smile returning.

"Rainbow Road," Falin announces. "Hope you're all ready to cry."

I pull her closer, breathing her in. "Bring it on, baby."

<hr>

"I HAVE A SECRET," I say, my head between Falin's legs. "I wanted you to win." I lap at her slick pussy, struggling to hold myself up. We may have gone a bit too hard on the tequila after my little game.

"Always talking," she says, lifting her hips and grinding against my face. "More of that."

"That? You mean more eating your wet cunt like it's my last meal?" My head swims but all I want is to make her come with my name on her lips.

"Yes. Oh God, keep going."

And I do. Or at least I try... things are a little *uncoordinated* at the moment. When I lose my rhythm for the third time, I roll over, pulling her up and onto my chest. "Sit on my face, baby."

She gets into position, her thighs on either side of my head, her round ass in my hands, her pretty pussy hovering over my lips. I hold her down, rocking her hips, drenching my face in her juices. Falin's not shy about what she needs. She takes control—grinding, bouncing, rocking —and I'm addicted to every movement.

"Fuck, Jasper, I'm close." Hell yeah, exactly what I need to hear. She keeps up her pace while her muscles tense around me and her moans echo off the walls. My hips arch and buck, my hard cock searching for relief. I need her to come so goddamn badly. I'm desperate for it.

My hands travel up her body to play with her tits, rolling and pinching her nipples. She throws her head back and cries out and fuck... she's so hot. My vision blurs, lungs burning for air but the sight of her like this is everything.

"Oh... my... fucking... God," Falin yells as she comes all over my face. I'll never get enough of hearing her screaming in pleasure. Her pussy's still pulsing as she climbs off on shaky legs, and straddles me.

"You don't waste any time, do you, baby? Is that greedy cunt ready for my—oh fuck," I groan as she seats herself all the way down, her pussy taking every inch like she's made for me. She leans over and I pay extra attention to her nipple, nibbling it until she gasps. "You feel so good... so tight."

"Yes... so deep." She rolls her perfect hips, rocking, chasing her pleasure. I help her bounce, lifting her up and slamming her back down, arching my hips with each roll of hers. She leans over, sucking my lip, sliding her tongue in to massage mine. I'm so lost in her, I can barely breathe. "I want..." She kisses me while her pussy suffocates my cock. "I want you everywhere."

"Whatever you want, whatever you need," I groan. She shifts to the side, reaching for something in the drawer. I barely register the loss of her wet heat, before she's squeezing lube all over my cock, pumping her fist to spread it along my shaft. "Baby, you're so wet already."

She straddles me again, holding onto my cock, and slowly guiding it into—holy fucking shit. My eyes roll back in my head as my cock notches her ass. As soon as I'm past that tight ring of muscle, she seats herself slowly, torturously... taking me so completely, I might die.

"Baby, holy fuck... You're gonna kill me. That perfect ass... so fucking tight." I wait until she's comfortable, as difficult as it is, and when she rocks her hips, her eyes closed and mouth parted, I lose myself. Every little inch she moves is pure heaven. Her muscles clench around me, choking my cock, and I see stars.

"Come in me, Jasper." She rides me deeper, taking every inch I give her. "Fill me until I'm dripping."

"That's my good little slut. So fucking filthy for me," I pump into her, praying to every God I know that I get to keep this woman forever. "Rub your clit for me. Show me how you make yourself come."

"Yes," she cries as her fingers rub tight circles over her clit. I won't last, there's no way in hell.

"Shit... I'm gonna come." That only makes her ride me harder. I inhale as everything in my body tightens. My eyes clench shut... or maybe I black out. I don't fucking know anything past the pleasure that shoots through my entire body. My hands grip her hips as I drive my cock in balls deep, shooting every last drop of cum inside her. She takes it all, sucking me dry until there's nothing left.

I pull her against my chest, kissing those beautiful lips, and whispering every praise I've ever known against her skin. "That was..." she says between heaving breaths.

"Intense," I say. As soon as she shifts, her muscles push me out and a husky laugh leaves her lips. "I was so not expecting that." I reach for the bottle of water on the side table, chugging some.

"What can I say, you're not the only one who loves to

get their ass fucked." I choke, sputtering water all over her and the bed.

"Christ, you can't say that while I have a drink in my mouth." I swallow it down, wiping my mouth, unable to hide my laughter. "Like I said, you're trying to kill me."

She kisses my cheek, before she climbs out of bed, showing off her gorgeous curves. "I don't see you complaining."

"And you never will."

She continues to surprise me every damn day. I'm the luckiest bastard alive.

CHAPTER THIRTY-TWO

FALIN

Two days. I've been staring at this screen for two freaking days—my eyes fuzzy, butt imprinted into my rickety chair. At this point, the data blurs together, one massive line of numbers and letters. It's the photos that I've been avoiding. I can't bear to look at their faces. Not until I have something useful to help save them.

Empty Red Bull cans and half-eaten chip bags litter my desk, and I don't even care. Leon, who came to camp in here with me a few hours ago probably feels differently, considering the raised brow glances he keeps giving toward my trash. Neat freak.

If he cares so much, he can clean it up. We're in crisis mode here. I'm so close to cracking this, I can feel it in my bones. Between the flash drive, Brennan's files, and the info Leon's been able to drum up, there's so much to cross reference, but every day we're closer and closer to finding a concrete location for those victims on the flash drive. *If they're still able to be found.* I push that thought far out of my mind. There's no room for negativity, not when my brain is already close to shorting out.

"Look at this," I say, pointing to a list on my screen. "These victim numbers seem random, but there's something weird about how they're documented."

Leon leans over, squinting at my screen. "I've seen inventory systems before. It seems pretty standard."

I huff, frustrated that he can't see what I do. "But when we line up these ID numbers with Brennan's container manifests, there's a pattern in how they move people through the ports."

He takes a few minutes to digest my words, his eyes darting between both our screens. "The container numbers aren't random. They're a victim count in each shipment."

"That's what I think too."

He clicks through a few screens, biting his lip ring. "They're tracking them like fucking cattle." He sounds as disgusted as I feel.

I point to my screen. "And look here. Fairfax didn't give us much, but this..." I scan the rows of money transfers, hundreds of thousands of dollars. "The transfers line up with the shipment dates."

"You're right," he says, sitting back in his chair. "And there." He points to the coded word at the end of each row. Some kind of shorthand system they used. Most of them repeating.

"Wait," I say, grabbing his hand. "There!"

One word stands out from the rest.

QNS4721ASTIND

"This entry's different." I highlight the text. "See how the other codes are all six characters? This one's longer, and it only showed up in the most recent transfers."

My hands shake as Leon moves his chair closer. "It

could lead us to an address. Let me run it against a few of the property records I was able to find under Orlov's shell companies."

I crack open another can of Red Bull, ignoring my already racing pulse. Jasper comes to the door, poking his head in, but I don't bother turning to look at him. I can't lose this train of thought.

"You need anything?" he asks. I know he's feeling antsy, which often leads him to trouble. I glance his way for a moment.

"We'd love a pizza," I say. "Right, Lee?" Leon nods, face still glued to his screen.

"I can do that. Anything else?" The happiness in his voice at being given a task is endearing.

"I think the girls are low on food too," I add. If I can get him out running a few errands, hopefully by the time he gets back, we'll have good news.

His arms wrap around me from behind, and I melt against him. He brushes a quick kiss along my jawline, before reaching my lips. "I'll be back in a few. Text me if you think of anything else."

Before he leaves, I hold my arms out for another hug. "Grab my credit card from my wallet." I can see him wanting to argue, so I narrow my eyes until he relents. Good boy.

Now that Jasper's gone, I go back to the task at hand. With the amount of property records, it's a shock we haven't found any of them occupied. They're all broken down homes, or warehouses, most scattered throughout the country.

My fingers stop mid-scroll. "Holy shit."

"What is it?" Leon asks.

"I found a possible match." I pull up a map of the property. "It's a warehouse in Queens, owned by one of their dummy corporations. QNS, must stand for Queens, the numbers are streets, and AST IND..." I zoom in on the photo. "Astoria Industrial."

"Fucking hell," Leon says, dragging a hand over his face.

"But look." I scroll through the records. "This property doesn't show up anywhere else in their system. Not on Brennan's manifests, not on the inventory records. They're keeping it separate from their usual operation for some reason."

"Go back to the original inventory listing. Is there a name listed with that particular code?"

I jump pages, my mind scrambling to keep up. "Interesting. There's a photo, but nothing else."

"They're definitely hiding something there." He stands, pacing the length of my bed.

I open another window, finding Bailey's photo in the database. #521. My heart clenches as I study her face. Somewhere in all this data is the key to finding her. We just have to keep digging.

"We should tell the others. Call Ray. I have a feeling this place is going to be it. Fuck, I want to hop on my bike and go there right now."

"No," I say. "We need to map this out." I start backing up all my data to a secure drive, my mind swimming with different possibilities of what we'll find there. "Why don't I tell Blake and Damon, and you call Ray?"

"Yeah, okay." He's out the door before I look away from my screen.

I pull up the street views and schematics of the warehouse, and try to piece together the best approach. Something about the location makes me pause. It almost seems too convenient. All the puzzle pieces connect, but still, my gut tells me there's something we're missing.

I only hope I can figure it out soon.

"Don't worry Bailey, we'll find you."

THERE WAS no stopping the guys last night from doing a quick drive-by in Damon's car. They promised they wouldn't try anything, and surprisingly they kept their word. The place was exactly how it looked from the images I pulled up online. Quiet. Vacant. After watching for an hour or so and seeing no one coming in or out, they called it a night.

This morning though, they're like wound up spinning tops ready to be set free. Ray and his crew are meeting us at the address at eight, and we'll find out for sure what the hell is going on in that warehouse.

With the energy in the apartment feeling suffocating, and my head fuzzy from looking at screens for days, I figured a nice walk and some caffeine would do me some good.

I grab my jacket from where it's slung behind a chair, feeling Jasper's eyes on me from across the room. He's messing around with his guitar, shirtless on the couch. It's hard enough to leave with him looking so damn good, but he's gotta give me the eyes too. "I'm just going to grab some coffee. Don't give me that look."

"What look?" he asks, giving me his golden retriever eyes. I sigh, unable to hide my smile.

"Want anything?" He raises his brows and I know exactly what he's about to say. "Not sexual," I tease.

"Let me grab a shirt. I'll come with you." He meets me

by the door, kissing me like he can't go another second without it.

I'm still getting used to all this open affection between us. Not that I've been cold before, but this is different. The constant checking in, the touching, the kissing. I like it more than I want to admit.

We walk hand in hand to the coffee shop a block away. It's relatively quiet this early in the day. Somehow, even after the plans we have tonight, this small moment feels normal.

"You look all deep in thought. Let me guess, you're thinking about me naked?" Jasper asks, slinging his arm around my shoulder and pulling me tight against his body.

"How'd you know?" I say, my voice oozing sarcasm. "I can't go five seconds without picturing your bubble butt."

He glances over his head. "I do have a nice ass, don't I? I'd picture my ass too."

"Oh my God, I can't with you." I laugh and give his ass a light smack. "If you must know, I'm thinking how weird it is to do something so... ordinary. Getting coffee with my boyfriend while we plan to raid a warehouse full of traffickers later tonight."

He chuckles. "Boyfriend, huh?"

"Oh, shut up." I glare up at him. "What would you prefer? Plaything? Fuck buddy?"

He lets out a low rumble that brings heat to my cheeks. "I can work with those." His thumb traces circles on my upper arm. "But I gotta say, being your boyfriend has some pretty awesome perks."

"Like what?"

"Well, for starters—" He's cut off by the sound of screeching tires. We both tense, hands instinctively moving toward our weapons, but it's just some asshole running a red light.

"Fuck. We're on edge, aren't we?" I try to sound like I'm joking, even though my heart's still racing.

"Can't help it." He scans the street as we walk. "Keep thinking about tonight. About Bailey."

I squeeze his hand. "We're going to find her."

"I know." He brings our joined hands to his lips, pressing a kiss to my knuckles. "Because I've got you."

The coffee shop is just ahead, promising caffeine and a few more minutes of pretending we're a normal couple on a normal morning. But we both know better. After tonight, nothing will be the same. I can feel it in my bones.

While Jasper finds us a table, I order our usuals. Latte for me, and caramel frappe with extra whipped cream for him. My boyfriend has the taste of a teenager, but somehow it makes me like him more.

My phone buzzes in my pocket, and I pull it out, tapping the screen. It's another DNA match notification. Since helping to find Bailey, I've joined two new sites. The results rarely pan out, but I can't help checking anyway.

The barista calls our order and I step over to the counter, but my eyes are glued to my screen. Twenty-five percent match. My hands shake as I put my phone away to grab the coffees.

What does this mean? Did I actually find someone?

"You okay?" Jasper asks as I set the coffees on the table.

"Yeah, just need to use the bathroom real quick." I force a smile, needing a moment alone to process this. If I say something to Jasper before I've even had the chance to look at it, he'll be so happy for me, jumping up and wrapping me in his arms. I couldn't bear that if it turns out to be a hoax somehow.

The hallway to the bathroom is narrow and dimly lit. I grab my phone again, swiping open the app. A woman, an aunt, maybe? I round the corner, clicking on her photo to open up her profile, but stop short as I almost collide with a man stepping out of the shadows. "Oh, shit. Sorry," I mumble, pushing past him.

"No harm done." The man's voice is smooth, but something about it gives me the creeps. I glance up to find his dark eyes studying me intensely. "I've been waiting for you, Falin."

I reach for my waistband, where I always keep my switchblade, especially lately, but his hand shoots out, wrapping around my wrist and squeezing. "What the fuck?" I seethe. "Let go!" I turn to call for Jasper, but his other hand covers my mouth, his expensive cologne wafting up my nose, making me gag.

"Don't make a sound or I'll kill you and he'll never find your body." I feel my legs shake, wanting to give out, but I force strength into them. "Do you understand, Falin?"

Without any other choice, I nod, and he slowly removes his hand from my mouth. I've never seen him, but my body knows who he is. Every nerve ending screams danger. *Alexander Orlov.* He has to be.

"Quite the happy little family you've built here in New York." He pulls out his phone, showing me photos that make my stomach drop. Blake and Damon walking to the deli. Leon getting on his bike. Jasper and me opening the door to the apartment building. "It would be a shame if anything happened to them."

"What do you want?" I keep my voice low and steady. The exact opposite to how I feel.

"A little meeting. Me, you, and your friend, Blake. We have business to discuss." His grip on my wrist tightens, and

I bite my lip to hold back a wince. "Don't think about telling your boyfriends. I'll know if you do."

"If you think I'd be stupid enough to meet you—" He moves so his face is nearly an inch from mine. His spittle hits my lips as he speaks.

"You will, because if you don't, I'll have my men grab Jasper Shea and he won't be as comfortable as his pretty little sister."

My eyes widen, but I school my lips into a neutral expression. I don't want to give him the pleasure of knowing he's gotten to me. Fuck. We've been right all along. I knew it, but hearing it from his mouth. Knowing he's put the pieces together, that's something different entirely.

I spit in his disgusting face. "Fuck you."

He lets my wrist free to wipe his face with his pocket square as a small laugh leaves his lips. His eyes are still cold as ice.

"Eight o'clock. The address will come by text. You and Hyland only, tell no one, or start planning funerals." He folds the cloth, shoving it into his pocket. "And Sinclair? I'll be watching. One wrong move and they all disappear."

He's gone before I can respond, leaving me barely able to stand. I rush into the bathroom and lock the door, sliding down onto the floor. Tears threaten to come, but it's like they're stuck. I force air into my nose and out through my mouth, cursing under my breath.

How did he find us? What the fuck am I going to do?

My phone buzzes again and I already know it's him before I even look. There's no way I'm bringing Blake to him. I'd rather die than put my best friend in harm's way. A notification pops up again from the DNA site, and I can't bring myself to care anymore. Not now. There's no use in finding my missing family if I'll be dead in less than twenty-four hours.

I splash some water on my face and will myself to breathe normally. Jasper can't know what just happened. *You got this. Get home and figure something out.* But what?

When I return to our table, Jasper's scrolling his phone, smiling at something on the screen. He sees me, and his face falls.

"You okay? You look pale." He reaches for my hand.

I force a smile, hating myself for what I'm about to do. For lying to him when I've asked for nothing but honesty. "Just tired. Tonight's got me on edge."

"Me too, but these kitten videos are helping." He kisses my palm and goes back to watching his phone while I sit there thinking about how fucked I am.

How am I going to keep them all alive?

CHAPTER THIRTY-THREE

JASPER

Something's wrong with Falin. I wish I could figure out what it is. If I did something wrong, she's usually the first person to tell me—loudly and unapologetically.

She's been off since the coffee shop—distant, barely meeting my eyes, answering in one word responses even when I'm being a smartass.

When she said she was too sick to come tonight, that really tipped me off. This is the woman who worked through three days of no sleep, barely eating because she was close to cracking that code. Tonight wouldn't be happening if it wasn't for her. I've only known her for a few months, but I know she'd have to be halfway to the grave to sit this out.

"Maybe I should stay," I say, hovering by her bedroom door. She's curled up in bed, kittens on her chest, but her posture is too stiff for someone who's supposedly sick. She pets the kittens, barely meeting my eyes.

"No," she answers quickly. "You need to be there. For Bailey."

She knows bringing up Bailey's name directly will have me by the balls. Well played.

Blake pokes her head in, jacket on and ready to go. "I can stay with you, Fal. The guys can handle—"

"Absolutely not." Falin sits up and the kittens bolt from her sharp voice. "You both need to go. Please."

Fuck. My chest tightens again. It's pretty much been that way all day. Pent up adrenaline mixed with anxiety. Her tone isn't helping the situation. It's like she's begging us to leave. I've heard Falin beg before, usually with my head between her thighs, but this is different. Desperate.

I finally relent, kissing her goodbye, and leaving her with a glass of water and a bottle of ibuprofen. "Call me if you need anything," I tell her. She waves me off, assuring me she'll be fine, she just needs rest.

Leon hops on his bike, and Damon, Blake, and I pile into Damon's car. My leg won't stop bouncing, my head swimming with alarm bells. We make it fifteen minutes before Damon shoots me a look, asking me what the hell was wrong.

"She'll be fine," he says, but I barely hear him over the roar in my head. "Ray's probably already there. This will go smoothly, I can feel it."

Blake pokes her head through the middle console. "Falin's tough, she'll be okay. I'm sure she's super bummed to miss out on tonight."

That's just the thing.

At the next red light, I make a snap decision. "Pull over. Drop me off here."

"What? Why?" Damon asks.

"Something's not right. I need to check on her."

He starts to argue, but I open my door before he gets the chance to pull over. I don't have time for this. "Goddamn, brother." The light turns green, but before he hits the gas, he yells out the window. "Be careful. Text if you need us."

I pull out my phone and hit call on Falin's name. The line rings and rings before her voicemail picks up. I try again and leave her a message.

"I'm heading back home. Be pissed at me if you want, but I don't want you there alone."

I sprint all the way back, my pounding heart louder than my rushing thoughts. The apartment is dark when I get there. Empty.

"Fuck!" I knew something was off. After checking her bedroom for a note, or any sign of a struggle, I call Leon. He answers on his helmet's bluetooth. "I need you to track Falin's phone."

"What? Why?" he asks.

"Don't ask questions... please. Just do it."

He must hear the desperation in my voice because the noise from his engine dies down. "I pulled off the road. What's going on?"

"Where is she?"

He sighs, but doesn't ask any more questions. It takes a few seconds where I pace the length of the apartment, grabbing another gun from my dresser drawer and tucking it into my waistband. "She's in midtown. Looks like an office building, a high-rise. Sending the address now."

A chill rushes through me. "Something is wrong."

The text comes through and I'm already running. "Jasper, wait for us. I'm turning around now."

"No, you go on ahead. If I need you, I'll call you."

There's no time. I have to get to her. If she's hurt, I'll never fucking forgive myself.

THE SECURITY DESK is empty when I push through the glass door into the lobby. I glance at the elevator, but decide against it. There isn't time. I have no idea where she is in this massive building, but I won't find her in this lobby.

I head for the stairs, taking them two at a time until I hear footsteps above me. Pressing my frame against the wall, I draw my weapon, forcing my heavy breaths to slow. My phone vibrates and the sound is amplified in the massive stairwell. I don't have a chance to check who it is, or to quiet the damn thing. Whoever's above me knows I'm here. I take a step, craning my neck to see what I'm dealing with. It could be Falin, but my gut tells me it's not her.

"Stop right there," a man's deep voice echoes. I spot him, a big guy. Something about him looks familiar. He's aiming a gun down at me from two flights up.

"I don't have beef with you," I say. "I'm just trying to find my girl." I keep my gun drawn, but take a better look at him. For a guy aiming a gun, his posture seems pretty slouchy. Is his hand shaking? It's hard to tell from this far away. "Where is she?"

He's quiet at first, clearly weighing his options. When he finally opens his mouth, the words come out slow. "Just leave." There's no force behind what he says, nothing menacing in his tone. "Please. I don't want to kill anyone else."

"No shame in that. I'd very much like to keep breathing too." I climb a few steps, keeping my weapon aimed and eyes on him. "What's your name?"

"Don't come any further," he yells, his voice trembling.

I don't need to. I'm close enough now to take him out without a problem. "Looks like we're in a situation here, big guy," I say.

"It's Bruce," he says, correcting me.

"Ah, Bruce. Well, Bruce, since neither of us want to kill each other, maybe we can help each other out instead?"

Bruce's hand lowers, and I suck in a breath. "He killed him. Beat him to death right in front of me." His voice cracks. "Over nothing. A fucking mistake anyone could have made."

"Who did, Bruce? You can tell me, I'll help you." I chance a few more steps forward, now seeing moisture shining in Bruce's eyes. I remember him now. He's the fucker who grabbed Blake. Karma is a bitch, Brucey boy. But now I know for sure who has Falin and my chest tightens. *Orlov.* "Come on. Promise it'll help to talk about it."

That gets him to look at me directly. He's thinking about telling me what I need to hear. I can see it in his eyes. "He'll kill me too. Slowly. Painfully."

"Not if we get to him first." I'm close enough now to see the tears on Bruce's face. "Where are they?"

His eyes widen, his mouth opening like he's going to ask me a question, but he closes it just as quickly. "The roof. But you should know—"

I don't hesitate. I won't make the mistake of letting any of them live again. The bullet catches him in the chest and he slumps against the cement wall. As he slides down, a crimson trail spreads beneath his body, and his wide eyes meet mine.

"Thank you," he whispers.

I kick his gun aside and run. His words echo in my head, but I can't dwell on that. My legs burn but I don't slow down. I barely think. Twenty-seven floors worth of stairs and my heart's about to explode, but none of that matters. She has to be okay. *Please don't let me be too late.*

The roof access door is ahead, close enough that I hear voices coming from outside. Through the small window I see them. Falin standing near the edge, Alexander a few feet away with his gun aimed at her head.

Panic squeezes my throat, choking the air from my lungs. I hear him raising his voice over the cool night breeze. "You're trapped, stupid girl. Should have ran down the stairs, but I wouldn't expect smart thinking from you."

"How do you know this isn't exactly where I wanted you?" she says. She's standing tall and strong. I need a fucking plan, but every way I look at it, there's no being stealthy here.

Orlov snickers with cold indifference. "Corner me on my own roof? Like I said, not much going on upstairs. Good thing you'll make up for it in other ways. If I decide to let you live." He takes a step closer, his gun trained on her head. "Where's Blake? I told you to bring her."

"Like I'd hand over my best friend to a piece of shit like you. Who's the stupid one, now?"

A gust of wind rattles the door. I use the distraction to quietly crack it open, so I can hear better.

"Such fire." He clicks his tongue, pacing back and forth. "Too bad it won't save your boyfriends. That warehouse you're all so interested in? It's wired to blow the moment anyone breaches the door. Your friends will be dead before they realize what hit them."

Oh my fuck. I have to warn them, but I can't bring myself to look away from Falin. One distraction and she could be gone.

"You're lying." She holds her chin high, but her tense body betrays her.

"Am I? You really think you're in control here?" He moves closer. "That's your problem, isn't it, you dumb whore? Always needing to control everything, everyone.

That's why you came here alone. How's that working out for you?"

"Better than being a piece of shit who trades in human lives. No one loves you, let alone *likes* you. Brennan did your job better and you know it." She inches closer. The fucking balls on this woman. "You're a pig. A disgusting middle-aged white man who can only get it up when he's raping a woman."

He grabs her by the hair, yanking her down. As I'm about to sprint forward, his words hit me like a tire iron to the back of the head. "Like that pretty brunette? What was her name? Oh, that's right. Bailey Shea."

I freeze, my hand gripping my weapon so tightly, my fingers go numb.

"Fuck you," Falin seethes.

"She begged for her brother at first. Cried for him. Cried to go home. But now?" He smiles. "Now she won't even remember his name."

I burst through the door, my gun raised. "You fucking bastard!"

"Jasper, no!" Falin meets my gaze. Fear shines through her smokey wide eyes.

Orlov spins, still keeping his gun aimed at Falin. Adrenaline pumps through my system, every nerve ending wanting to fight. To kill. "Ah, the boyfriend arrives. The failed hero. This is getting to be so much fun."

"Let her go," I say as calmly as I can muster.

He laughs again, the sound making the hairs on my arm stand up. "Why would I do that? She'll make me a lot of money. Just like your sister."

"Shut your fucking mouth!"

"I did my research on you, Shea. You think you can fuck

up my life and walk away scot-free. I'm afraid I'm not that nice of a man."

"Don't listen to him," Falin pleads. "He wants to watch you squirm."

"He should listen. I have so much to share. Like how she screamed in that London townhouse. How she—"

I hear it before I see Falin move. Her gun aimed, the shot hitting Orlov in the chest. He staggers but somehow stays on his feet, his gun swinging toward me.

"No!" Falin moves faster than I've ever seen her, throwing herself between us as Alexander's gun goes off. I sprint forward to grab her, spinning us both as a familiar white hot pain tears through my abdomen. I roar through the pain, holding Falin tight.

We stumble, landing on our knees just as Orlov loses his balance near the edge. His eyes bulge as realization hits him. His arms windmill but there's nothing for him to grab onto. Only air. He screams as his body careens off the edge, echoing all the way down.

Falin clutches me as I sink down, both of us shaking with released adrenaline. My body burns, and blood soaks my shirt. She presses her hands against my wound, tears springing from her eyes. "Why?" she cries. She grabs her blade, tearing off the bottom of her shirt to hold onto my wound. "You dummy of a man. Beautiful, idiotic, frustrating... You weren't supposed to come!"

"Baby..." I try to reach for her, but she holds me down.

"Don't move," she says, pulling out her phone. "I'm calling 911."

I grab her face with trembling fingers, kissing her like it's the last time I'll ever get to taste her lips. "I knew something was wrong. I—"

"Shh," she says between giving the dispatcher our location. "Save your strength."

"Bailey... London. We have to—" I can barely think straight. The pain is making me want to throw up right then and there. My eyes can hardly stay open.

"It's okay." She presses her forehead to mine. "We'll find her. Together. But first we need to get you help. The paramedics are coming. And I need to warn the others about that warehouse." She keeps one hand pressed firmly on my wound while texting with the others. "Shit. I'm fucking scared."

I try to focus on her voice, but everything feels distant, like I'm being pulled underwater. Is this how it would have felt if I let the river take me?

Orlov is gone. We fucking killed him. Bailey's in London. Or at least she was. Oh God, it hurts. I close my eyes and sink into that dark place where pain consumes me.

I don't know how long I stay like that, lying on my back on the cold, hard ground. Falin's voice pulls me back. She's hovering above me. An angel to break through this hell.

"I'm sorry I wasn't good enough. That I couldn't save her. You can leave me here... I'll—"

"I'm not going anywhere. Just stay with me," she whispers. "Keep those beautiful eyes open for me."

I blink hard, fighting to stay conscious. "The guys?" They better be okay. I won't live with myself. She's quiet as she keeps pressure on my wound. Too quiet. I ask again. "Did you get them?"

"They're okay," she finally answers.

Then why does she sound like something's wrong? I force my eyes to focus on her face through the haze of pain. "Baby? What happened?"

"It's Ray and his guys."

I hear sirens in the distance getting closer. Falin's hand trembles against my stomach but she keeps steady pressure. "Just hold on. Help is almost here."

CHAPTER THIRTY-FOUR

FALIN

Jasper's in surgery. Fucking surgery. This waiting room is purgatory. Every step I pace along its stark-white floor brings me one minute closer to seeing him. To knowing he'll be okay. Hours have passed, I think, marked only by the change of old comedy reruns blaring from the TV across the room, their laugh tracks taunting me.

The blood is still under my fingernails despite scrubbing them raw in the bathroom. I don't know what the bullet hit. How deep. If it tore through organs or severed nerves. There was so much blood. God, I can still smell its coppery tang in the back of my nostrils. And he's already been shot once in the past year. It should have been me. I deserved it for thinking I could take Alexander alone.

Alexander's words echo in my mind. *Always needing to control everything, everyone. How's that working out for you?*

Not fucking well at all.

Was that what I was doing? Trying to control the situation? I don't know anymore. I wanted to keep them safe, and look where that got me. At least Alexander's dead... but I know he's only a small part of this web. His uncle is who we need.

"Falin!" I freeze to find Blake rushing through the emergency room doors with Damon and Leon close behind. I've never felt relief this strong before.

I run to meet them, tears springing to my eyes. They wrap me in a hug, all of us in one giant heap of arms and murmured words. "You're okay," I repeat. "We're okay."

When we pull apart, I take in Blake's tear-stained face. "It was—"

Damon pulls her against his chest. "It was bad."

A weight sinks in my gut. "Tell me everything."

"We will," Leon says. "But how is he? We raced over here as fast as we could. Cops everywhere, we couldn't move. Fuck. We had to get out of there."

Shit. If cops are involved...

"He's in surgery, that's all I know. The bullet hit his abdomen. It all happened so fast."

Saying the words out loud, seeing their panic-stricken faces, makes this all too real. Blake sucks in a breath. "I'm going to see if I can get some more information. Maybe if I use my big med school words, someone will give me something."

I nod, watching her back as she retreats toward the check in desk. "Ray?"

Damon's face twists, like hearing the name causes him physical pain. "They got there first. We didn't know."

Oh God. All those guys... dead. They were there for us through all of this nightmare. They had families and lives. I close my eyes as a wave of grief washes over me. It quickly changes to anger.

Blake hurries back over. "They said we can see him. I had to argue with a nurse, and a doctor," she smiles, "but I wasn't taking no for an answer."

I follow Blake down the sterile hallway, trying not to focus on the sharp antiseptic smell or the way my hands won't stop shaking. The others trail behind us, their footsteps echoing against the linoleum floor. I need to see his face. To know he'll be okay.

Jasper's recovery room is dimly lit with different machines beeping steadily beside his bed. Seeing him lying there, pale and still... my chest cracks in two.

Blake explains what little information she was able to get. "The bullet tore through his abdomen, causing internal bleeding." It was four hours of surgery. Four hours of me pacing the waiting room, convinced I'd lose him before I got the chance to tell him how I feel.

She comes to stand by my side, squeezing my hand. "The surgeon said everything went well. They repaired the damage. He'll be in pain for a while, but there shouldn't be any lasting effects. I'll go see what else I can find out." Her hug envelops me before she heads back out into the busy hallway.

I sink into a crouch beside his bed and carefully take hold of his hand. His skin is warm despite how pale he looks, his pulse a steady drum beneath my fingers. Tubes and wires snake from his body to all of those machines. For a brief moment, I remember how my mother looked as she lay in her hospital bed, right before she died. I was so young, but the steady beeping brings me back. It's both comforting and terrifying. Those beeps mean he's alive, but seeing him like this, so vulnerable. I wish I could kill Alexander all over again.

Leon and Damon hover near the doorway, their faces

grim. I know they're thinking about Ray and his men, about the cost of tonight's mission, about Jasper barely escaping with his life. The weight of it all is heavy in the room.

"Hey," Damon says softly. "We never found out exactly what happened."

I stroke my thumb across Jasper's knuckles, drawing strength from his steady presence even in unconsciousness. Taking a deep breath, I turn to face them.

"Alexander is dead," I whisper. "I shot him and he fell off the roof."

They stare at me, stunned. Finally Damon lets out a short laugh, the sound startling in the quiet room. "You killed Orlov? *You?*"

Okay, now I'm getting pissed. I cross the room so they can hear me clearly. "Yes, me. Why is that such a surprise?"

Damon's jaw hangs slack, his eyes wide as he looks at me like he's seeing me for the first time. Leon cracks the slightest smile, and squeezes my shoulder gently. "Wouldn't expect anything less from our girl."

Our girl.

Two simple words, but they reach into my body and fill every hollow space that years of loneliness had claimed. I'd forgotten what it felt like to belong somewhere, to have people claim me as their own. The fierce protectiveness in Leon's voice, the pride in their eyes. It's everything I never knew I was missing. I blink rapidly, fighting back tears.

"Thank you," I whisper, "for letting me in."

"You're Jasper's girl and Blake's sister. That makes you ours."

A family. It's what I've craved for so long that I don't even know how to process their words. For years I kept my walls up high, convinced that control meant safety. That if I never let anyone close enough to hurt me, I'd never have to feel that crushing sense of abandonment again. My parents left. My mother died. My father chose a life of liquor and law. Never staying in one place too long, staying busy. It kept my heart from breaking.

But looking at these men, at Blake, at my family, I realize control was just another wall I built. Another way to keep myself from the terrifying, wonderful feeling of belonging. Of being claimed and loved exactly as I am.

Jasper. Please God, if you ever cared about me, make him pull through. I can't lose him. I make my way over to the side of his bed again, taking in every detail of his face. His perfect jaw, lined with stubble. His straight prominent nose leading to full lips. Those dark lashes and thick brows. This face I've grown to need more than air.

I don't know how it happened. How this insufferable, beautiful man slipped past every defense I'd so carefully constructed.

The weight of it has me sucking in a gasp. *I love him.* I love him in a way that pulls the air from my lungs. I love him the way I swore I'd never love a man. The type of love that means giving up control. Being vulnerable. Risking everything. Somehow the only thing that scares me is not being able to tell him.

I brush a kiss across his cheek as my heart races, and cross past the guys to get some air. They ask if I'm okay, but I can't find the words to tell them that despite this situation, I'm great. I finally feel whole.

Blake, Damon, Leon, *him*—they're the family I need.

I want it all. To fight, protect, and love each other without any guarantees.

My whole life, I've been searching for my birth parents, desperate to understand where I came from. But maybe finding where I belong matters more than finding where I began.

"Hey, you alright?" Blake's eyes widen as she heads toward me. I must look like I lost my mind as a smile lifts the corner of my lips.

"Yeah," I say, swallowing the emotion clogging my throat. "I love you, Blakey." I wrap her in a hug, feeling the overwhelm of gratitude for my best friend.

"I love you too." She pulls back to look at me, and feels my forehead with the back of her palm.

"I'm fine, I promise." I smile to show I mean it.

"Just checking. You went through it tonight. We all did." She's quiet for a moment while the events of the night must play through her mind. "But good news," she forces her tone to sound upbeat, "they're moving Jas to a different floor soon. He'll be here for a few days, but the consensus is that he got super lucky."

"We all did," I say.

Not Ray or his guys though.

Now that we know Jasper will recover, some of that anger comes to the surface again. Realization hits me—*Bailey*.

I hurry back into the room with Blake close behind. "I forgot to tell you." The words stumble out of my lips faster than my brain can conjure them. "Alex—he said, before he fell—he—"

"Take a breath, we're right here," Blake says. I glance between Blake and Jasper's unconscious form and blink.

"Bailey's in London. Or at least, she might be." All three sets of eyes widen, urging me to go on. "Before Alexander fell, he said some things... about her. We were right, Orlov is involved. They have her, or had her... I don't know."

"London?" Leon asks. "You're sure?"

"Yes." My head swims trying to think of Alexander's exact words, but most of it is a blur already. "I wish I could have pushed for more but—"

"I've been thinking about this since you told us he's dead. His uncle won't let this go," Damon cuts in, his voice low. "You realize what killing Alexander means? Ivan Orlov will burn the world to get revenge."

Blake grabs his hand. "With everything that happened, I hadn't thought of Ivan."

"Ivan built his empire," Leon begins. "Politicians, judges, traffickers across the world. They all answer to him. Alexander was just a small player compared to his uncle."

My body goes cold as Damon adds, "And now we've killed his blood. His heir. On top of everything else."

"So we go to London," I say. "Find Bailey before he moves her or worse."

Leon shakes his head. "We need to be smart about this. Ivan's reach is global. One wrong move and..."

He doesn't finish the thought. He doesn't need to.

"We can figure this out later, okay," Blake says. She turns to me. "You did amazing, and you're here, in one piece, and Alexander's dead." Her eyes drift to a spot on the wall as she lets her words sink in. I'd almost forgotten what Alexander's death would mean to Blake. The man who killed her brother. Who kidnapped her. Who ruined her family.

Damon pulls her back against his chest, wrapping his arms around her. "That fucker will burn for what he's done, Angel. And Ivan, we'll find him too."

"One monster dead, but so many more still out there." Her solemn voice hits me deep. We know the truth. We'll never find them all, never drag every monster from the shadows and into the light. Some creatures just won't die, no matter how many heads we slice, or how much blood we spill. But I intend to fuck up as many as I can—as *we* can—starting with Ivan Orlov.

"We will," I say, already feeling my body buzz at the thought.

Leon meets my gaze, his hazel eyes filled with intensity. "And end them."

Jasper's low groan pulls our attention and I rush to his side. His eyes open slowly, those blue irises just as bright as always. "Jas? I'm here, we're all here."

"I'll go tell the nurse," Blake says.

"Hey, Trouble." His voice is like sandpaper, but holds the same flirty tone as always, and my chest swells. "What happened?"

My fingers push strands of hair behind his ears, rubbing his forehead gently. The guys lean in, patting his shoulder, saying their own versions of hello. Jasper tries to move but hisses. "Don't move. You had to have surgery."

Realization hits and his lips part. "Fuck... I remember. Orlov. The roof." His eyes meet mine, relief swimming in them. "You're okay?"

I squeeze his hand. "I'm okay." He releases a breath, and turns his head toward the guys.

"Ray's team..." Jasper starts.

"Gone," Leon says, his voice hollow. "They beat us to the warehouse. It was... wired to blow."

Jasper closes his eyes, taking it in. "Fuck."

The nurse comes into the room, cutting off our conversation. She looks between Damon and Leon and swallows hard, taking a moment to compose herself.

I get it, sis. They have that effect.

"I'll need everyone to clear out for the night. Visiting hours are long over, but we bent the rules until he woke up."

She checks his machines, pressing buttons, and pulling supplies from a drawer.

The guys say their goodbyes, followed by Blake. "We'll meet you in the lobby," she whispers to me on her way out the door.

"Do you think I could get a minute alone with him?" I ask the nurse. She darts her gaze between us, her expression softening. "Just one?"

"I'll go let the doctors know he's awake." Her tired face lights up for a moment before she leaves, closing the door behind her.

Jasper tries to shift in the bed but winces again. "Come here," he says, patting the tiny space beside him. "If we only have a minute, I need to spend it holding you."

"I don't want to hurt you." But I carefully perch on the edge of his bed anyway, unable to deny him. My heart thunders against my ribs as his hand finds mine.

"You scared the hell out of me tonight," he says softly. "When I got back to the apartment and you were gone..." His voice cracks. Oh God, I hate that I caused him pain.

"I'm sorry. He threatened to kill you all if I didn't meet him. I couldn't—" My words get stuck in my throat as tears spring to my eyes. Just thinking about Alexander hurting him again is too much to bear. I stare down at a loose thread on the blanket. "I couldn't let anything happen to you."

"Hey." He squeezes my hand. "Look at me, Trouble."

Swiping my hand across my eyes, I meet his gaze. The pain meds have him groggy, his eyes slightly unfocused, but otherwise full of warmth. There's no anger in them. No plan to scold me for needing control.

"I love you," he says. "And I'll always come for you. No matter what."

Simple and assured. Those three words spill from his

lips like they took no thought at all. Like saying them was as natural as breathing.

I hold my breath, waiting for the fear to kick in, but it doesn't come. There's no urge to run. No need to fight. I smile, breathe, let his love flow through my veins, strengthening my bones.

"Even when I'm being stubborn and reckless?"

He grins that crooked grin I'll never get enough of. "Especially then. Your stubbornness is like, thirty percent of why I love you. The other seventy percent is your cooking skills."

I laugh despite the tears in my eyes. "I've never cooked for you, dummy."

"Oh. Must be the painkillers talking." His expression grows serious again. "But I meant what I said. I love you, Falin."

"I love you too," I whisper, the words feeling so natural on my lips. "So much that it's kinda scary."

He tries to pull me down, but I put my hand on his chest to stop him from moving and rest my head against his forehead. "Good thing we're both pretty brave then."

I smile against his skin, brushing a soft kiss on his lips. "Good thing."

I CAN'T SLEEP without Jasper here. Damon and Blake have gone to bed, but I doubt sleep will find them either. We're all feeling the pain of so much loss. When I close my eyes, I see the bullet striking Jasper, blood soaking through his shirt. Knowing her like I do, Blake must be reliving the explosion that took Ray and his men. She didn't witness it happen, thank God, but I'm sure seeing the building overtaken by flames was horror enough.

Throwing on a sweatshirt to combat the chill in the air, I head to the kitchen. A cup of tea would be a good idea, if we have some. None of us have been great with keeping up on grocery shopping.

I hear clicking from the kitchen... Leon. He could use some tea too. Carrying both mugs, I find him at his desk, the blue glow of his screens casting shadows across his face. His shoulders touch his ears as he types, and he doesn't acknowledge my presence.

"You okay?" I ask, setting the mug of chamomile beside him.

He pauses, but his fingers stay on the keyboard. "Fine. Working on finding the London connections."

"Fine." Yeah, okay.

He's nowhere near fine, but I pretend to buy it. "So London? Kind of hard to believe?"

"Not really." His jaw clenches and eyes stay fixed on the screen.

Hint taken.

I shuffle my feet on the hardwood floor. "I'll quit bothering you. Hope you get some sleep tonight."

As I turn to leave his hand catches my wrist. "Sorry, I'm just..." He sighs and drags his palm down his face. "This is just a shock, is all. Everything..."

I know exactly what he means, no explanation needed. "We'll find her," I say softly.

His expression doesn't change from its blank mask of exhaustion, but his hands tremble slightly as he reaches for the tea. "Thank you for this."

Before I can respond, he turns back to his screen, effectively ending the conversation.

As I head to bed, I glance back toward his open door and see him pull something from his desk drawer. A piece of paper, or maybe a photo. He stares at it for a long moment before quickly stuffing it away.

Back in my room with my tea, I close the door. We each need space to deal with our demons tonight. Whatever Leon's fighting, I hope he finds some peace.

CHAPTER THIRTY-FIVE

JASPER

Refusing painkillers after getting shot may not be my best decision making, but I'll be damned if I'm going to let this fuckery drag me back down the dark path I've worked so hard to end. "When can I take more ibuprofen?" I ask Falin. She's been at her desk monitoring the police investigations. All of them—the warehouse, the fire, Orlov's death. She's kept tabs on Fairfax too. So much work that I can't keep it all straight in my fuzzy head. Thankfully with her and everyone else on top of things, I don't have to.

"Not for another two hours." She sinks onto the bed beside me, and I clench my jaw against the pain that ripples through me at the slightest movement. "Do you need anything else? A drink or a snack?"

I know she hates to see me in pain. If I wasn't such a selfish bastard, I'd tell her to leave me here alone, not that she'd listen, but I'd try.

I gesture toward the end table where a Gatorade, a water, and a lukewarm cup of coffee sit untouched next to a box of protein bars and package of Oreos. "I think I'm all good there. Come closer, I want to feel you."

She hums and as gently as possible, inches closer, resting her head on my chest. Her fingers trail circles over my pecs, and down until she reaches my upper ribs. "You don't have to be so hard on yourself. If you need them, you need them. We'll work through it when you're healed."

Her gentle voice and matching touch almost makes me want to relent. "No. I'll be fine. The pain's less every day." She moves to kiss my jaw but I hold her cheek, kissing her sweet lips until I groan with need. "The worst part is not being able to fuck you like I want."

"Just because *you* can't doesn't mean *I* can't," she says with a devilish gleam in her eye that makes my cock hard in spite of the pain. "You just lay there and let me take care of you."

"Fuck, baby, don't look at me like that. You're going to kill me." She sits up and pulls her shirt over her head, baring her gorgeous tits. My mouth waters as she trails her fingers over her nipples, toying with me. She crawls down the bed, slowly so she doesn't jostle me. Not that the pain matters right now, I want her too badly.

She arches a brow. "At least you'll die a happy man." Her fingers gently reach beneath the waistband of my shorts, shimmying them down just enough. "With your cock in my mouth."

Fucking hell. "You don't have to—"

"Shh. What makes you think I don't want this as much as you?" She wraps her soft hand around my length, pumping up and down. "That I'm not soaking wet picturing the taste of your cum running down my throat?"

Her mouth. Christ. It's a miracle I don't come on the spot.

"Trouble," I groan. "You're so goddamn hot."

She spits on my tip, getting it nice and wet, before

pressing her tits together and sliding my cock between them. So soft and warm and oh fuck… I can't lift my hips like that. I must wince because she stops, sitting back with worry in her eyes. "Did I hurt you?"

"No. Never, baby." I breathe through the pain. "I'm an idiot and moved my hips and—"

She holds my hip down with gentle firmness and I see the shift in her eyes, the intensity. Her other hand starts to fist my cock again, but her eyes hold mine. "If you move, I stop."

My chest heaves. I love this side of her. Bossy and in control. I nod, knowing staying still will be even harder now. She hovers over my cock, spitting on my head again, her warm saliva dripping down my shaft. I fight between closing my eyes and keeping them wide open, watching her every move.

"Good boy." The second my cock slides between her plump lips, I almost lose it. Grabbing the sheets to stop from moving, I groan. Her head bobs as she takes me deep, humming and moaning like she loves every single inch of my length hitting her throat.

Her cheeks hollow as she sucks, her hand pumping my shaft. "Baby, your mouth is too good. I'm gonna come."

She ups her pace and I feel it all at once, my balls tighten, my hips instinctively lift, and I spill every drop down her throat with a groan that could wake the dead. I don't care if I'll be sore. I don't care if I might have pulled my stitches. Her sucking me dry is worth every second of pain.

I watch her swallow, her tongue darting out to catch an escaped dribble and my chest swells. How'd I get so lucky? "Have I told you how much I love you?"

Pulling up my shorts, she laughs. "Just a couple times."

She kisses my chest, right over my heart. "I love you too, dummy."

"There she is. My Trouble." I pull her in, too in love to care about the pain as my abdominals clench, and kiss her like she's mine.

———

AFTER THREE WEEKS of laying low and healing, one of the first things I want to do, now that I've gotten the all clear to move around, is check in on the victims we saved from the house in the Bronx. I want to see their faces as we tell them the bad man is gone forever.

They don't need to know about the others yet—the countless monsters still out there. That knowledge will come soon enough. They've been through unimaginable things... the kind I can't even let myself picture Bailey enduring without bile rising to the back of my throat. They deserve whatever childhood they have left. Before we go to London and continue our search, I need to know they will be okay.

"Are you sure you don't want to come?" I ask Leon. He's been on the computer nonstop since that night, which isn't out of character for him, but he's been quieter than usual.

I know he blames himself for Ray's death, for the deaths of the four others. It's no more his fault than it is any of ours, but he's Leon. It'll take time until he sees that.

"I've just been going over those financial records again," Leon says, his voice rough from lack of sleep. The harsh computer light shows every minute of insomnia under his eyes as Falin sits beside him.

She peers at his monitor. "What did you find?"

"It's all right here." A slight smile curves the corner of

his lips, the first one I've seen in days. "The money trail. I'm going to take him down."

I hover next to him, trying to see what they see. "Talk to us."

"Look at this." He clicks away on his keyboard, pulling up account statements and wire transfers. "Every shell company, every front business like that club we took out, they all lead back to these three accounts. And the beautiful thing?" He highlights a line of transactions. "They're all right there. Not hidden. Or at least, not hidden *well.*"

Falin leans closer. "You found a vulnerability?"

"More than one." Leon locks in, his voice grows louder as he explains. "Their entire system relies on moving money through a series of go-betweens before it reaches its final destination. But they got sloppy. Started reusing the same paths, same timing."

"Can you get in? Move that money?" I ask, trying to understand even a fraction of what he's saying.

"Working on it, but yes." His eyes meet mine, focused and intense. "And I'm going to redirect every last penny. We can help those girls, Ray's family, all his guys too. What- ever else, I'll make sure to send to other organizations."

Falin squeezes his shoulder. "You're kinda brilliant, you know that? In a Bond villain sort of way."

"It won't bring them back," Leon says quietly, his hand rubbing his tired eyes. "It won't change what they've gone through."

"No," Falin agrees. "But it's a start."

"Do your thing, you British mastermind," I say. "Let's make Orlov wish he never touched Bailey."

We sit in silence for a moment, watching as Leon's code slowly dismantles the empire Orlov built, piece by digital piece. I have no fucking clue what he's doing, or how, but damn if I'm not blown away.

I think about Bailey, and every other victim we couldn't save. The ones from the gala... the photos on the drive. We have to find a way to help as many as we can.

Falin grabs the cat carrier from the bedroom, breaking me away from my thoughts.

"Did you say your goodbyes?" I ask Leon, pulling my gaze away from the screen. He raises a brow. "The kittens," I add. "You know we talked about this last week."

"Shit." He drags his hand down his face with a sigh. "Completely slipped my mind. You're certain about this?"

No. They're my children. I saved them from death, nursed them to health. They carried me through my darkest hours. "I am. If we're going to London, we can't bring them with us."

Leon rises and stretches, scooping Havoc from her spot on the cat tower. He hugs her close to his cheek, inhaling her kitten scent. I swear it's better than drugs. "About that."

"About what?" Falin asks, coming to our side.

"I was thinking I should head to London first, scope things out. Stay with my mum while I hunt down a decent flat. Reach out to some contacts there."

He returns Havoc to her tower and she curls up, a perfect little puff ball. "What are we supposed to do here?"

I can't stand more waiting, especially knowing Bailey's most likely not even in this country anymore. Leon glances between Falin and me, a knowing smirk playing on his lips. "I'm sure you two can keep busy."

"You really shouldn't travel that far yet," Falin says. "Plus, you have another follow up with the surgeon in a few weeks."

"Have you run this by Damon?" I ask. These decisions

usually involve all of us. The thought of Leon across a damn ocean alone, potentially getting into trouble, doesn't sit well with me. Yes, he can handle himself, but he prefers to keep to his desk, managing things from behind his screen. I don't know if he has what it takes to kill if he needs to. Not like me or Damon.

"Spoke to him earlier, before they went out." He exhales. "Look, I'll be honest. The atmosphere here is getting a bit too... coupley. I need some space... just for a few weeks."

"We get it," Falin answers for both of us. And I do understand. I'd feel the same way living with two couples who can't keep their hands off each other.

"And Jas, finding her will be my only priority the moment I land. I promise you that."

"I know, brother." I nod. "If that's what you think is best, then you have my blessing. As soon as you're ready for us, we'll be there."

Falin pets the sleeping kittens. "So, does this mean we can keep them?"

"I guess so." I can't help but smile. "For now."

"Probably for the best, considering we didn't even ask Bella's family if the girls could have them." She moves the cat carrier to the side of the room.

"True," I say. "For all we know, they could be allergic."

"Better give it a few weeks before we ask," she says with a smirk.

"Get going," Leon says. "You'll be late, and I have loads of work to do here."

I wrap my arm around Falin and wince as I bend to grab our bags. She swats my arm away, slinging them over her shoulder before I do something else dumb and fuck myself up more. "No lifting! You better behave this weekend or you'll get it."

I waggle my brows. "Is that a promise?"

"Fuck's sake, get out of here already," Leon groans, throwing a couch cushion at our retreating back.

We get settled in Damon's car, which he repeatedly told me I'd face sudden death if anything happened to. Attachment issues, I swear. "Are you ready?" I ask Falin.

She gives a half smile. "I think so?"

Not only are we taking a little trip into Jersey to see Bella and Ruby, the strong as fuck teenager labelled number two, but we're also meeting Falin's biological aunt for the first time.

"It's going to be great," I reassure her. The engine rumbles to life and Pierce The Veil sounds through the speakers. "And hey, maybe you'll get some answers about your parents. If not, at least you're laying to rest a part of you that's been searching for so long."

"When that match first came through I never believed I'd be alive long enough to actually speak with her, let alone meet her. Alexander had me by the throat," I tense, my jaw clenching as she says his name. She notices, and covers her palm over mine. "Metaphorically, and... Well, you know the rest."

"You're here and she's the luckiest person alive to get to meet you," I say. "If she doesn't love you, do I have your permission—"

"Don't even finish that thought," she says, laughing and shaking her head. I rest my hand on her thigh and head out of the city, already feeling homesick for our little apartment with our kittens and our best friends.

"I'm going to miss the babies," I say. "But it'll be nice to get you all alone in a hotel room."

"Why would that sound so creepy coming from anyone else? Major Norman Bates, shower scene vibes."

"Oh yeah?" I drop my voice. "I can think of another shower scene I'd like to recreate."

"But your stitches?" she asks. "Also, cheesy... What am I going to do with you?"

"I got the all clear from the doctor this morning. I was going to keep it a surprise and do a whole scene later where I get naked and fill the tub and—"

She grabs my face, shutting me up with a quick kiss. "I think we should check into the hotel *before* we visit the kids."

Her hand drifts over the bulge in my pants and she gives a soft squeeze. "Yup. You're right."

"Always am."

She's not wrong.

CHAPTER THIRTY-SIX

FALIN

It's been one month since killing Alexander Orlov. Seems like so much longer though. I don't think I'll ever stop looking over my shoulder, and I sure as hell won't go out without my switchblade. Like I keep reminding myself, Alexander may be dead, but there's so many more monsters hiding in the shadows.

But tonight, I put that out of my mind. Walking hand in hand with Jasper down a busy Manhattan street, I feel something I haven't felt in years. Peace.

"You're doing it again," Jasper says, giving my hand a gentle squeeze.

I glance up at him. "What?"

"Hiding somewhere in your head. I call it your emo time." He pulls me against his side and wraps his arm around my shoulder. "What's going on in there?"

"My emo time, huh?" I laugh, soaking in how nice it is to feel his warmth against my skin in the early spring breeze. "I don't know, just thinking about how different everything feels lately. How different I am."

"Different good or different bad? If it's bad, just tell me

what to do and I'll do it." I know he's kidding around, but also, deep down, if I needed something, he'd seriously do it. Anything.

"Good. Definitely good." We stop at a crosswalk and I turn to face him. "A year ago I would have run from all of this. The commitment, the family we've built, the messiness of letting go of what I can't control."

His blue eyes soften as he brushes his thumb across my cheek. "And now?"

"Now I can't imagine running from any of it. Even when it scares the hell out of me." I rise on my tiptoes to kiss him, not caring that we're blocking pedestrian traffic. "Even when you drive me absolutely insane."

"I am pretty good at that, huh. Some may say it's my special skill." He cocks his head and grins. "Actually scratch that... I have other, better, skills."

"Speaking of skills," I say. He smirks, but I bump his shoulder. "Not those kinds. Keep it in your pants, sir."

"Sir? That's not helping," he jokes.

"I was saying..." I narrow my eyes, but with none of my usual annoyance, just playfulness. "Aunt Sarah called me earlier. She asked about you. Said and I quote, 'That man can talk his way out of hell with the devil himself.' I laughed but damn if she didn't peg you right away."

"Peg me?" He waggles his brows and I roll my eyes. "Kidding." He laughs, full and deep. "It's a gift. Got me out of trouble more times than I can count. Even got me the hottest woman in Manhattan, quite possibly the world."

"Damn straight," I say, squeezing his butt. So round and firm... I'm jealous. No man should go around with a butt this good.

"How are you feeling with all that?" he asks. I chew my lips, thinking of a way to put it all into words.

"It's wild. Kind of like finding a missing puzzle piece you didn't even know was missing. She has my eyes, or I guess I have hers. And she totally flings her hands around when she talks." I start doing it without thinking and Jasper reaches for my hand, kissing my palm.

"You are a hand flinger when you talk," he says.

I shrug. "Blake's told me the same thing. Guess I never noticed before." I smile remembering how my new aunt, my mom's sister, embraced me like she'd known me her whole like. It's still so surreal. She doesn't have answers on where my mother is, but at least I can find out more about her past. "She wants us to come for dinner in a few weeks. If we're not in London by then."

"We'll make it work either way," he says, holding me close. "You deserve to know more about where you came from. Even if where you are now is pretty damn perfect."

I lift up on my tiptoes to kiss him, not giving a shit that we're blocking pedestrian traffic. "Pretty damn perfect, huh?"

The sound of a horn honking and whistling breaks us apart. Damon pulls up in his precious Chevelle with Blake hanging out the passenger window. "Get a room, lovebirds!"

"Good idea," Jasper says. "Maybe we can use yours."

"Over my dead body," Damon says, smiling.

"Come on, we've got a going away dinner to get to," Blake says.

The apartment is quiet when we walk in, just Leon sprawled on the couch with his sketchbook while the kittens attack his shoelaces. When they hear us, they zoom down the hall, yowling and batting at each other. I get a pang in my chest as I look at Leon. It won't be the same at home without him.

"Are you all packed?" I ask. Blake and Damon head to the kitchen with the bags of takeout and bottles of booze.

"Almost. I have a few file transfers running, but once that's through I can pack up the rest of my computer stuff." His lips quirk up.

"No work talk," Blake says, bringing Leon a glass of amber liquid. "It's your last night, we're sending you off properly."

"By getting him drunk?" I ask. Although, I'm very much okay with this plan. I settle onto the couch, and Jasper claims his spot on the floor in front of me, leaning his head back between my legs.

"No," she says, crossing her arms, so her cropped shirt rides up. Damon's right behind her like a dog with a bone, wrapping his arms around her bare waist. She hums and leans into his embrace. "By being together. Everyone grab a drink, we need to make a toast."

Jasper hands me one of the glasses on the coffee table, and takes one for himself. We all hold up our glasses, trying not to get emotional.

Jasper clears his throat. "To Leon, the smartest dude we know."

"And the most stubborn," Damon adds.

"And the best artist," Blake adds, her lips quirking up in a small smile.

I think for a moment on what Leon's become to me. "To the brother I never knew I needed."

Leon angles his head, hiding his eyes. I catch the smile he doesn't want us to see. The emotion in his gaze too. We clink our glasses together, the sound louder than the music coming from Damon's phone. No one mentions how Blake wipes at her eyes, or how Damon's hand shakes slightly as he throws back his drink.

We load up plates of Italian food and spend the whole night talking, sharing stories and laughing at memories from the past few months. The kittens eventually finish up their witching hour zoomies and curl up in their tower, purring contentedly.

"Promise us you'll call every day," I tell Leon. "Even if you haven't found anything yet."

He nods, his brows drawing in. "Of course I will. And the second I have a lead on Bailey…"

"We'll be there," Jasper finishes.

"Just don't do anything stupid until we get there," Damon says. "That's our job."

Leon scoffs, and takes a sip of his drink. He looks at Blake and me, smiling. "You two better make sure they stay out of trouble. I'm trusting you."

I squeeze Jasper's thigh, and he chuckles, saying, "You know they will."

Leon holds up his glass, his eyes glazed with a far away look. "I've got one more toast." Jasper adds another splash to our cups and we hold them up again. "To Bailey." He swallows hard. "We're coming for you."

We take our drinks quietly, each of us in our own heads, until Blake clears her throat. "Who wants dessert?"

Later, after Damon and Blake head to bed, and Leon disappears to finish packing, Jasper pulls me against his chest. His body is tense against mine, and I know he's thinking about Bailey, about London, about all the time that's passed. I can tell when he goes to that place in his mind. "You okay?"

"Just want to be there already." I smell the whiskey on his breath, hear the emotion in his words. "Every day we wait…"

"Hey." I stand on my tiptoes to look him in the eyes.

"We'll be there soon. Leon will do whatever he can, I know it, and if he finds her sooner, we're on the first flight over."

He nods, pressing his forehead to mine. "I know. I just miss her so much. I want to call my parents, tell them we've done the impossible. They're so torn up, at this point they've lost hope. I don't want to give them anything yet, not until we have her."

"We'll get her back. You *will* make that call." I pour every ounce of conviction I have into those words because I feel them in my gut.

"Thank you," he whispers against my lips as he brushes his hand across my hair. I pull back, raising a brow in question. He goes on. "For loving me through all this craziness, for being there, for making our room feel like home even when my head's a mess."

He's right, I'm loving our room now that we've combined our stuff and moved into the bigger space. His guitar next to my desk. Our clothes mixed in the closet. His comforter on the bed, and my pillows. Our life together growing piece by piece.

"You don't have to thank me," I say. "That's what you do for the people you love."

We get comfortable in bed, pulling the blankets over us, as Havoc and May claim their spot above our heads.

"Love you too, Trouble."

Our life is far from normal. Police investigations linger unanswered, their questions a constant shadow. Bailey's still out there somewhere, waiting. Ivan's empire still needs dismantling, piece by corrupt piece. But tonight, I'm exactly where I need to be. With my family. With my man. Ready to face whatever comes next, as chaotic and unhinged as it may be.

I've finally found my place in the world—not just a place, but my people. And I'll fight like hell to keep them. With a switchblade, of course.

Want a little more Jasper & Falin? Check out my website now to get access to their special bonus scene! https://laurengreenebooks.com

Find out what happens next in *Love Bleeds Red* book 3 in the Vengeful Hearts Series!

ACKNOWLEDGMENTS

It's tough to not get emotional as I reflect on my time writing Bulletproof Love. It's been one of the easiest and most fun books to write while somehow simultaneously pulling every ounce of creative energy from my soul. Jasper and Falin demanded a lot of me—and they deserved every late night, every shed tear, and every piece of my heart. I hope I did their love story justice.

I couldn't have gotten here without the support of so many. Leah, you keep me going, and I love you so much! Havoc, thank you for loving these characters as much as I do, and making sure they get the stories they deserve. To my cover designer, Julie, you killed it with this cover. Thank you!

To my street team, beta readers, and ARC readers—thank you for taking time out of your busy lives to support me and my work. You're all the best!

Special thanks to Crystal, Yolva, Delaine, and MJ. Love you ladies!

To my family, there aren't enough words to say how grateful I am for you. Your constant support and reassurance lets me live my dream every day.

And my readers, without you I couldn't do this. Thank you so much for taking a chance on this series.

ABOUT THE AUTHOR

Lauren crafts angsty, steamy romances filled with complex characters and witty banter. When she's not writing, she's navigating life in Arizona with her busy family. Lauren's creativity is fueled by spooky season vibes, reruns of The Office, and copious amounts of iced coffee. A devoted animal lover, she surrounds herself with furry companions while dreaming up her next happily ever after.